Aurora's
WILDERNESS LOVE
Hot Girl Summer Love

Harmony Noble

TrueLoveWriters

ISBN 978-1-963074-49-9, 978-1-963074-63-5 & ISBN 978-1-963074-50-5

Story creation, cover, and illustrations by Melody Noble & Harmony Curtis

Thank you for choosing this book.
We hope the story
brought you as much joy reading it
as we had in creating it!

We'd love to hear from you! Feel free to reach out via email at TrueLoveWriters@gmail.com, and follow us on Instagram, Facebook, TikTok at @truelovewriters for the latest updates and behind-the-scenes fun.

Get access to exclusive offers, bonus content, new release updates, and recommendations for more great reads.

Sign up for our e-newsletter at HarmonyNoble.com.

To Alaska,

Thanks for your icy charms that send dates straight
to my cozy bed in search of warmth.
Your cold weather lets me live in layers
and puffy jackets
while I shamelessly eat comfort foods.
Who needs hot girl summer pressure when
when I look fabulous in a hoodie?
Here's to you—and the relentless long winters
that leave plenty of time for writing!

Aurora's
WILDERNESS LOVE
Hot Girl Summer Love

Harmony Noble

TrueLoveWriters

Chapter 1

The Crazy Alaskan Driver, Me

The traffic light finally shifts to green, and sweet relief washes over me. I quickly toss the sparkly lip gloss Lisa swore would make me 'absolutely irresistible' into my already stuffed bag.

Tonight's agenda? *Help a friend by surviving a blind date.* Oh, and enjoy a complimentary fancy dinner, not to mention the fifty bucks she's paying me for stepping in at the last minute—that's just icing on the cake. But let's be real. The thought of another awkward blind date is enough to make me reconsider my friendship with Lisa.

Lisa, with her wild job at Hook and Reel Dating Service—or as they call it, HARD—because apparently, "relationships shouldn't be HARD"—is always throwing these spontaneous, last-minute dates my way. She's the opposite of me, the kind of person who believes in love at first sight, and that love can happen to anyone at any time. And given my current dismal financial state and lack of a steady job, her little cash boost makes this gig feel like a golden opportunity.

HONK! HONK!

"Holy Mary, and moose antlers!" I yell, startled by the blaring horn. I might have been veering slightly into their lane as I checked my teeth for lipstick.

I swerve back into my lane, my ancient Subaru, affectionately nicknamed "The Rust Bucket," protesting with a series of increasingly alarming rattles. Racing by me, the muddy F350 is adorned with a "Happiness is a Warm Gun" bumper sticker. Of course, the driver I'd almost introduced to my insurance deductible is a hairy redneck, who probably knows how to hunt and field dress a caribou and carries the terrifying tool for that in his oversized pickup.

Mortified by my near-vehicular manslaughter, I hunch my too-tall frame lower in the driver's seat—a futile effort, as I'm pretty sure my red hair grazing the sun visor is still visible. I lift a hand in a sheepish wave, giving up on cowering.

He responds with a universally understood gesture of lifting his chin and spitting out his window—the spitting might have been unrelated to me, though.

My phone buzzes in the cupholder.

Lisa.

She's probably checking in to see how the date's going. "Date" is a strong word when it's a favor to your bestie. Still, I'm optimistic since most of the guys using the expensive dating service she works for are wealthy. Hooking a rich Alaskan guy means I won't need to continue job hunting. If we make a *real* connection, maybe he'd pay my university bills, too.

If I'm gonna dream, I might as well dream big.

I am *so* late.

Anchorage's sun slices through my windshield, a blinding reminder that Alaska's unique bright sky at eight pm certainly does make it live up to the tourist name of the "Land of the Midnight Sun." Of course, I lost track of the time—it looks like noon outside. I squint, jamming oversized sunglasses on my face, and floor it down the highway. Summer air bites me through the cracked window, cool and crisp. Even Mother Nature is judging me harshly.

My phone buzzes again. Darius, my best friend and moral compass, texts, "R u there? What's happening?" joining the *Hot Mess Express* group chat with Lisa.

Lisa responds before I can even blink. "Don't distract her. I need her to at least attempt to be on time."

I groan and quickly reply, "How am I even an adult?" Glancing in the mirror, I see my once-perfectly wavy auburn hair turning into a frizzy disaster, a few strands escaping my cute braid as if they, too, have lost faith in my life choices.

I glance back at the road. "What th—"

A moose. A literal, dumbass, suicidal moose lumbers onto the highway.

"Son of a—"

Slamming on the brakes, my car fishtails. Coffee cups from my floorboard launch into the backseat. My seatbelt nearly chokes me. The Subaru skids to a stop inches from the towering, indifferent beast.

The moose blinks. Chews. Flicks an ear.

I thump the steering wheel. The horn gives a sad, asthmatic honk.

A Jeep with a hairy mountain-man type passes me, honking and waving his middle finger as if this is my fault.

The only thing Alaska has more of than moose is jerks! Despite modern times, the ratio of men to women in Alaska is still two to one. Alaskan women say, "The odds are good, but the goods are odd."*And it's true.*

I groan, continuing and tossing my phone onto the passenger seat, where it lands with a soft thud against a pile of crumpled receipts.

My stomach growls in protest, a loud rumble echoing in the small car, just as I spot the neon Anchorage glow of Ronnie's Sushi up ahead.

Free dinner, here I come.

No matter how the date turns out, getting a night out is just what I need. And maybe this blind date wouldn't be a complete train wreck. Though, Lisa's track record with setting me up on these dates is questionable.

I smooth down my thrift-store dress, a vibrant floral number that probably looks more "Alaskan cruise tourist," than "sultry single," and tuck a stray strand of my hair behind my ear. "You got this girl," I mutter with a healthy dose of self-deprecating sass and a nervous wink in the rearview mirror.

My reflection stares back, unconvinced.

Almost as if on cue, my phone dinged with another message from Darius. "Happy hunting! Don't be too THIRSTY, girrrrrl!"

Then it dings with Lisa's response.

Except it's not Lisa.

My phone flashes a data usage warning, followed by an alert that my end-of-billing-cycle payment is ten days past due.

Perfect. Just what I need—another reminder of my financial situation, as if receiving all my university paperwork for the upcoming school year isn't enough of a reminder that I need cash.

I yell into my phone, "Message Lisa...*Please let Tim know that I'm running a few minutes late, but I'm parking now.*"

I slow down to a crawl, looking for a spot to park, and my phone pings again. "It's THOMAS. Hurry up! I can't lose another client."

Somehow, I get lucky and find the last parking spot, a weirdly angled spot involving several awkward maneuvers. I silently apologize to the car beside me and the pavers one tire is on top of. Exhaling a sigh of relief, a sleek, dark SUV–a fancy-pants Land Rover—pulls up too close, its headlights blinding me.

"Seriously?" I mutter, already bracing for the inevitable territorial battle over parking. Anchorage may be a city, but it still has the charm of a small town. And during the summer rush, mastering the art of parking becomes a vital survival skill, especially with tourists squeezing into every tight spot.

The driver's side door of the SUV swings open, and a woman unfolds herself with an air of effortless grace that I immediately envy and fear. I notice the sleek, black leather jacket giving her frame a powerful, commanding edge. She's striking even in the dim light, with perfectly tousled dark curly locks that look deliberate and windblown. And then I see her feet. Beneath tailored trousers that screamed "power lunch," she is wearing a pair of bright yellow checked Converse sneakers, the kind a kindergartener might sport with a matching lunchbox.

I suppress a grin. Unexpectedly quirky footwear for someone who otherwise exudes corporate chic and dines at expensive restaurants. *Interesting.*

She rounds the hood of her SUV, a frustrated sigh escaping her lips as she glances at the cramped space. “Excuse me,” her voice was low and controlled, making me instantly pay attention. “Are you planning on... inhabiting both parking spots, or will your vehicle eventually fit entirely within the lines?”

Heat rises, coloring my cheeks redder than my hair. Oversharing and rambling apologies are my super-secret talent, so she doesn’t know who she’s messing with.

“Oh my gosh, I am so sorry! Parking in this lot is always such a... adventure, you know? Especially when you’re running late because you almost had a vehicular disagreement with a few cavemen in pickup trucks and a moose. I mean, aside from bill collectors and this blind date, I didn’t think my night could get worse! You understand... I mean, *you* probably don’t have any of those issues...” I trail off, realizing I’m rambling and sound like a caffeine-fueled squirrel.

The woman’s lips twitch, and a small, almost imperceptible smile plays across her sharply sculpted face. Her dark eyes, sharp and intelligent, hold mine for long enough that my heart jumps into my throat to halt my babbling.

“Right,” she says, her tone dry but not unkind. “Well, ‘adventure’ or not, perhaps you could adjust your parking?”

“Absolutely! So sorry!” I babble, adding in my signature Aurora Thompson finger guns for good measure.

She blinks slowly, and an eyebrow shifts, rising slightly.

I scramble back into the Rust Bucket, my hands suddenly clumsy on the steering wheel. As I maneuver the car a few more inches to the left, I catch another glimpse of her. Even with a hint of exasperation in her expression, she’s undeniably stunning. There’s a captivating stillness about her, a confidence that radiated even in a parking lot showdown, and the unruly curls and quirky shoes add to her charm. My stomach does a ridiculous, completely unnecessary cartwheel.

Once my parking is perfect—or at least something resembling it–I turn off the ignition, my heart still hammering a frantic rhythm against my ribs. Gathering my bag, I glance up and see her watching me, an eyebrow cocked. Her head is tilted, which makes the pink neon sign shine across the planes of her face, creating a dazzling artwork for my eyes alone.

"Have a... eventful evening, Trouble," she says, a hint of amusement in her low voice before she strides towards the restaurant.

Eventful. That was one word for it. I watch her go, the yellow of her sneakers a hypnotic flash of color against the muted tones of the dusty parking lot and dimming evening light.

I smile and shake my head at her ridiculous highlighter-yellow shoes and no-nonsense business suit. If I were interested in a real date–if I had time to actually date—she'd be my first choice, no contest.

"Simmer down, libido," I say aloud to the random thought of having dinner with her and blowing off Tim. Heat blooms in my chest that I ignore and shake off with a giggle.

I take a deep breath and remind myself why I'm here: free sushi and to help Lisa. Nothing more. *Definitely,* nothing more. Especially not getting flustered by a gorgeous stranger with a talent for understated sarcasm and unexpectedly quirky footwear.

Nope. *Not happening.*

Chapter 2

Red Flag Sushi Date

Speed-walking into the restaurant, I exhale, shaking off my nervous energy. I have dinner and a date to survive.

Here I am, barely eighteen and already failing at my attempt at adulthood. I'm desperate, meeting a random stranger, driving on bald summer tires, and wearing my best thrift-store designer, wondering what I'm doing wrong and if there's anything I'm doing right.

Nothing says "I've got my life together," like being fashionably late to a blind date dinner at a restaurant I can't afford. By the looks of it, this place doesn't even have a happy hour deal.

I rush into Ronnie's—the most upscale sushi restaurant in Anchorage—feeling like a hot mess as I duck to avoid the dangerously low-hanging decor. The hostess greets me with an overly enthusiastic, "Welcome to Ronnie's—"

"I'm late for a first date," I blurt, cutting her off. "Tim... No, I think it's Thomas?"

"At the bar," she replies, pointing to the loud, crowded area behind her without missing a beat.

I pause, glancing around at the busy place with music hammering the entrance, and lean in. "You guys aren't hiring, are you?"

She shakes her head. "Sorry!"

Worth a try. I don't need a great job. I just need a consistent paycheck.

I glide into the bar, smoothing down my dress and adjusting my posture for my grand entrance. My glossy lips pout into a sultry smile as I strut in. A few guys look up to grin back. I'm the star of my very own Alaskan Sex and the City series, and I'm here to find my Mr. Big.

Only one guy is wearing a suit among the flannel and jeans-wearing crowd at the glass-topped bar. I slide onto the metal square stool beside him, ready to apologize. Still, the words die in my throat, with his odor overwhelming my senses.

Thomas glances my way, his chocolate-brown eyes scanning me as though he's looking *through* me, not at me. His gaze finally locks in, mostly on my breasts. *Classy.*

"Auuuuura!" he exclaims with the slurred enthusiasm of someone who's already had a few too many. "I ordered you a drink," he adds. He nods to the inked-up, yummy bartender who could easily moonlight as a moody Banana Republic model or play in a lesbian punk band when she's not slinging drinks.

Two hot girls in one night? The universe is tempting me back to team lesbian. Why did I let Lisa convince me to date guys again?

I bite my lip and remind myself that Lisa will kill me if I don't at least have a quick date with her client, and my bank account needs the money.

The extra-hot bartender, Slate, hands me a Coors Light bottle with a sad, wilted lime instead of a dainty cocktail or sake that everyone around me enjoys.

"Thank you for ordering," I purr, sipping the beer and trying not to grimace. I can't fault him for bad taste, can I? Maybe he's a misunderstood genius hiding behind poor beverage choices, and that's why he needs a dating service.

Slate, gruff and busy, meets my eyes and shakes her head at the disgrace that I'm drinking before tossing the menus in front of us and clearing away the empty Coors bottles Thomas has already accumulated. Looks like he started partying a little early.

I glance at the menu, stealing a few sidelong glances at Thomas. His sagging skin, tired eyes, and slight paunch don't scream millionaire or even I'd-trust-you-to-water-my-office-plants.

"So, Alliee," he slurs between gulps of Coors Light, "Do you have kids or a job?"

This is a *stellar* start. I shake my head and give up on trying to have a captivating conversation.

Just as I'm about to drown in awkward silence, the bartender makes eye contact and mouths, "You okay?"

I shrug, then nod. I'll give him the benefit of the doubt. I *was* thirty minutes late—he probably drank to calm his nerves.

"Aurora," I correct. I add this to my growing tally for Lisa, as part of my argument for why she should pay me extra for this date. *Red flag #1: poor drink choices. Red flag #2: calling me by the wrong name.*

"That's your kid?'

"No. That's my name. I don't have kids," I clarify, trying to salvage some dignity. "Right now, I'm focusing on finding a job and starting business school at the University of Anchorage this fall."

He nods, clearly not listening, and slurs, "Cool, cool. So, do you want kids or is this a sugar daddy situation?"

I cough, choking on my thin beer. My cheeks flame with embarrassment and outrage. This is *not* the date I signed up for. "I think there's been a misunderstanding. I'm looking for a casual date, not... that."

He laughs, shaking his head like I'm joking. "Good luck with that!"

"Excuse me?" I turn, ready to signal Slate that I need help, but she's at the other end of the bar.

He smirks. "I'm rich, and I could take care of you, but you have to take care of me, too. If you know what I mean."

My cheeks burn hotter than the wasabi on the sushi platter nearby. "Uh, so there's definitely been a misunderstanding--"

The bartender interrupts, "Did you decide on our dinner rolls or platters?"

Yes, I decided I'd rather not eat and leave. *Immediately.* I open my mouth, but Thomas answers first.

"The Led Zeppelin Roll and Last Samurai Roll, and we'll need two shots," he declares, pointing at a bottle and dismissively waving at the bartender without looking up from the menu. The bartender glares daggers at him before turning to enter in the order.

I absolutely *loathe* it when people act rudely to service staff. Having worked in retail and customer service, no amount of money can compensate for a lack of class. *Red flag #3: rude and condescending!*

Thomas winks at me like he's doing me a favor, sending a cold shiver down my spine.

"Um, okay. Those sound good," I answer noncommittally, tallying his cringeworthy behavior.

I glance around the bar, already planning my escape. Lisa may do a background check on every one of her company's clients, but Thomas' background isn't his problem.

Forcing a smile, I bat my lashes and glance at my phone. Fifteen more minutes, then I'm out of here. At least sushi is better than the stale ramen dinner waiting for me at my apartment.

I take a deep breath. This could be great practice for job interviews, particularly the pesky question of how I react in stressful situations.

"How about you?" I ask, trying to steer the conversation into safer waters. "What are your passions?"

"Not sure if anyone told you, but I'm a pretty big deal. I'm a Director for Ennis Oil's Anchorage Headquarters," he puffs his chest and says this like he's cured cancer.

He continues, his words slurring together. "I've had my fair share of long-term relationships. I'm ready to have kids."

With me? I take the shot that Slate sets in front of me. I mouth *Help*, but she's already helping someone else.

He pauses to down the shot, then gulps his beer. I cringe as he burps—not even excusing himself. "But women? Oh boy, they can be a handful—always wanting something serious! I want a wife but no commitments. Open relationship. I want the physical stuff, with no drama, you know?"

I let out a nervous laugh, praying this is a twisted joke. But no, he's dead serious. His unflinching seriousness makes my skin crawl. I want to run.

How many red flags have I counted so far? At least *ten?*

Luckily, Slate interrupts just as the conversation quickly delves into awkward territory. She clears our glasses, dropping down the fresh plates of sushi that, to my relief, looks delicious. I glance at my watch–*only five minutes!*

I shove a piece in my mouth, the delicate rice and savory fish melting together, and despite myself, a small moan escapes. His eyes light up, clearly excited to hear me moan.

And then, in true disaster fashion, Thomas stands up abruptly. "Going to the restroom," he mutters before stumbling off. His steps are so uncoordinated that I wonder if he's having a stroke or a medical emergency.

Am I the terrible person who should be getting him medical attention?

He burps again–*No, it's not me!*

He lumbers toward the restroom, hiccuping and tripping as he goes. The moose I nearly hit earlier has better grace than this guy.

I pop a piece of sushi into my mouth, savoring it as Slate drops off another plate of sushi—this one more gorgeous than the last. I'm too busy chewing to say anything, but in my mind, I'm already fantasizing about tasting the next sushi roll. The excellent sushi did make this date worthwhile.

"Can I get this to go?" I ask Slate, my mouth full. If this date is a bust—and let's face it, it already is—I'm at least going to take the food home and eat like royalty tomorrow.

Taking advantage of the brief moment of peace, I pull out my phone and start texting Lisa. "SOS! You sent me on a dating disaster!"

I glance up at Slate, who's watching me with amusement.

Great, even the staff recognizes what a train wreck of a date this is.

My phone buzzes again. "Babe, on paper he had potential. Are you sure? Maybe he can help you get a job?"

I consider it. Job hunting isn't going well. Maybe there's some merit in his boasting.

I type out my response, "Maybe? I thought this whole 'helping Lisa by dating clients' thing would be a step up from donating blood for free juice and cookies. I'd rather be selling my plasma–he's cringe."

Lisa's reply is instant, "I'm so sorry, babe! Most clients are fine, I swear!"

I sigh deeply, and Darius chimes in, "Aurora, you know my temp agency is always hiring. Just say the word, and no more dating disasters."

With a winky face, Lisa adds, "Omg, you can do both. Office temp by day, dating temptress by night. I have so many pencil skirts you can borrow."

Temp agency? I want consistency, not the chaos I grew up in, never knowing what to expect from my mom. I need a job that alleviates my stress, not adds to it. A temp job is a last resort, but I'm seriously considering it.

I quickly text Lisa one last thing, "Gotta go. Prince Not-So-Charming will be back soon. Send a search party if you don't hear from me in an hour."

I add, "Ronnies is a great spot and you should come check out this bartender, Slate. She'd be great for your dating agency, a real alternative, butch vibe."

"I need more women for these guys, not lesbians!" she replies.

I ponder why lesbians don't use dating services. Are there not enough of us? Or do we all eventually give up on love and start dating men until we pick the least disgusting one to marry?

As I tuck my phone away into my bag, Slate slides something across the table toward me. "I guess you're handling this one," she says, casually.

I freeze, sushi poised halfway to my mouth, as I catch sight of the bill on the tray: $183.29. *Are you kidding me?*

I glance over at the restrooms, my mind racing.

"Your friend just jumped into a cab," she states, completely unfazed.

I blink at her in shock, sushi still hanging in mid-air. *Wait, what?*

"Um, here's my card," I say, hoping it doesn't bounce. "I'll be right back—just need to hit the ladies' room," I add with a smile that's probably more of a grimace at this point.

Can you really wash dishes at a restaurant to settle a bill?

Chapter 3

Trapped!

I bolt. Not gracefully, not coolly. This isn't some James Bond escape scene. This is a full-on, heart-pounding, do-I-hate-my-life-yet sprint to the bathroom. The hostess watches me with pity and makes me feel like a distressed kitten in need of adoption.

And honestly, she's not wrong. If she knew about the bar tab and the towering stack of overdue bills in my inbox, she might actually toss me a spare mint and offer me a hug.

I slam the bathroom door behind me, its sound echoing in the otherwise quiet space, and press my forehead against the cool wood. I inhale deeply, willing my pulse to slow. *Okay. You've got this, Aurora.* The words feel like a desperate prayer as I look at my reflection in the mirror, which is staring back at me with as much disbelief as I feel. If my reflection could speak, I imagine it'd say, *Girl, you are so not okay.*

Shaking hands, I reach for my phone because maybe—just maybe—I can perform some miraculous financial trick, and the money will appear. But instead, I'm greeted by a flashing red alert.

"Service Suspended: Please Contact Your Carrier."

"No, no, no!" I gasp—my voice cracks, as a whimper escapes. I jab furiously at the screen as if I can command the universe to right this wrong with sheer willpower. But it doesn't work. The screen stays stubbornly frozen, mocking me.

I am cut off. Completely. Not just from the world—*that* would be bad enough—but from *help*. My friends, the only ones who could save me, are unreachable. The only number I have memorized—my mother's. I'd rather face off with a pissed-off bear than call her for help. I can already hear her, "I told you so." I won't call her. That is *not* happening tonight.

What do I do now? Should I go back to see if the cute bartender will be able to help? Or maybe the restaurant will give me until tomorrow to pay.

No. I straighten my spine and channel all the wisdom from my advanced placement classes and college-prep track. *I can handle this*. I'm practically an adult. And I can negotiate my way out of this nightmare, just like a capable, professional, almost-adult.

With renewed—delusional—determination, I reach for the door handle, yanking it ready to talk with Slate. The handle comes off in my hand with a sickening *clunk*.

I freeze.

Stare at it.

Blink.

Am I... am I hallucinating? There's no way I just broke a piece of the *restaurant*—a restaurant that I'm about to beg to forgive my bill.

"What god did I offend?" I mutter to no one, shoving my shoulder against the door. It refuses to budge.

Panic claws at my chest.

Nope. Nope, nope, nope.

I'm trapped. In this trendy, minimalist-designed bathroom. With no way to pay my bill. No way to call for help. And the horrible realization that if I'm not out there in five minutes, Slate will assume I dined and dashed—or worse, call the police. How hard will it be to get a job when I have no experience, and I'm a criminal?

"HELP!" I bang on the door like I'm a contestant on a game show, and this is my final lifeline. "I'M STUCK!" My voice cracks in a helpless, terrified way.

Nothing.

Nothing.

I blink at the door again, half expecting it to open out of sheer mercy. But no. The silence stretches for an eternity.

Oh my god. I'm going to die here. Alone. In a bathroom.

My obituary will practically write itself. *Aurora Thompson, 18, perished in a bathroom after unsuccessfully trying to dine and dash. The cause of death appears to be underage drinking, financial ruin, and bathroom-induced despair.*

I slump against the door, wishing to evaporate into the air. But no, I'm still here. Still stuck. Still panicking. And I haven't even hit the worst part yet—trying to figure out how I'm going to explain this mess when I finally get out.

Then, a voice slices through the bathroom door, like strumming a guitar, vibrating my soul.

"Hang tight, Trouble."

The door swings open before I can process the words, and I stumble straight into her. She catches me in her steady, strong arms, immediately making me think I should have followed my impulse to skip out on Thomas and dine with her.

The woman from the parking lot—the one with the high-powered, boss-lady energy, the tailored suit that costs more than my rent, and those *shoes*. The yellow ones. The ones that scream, *I've got style and my life together* while I'm here wondering if I can wash dishes or fit through a bathroom window.

Up close, she's even more stunning than I remembered. The sharp angles of her jaw and cheekbones are enough to make the gods jealous. Tattoos—intricate black designs that start as trees and twist into birds—are inked along her forearms. They're... beautiful. Unfathomably cool. And I somehow didn't notice them earlier.

Her scent hits me—citrus, leather, and a smoky, deep, earthy aroma that makes her even more attractive. It's intoxicating. *She's* intoxicating.

"Are you okay?" she asks, steadying me with a firm grip. Her voice is firm and capable—ugh, *too* capable, which makes me feel even more like a mess.

"Yes! No... I mean, thank you," I blurt out, stepping back as quickly as possible before my attraction to her overloads my circuits and I combust.

She takes the broken handle from my hand, reattaching it without hesitation. She doesn't even break a sweat. She clicks it back into place with one smooth motion, and I can't stop staring at her hands, moving with the precision of someone who knows what to do in any given situation.

I twist the handle, and it works. The door handle is fixed, just like that.

"You're my hero," I whisper before I can stop myself.

Oh god, did I just say that out loud? And did it sound *exactly* like something a drunk horny person would say?

She looks at me, sliding her hands into her pockets with effortless swagger. Her yellow Converse sneakers stand out against the sharp, tailored look she's somehow pulling off, and my brain glitches.

Who is this woman exuding a cool, untouchable businesswoman vibe?

Her lips curl into a slow, knowing grin. "I heard you." She sticky eyes me for a moment—*tasting the sight of me*—and the heat rises and licks my entire body so even my toes are blushing under her gaze.

Is she flirting with me?

No, no way. My brain's foggy, and I can't figure out the difference between her being polite and her being interested.

Before I can untangle my thoughts, another voice—smooth, impossibly deep with the tickle of a Spanish accent—calls out. "You coming?"

Oh no. Oh no, no, *no.*

I turn, and my stomach drops.

She's with someone, and the man standing in the doorway is... *unbelievable*. He looks like he stepped out of a Latin telenovela—tall, broad-shouldered, impossibly handsome. The kind of man who doesn't wear a button-up shirt so much as paints it on. Of course, the top two buttons are deliberately undone. Because why wouldn't they show his tanned and muscular chest?

And then I notice it—the warm and easy vibe connecting him.

She's with him because, of course, she's not single or a lesbian.

She flashes him a grin, tilting her head in a way that says she doesn't need to say a word. There's an intimacy in how she moves. They've been dance partners for years, and I'm the clumsy beginner trying to cut in.

I step back, away from her and her intoxicating scent.

"Yeah, one sec," she says to him, her tone easy and casual.

I want to curl up in a ball and disappear. I mistook her pity for interest. She's not just *taken*. She's taken by the kind of man who would be cast as the lead in an action movie. I know this sinking feeling. It's the realization that you don't stand a chance.

"Come on, let's get out of here," he says, not noticing me and pulling her gently toward the door. She stops to hand the hostess some bills. Then her arm slips into his, and my heart drops even lower.

My mouth is suddenly dry, watching as they exit the restaurant like they're in a perfume ad. Meanwhile, I'm standing here, feeling like a raccoon caught rummaging through trash.

As if on cue, the hostess steps forward and blocks my view. "You must have made a friend—she paid your bill."

I freeze, a cold shock running through me. I try to laugh, but it comes out as a strained sob. Then I just go back to the bathroom to cry.

I catch my reflection, tired eyes, and smeared lip gloss. I'm a mess. The sun might never set here, but I know when to call it a night.

I wipe my face and stop by the bar before leaving.

"Thanks for offering to help on my bad date," I tell Slate.

She shrugs. "I've seen worse, but that one was a doozy. Maybe you should google them before meeting," she suggests.

I swallow. "It was a set-up, but I'll let my friend know that he wasn't my type."

"Hey," she says, leaning forward so I can see she's not wearing a bra. "I'm off at ten and you seem like my type," she teases with a pout of her lisp and a sparkle in her eyes.

After meeting my mysterious parking lot stranger, I'm ruined. I guess I had hoped after she saved me from the bathroom, I'd go home with her and live happily ever after. I should know better than to believe in fairy tales.

With Slate's proposition, I smile and nod, not wanting to be rude.

"Maybe I'll see you later," she says, and I nod as I leave, feeling even worse than I did before.

Dating for real? It's a luxury I can't afford. I don't have time for distractions—especially not when I run into someone who makes my pulse race and my heart skip a beat from just their scent.

I can't keep pretending everything's fine when it's not. I can't afford to waste time. My priorities are survival—a job to pay my bills, rent, and university costs—those things matter. The rest is background noise—wasted effort.

Nodding with my decision, I decide to drive directly to Darius' place. I hate to ask for help, but I'm out of options.

Chapter 4

Walk of Shame

I knock on Darius's door, starting soft, then building to a more insistent rhythm. After twenty seconds, I hear the unmistakable sound of his footsteps rushing toward the door. I exhale, bracing myself. This means I really do have to ask him for a job now.

"Fine," I say, practically bursting with defeat the second he throws open the door. "You win. I'll work at the temp agency."

His eyes go wide, his grin almost too much to bear. "OMG, was it *that* bad of a date that it broke you? Girl, spill it!"

I let out a long, exasperated sigh and followed him into the living room. I drop onto his couch with an exaggerated flop. "The universe just hates me. And it sent me a sign that I'm definitely more into women than men. Poor Lisa. I'm clearly dating her worst clients, and I don't need money that badly. But I still need to pay my rent and phone bill." I wave my phone in his direction.

"You can do both," Darius says, sitting beside me, his tone light but serious. "I know Lisa's got a lot on her plate with the agency and trying to launch the dating app, but your real problem is the stress from your bills. Dating Lisa's work rejects might be fun... as long as you can avoid the crazy ones." He flashes a grin.

I snort. "Yeah, not sure I'm up for *that* kind of fun."

Darius pauses, thinking. "Wait—did you go to Ronnie's Sushi last night? Did you hook up with Slate? I think Lisa dated her last year. She seems like a lot of fun, bi-sexual, and very flexible. The brooding, intelligent type, just your speed."

"*No!*" I say, shaking my head in frustration. "I'm in crisis mode, Darius. *I need a job*, not a date."

He looks at me for a beat, a soft understanding in his eyes. Then, without missing a beat, he pulls out a blanket and pillow. "You get some sleep. I'll help you with your resume tomorrow. I've got an interview slot on Monday with the boss at the agency. You'll get it, and then I'll assign you short-term jobs to help you get back on your feet. Who knows, it might even turn into something you like."

I collapse onto the couch, grateful, even as a little voice questions how I got to this point. The sofa feels like an old, familiar friend—a safe place I've crashed on more times than I care to admit. Since high school, Darius and Lisa have been my lifelines when my mom's parade of dates and lack of interest in me became too much to handle.

Darius nudges me lightly. His voice is soft but sure. "Get some sleep, everything will look better in the morning."

He flips the light off, and the sound of the front door locking signals that he's heading back to bed. The warmth of the house and the rhythm of our friendship lulled me into sleep faster than I thought possible.

I walk into my apartment the next afternoon, bleary-eyed after sleeping in until noon at Darius's. He made me breakfast, packed me off with coffee, and texted me a reminder to email him my resume.

I rummage through the junk drawer until I find a stash of unused VISA gift cards from birthdays and holidays I've long forgotten. With a sigh, I use them to pay my phone bill. My phone flickers to life, bombarding me with missed notifications.

I eat the leftover sushi for lunch, savoring it more than I probably should. At least I got *something* good out of that disaster of a date last night. I've already sent Lisa the red-flag notes and the extent of her client's significant issues. She sent me a hundred extra dollars for my trouble. She also apologized that the guy left me with the bill—apparently, the first-date rule is that dinner is on *him*. At least Lisa's dating service is thriving. I guess everyone is looking for someone.

I spend the rest of the afternoon working on my resume and sorting through my budget. The college tuition reminders sit untouched on the desk, easy to ignore for now. I printed out the list of books I needed. Those bills can wait.

My phone pings. It's a text from Darius.

"Lisa's in trouble. Go to O'Malley's," he types.

I frown. The message is too short for someone who once texted me a 700-word rant about the wrong matcha latte shade.

"Elaborate??" I reply, my fingers hovering over the keys.

"Double-booked herself. She's not texting because she's drowning. Please go save her. Or at least save her social credibility."

I stare at the screen, then shrug. Why not? The night is young, and I do love a fancy cocktail. It can't be worse than Thomas.

I send a thumbs-up emoji and glance at my clothes, which are sitting on my bed from last night. I can't be bothered to put together another fantastic dating outfit, right? Who *will* notice if I wear the same outfit from last night?

Chapter 5

Canadian Date, eh?

Fifteen minutes later, I push through the swinging wooden doors of O'Malley's, a busy local bar that smells like cedar, whiskey, and bad decisions. I spot Lisa immediately—her blonde waves bouncing as she practically floats toward me, flashing her *frozen* smile in the whirlwind of floral perfume and "help me, help me" energy.

"Aurora, my beautiful, talented, soon-to-be-rich best friend!" she coos, grabbing my hands like I've agreed to donate a kidney.

I narrow my eyes. "No. Whatever this is, *no*."

She pouts. "But you don't even know what I need."

"I don't care. Darius texted me."

Lisa groans dramatically. "He has no faith in me."

"He's trying to save you from a meltdown," I say, folding my arms. "Spill."

She exhales like she's just been hit with a wave of dread. "Okay, so... maybe I was supposed to confirm a date for the matchmaking part of my job. And maybe that date fell through. And maybe I told the client that Summer—their assigned date—is totally still on so I didn't lose him as a client. Also, maybe I need you to pretend to be Summer for an hour." She gives me her *wide, pleading eyes*.

I blink. "Summer?"

"Yeah! The fun Canadian yoga instructor," she says, scrolling through her phone. Just then, my phone pings.

A hundred dollars appears in my cash app.

I stare at her.

"There. You help me out, you get a hundred bucks, it's practice for Darius's temp jobs, and you get to cover your date expenses. Thanks," she says, pulling me into a hug that's half gratitude, half triumph.

"Lisa, I failed my gym class stretches."

She waves a hand dismissively. "You don't have to actually *do* yoga. Just say you do yoga. Please. I like my job and I can't afford to lose this client. You've seen the kind of *clients* I've been getting lately." She gives me a look, and I picture Thomas from last week. My stomach sinks.

I tilt my head. "And the Canadian part?"

Lisa pulled a red beret from her bag and handed it to me with a flourish. "Here, wear this. Just apologize a lot, pronounce 'about' like 'a-butt,' and order gravy with whatever you eat."

I open my mouth to reject this entirely, but my finger itches to move the money into my account. I could work one hour for a hundred bucks. My Subaru needs gas. My fridge is a sad collection of expired ketchup packets. And, oh yeah, I need to pay my rent. The universe is testing me, and I'm failing spectacularly at being an adult.

"Fine," I say, grabbing the cash app receipt like it's a contract. "But I want a backstory. Summer's got *layers*."

Lisa claps her hands together. "Yes! Okay, you once met a bear, stood tall, and scared it off. It was life-changing. And you *love* hockey and French fries smothered in gravy."

I groan. "This is going to be a disaster."

Lisa pushes me toward the door with an over-the-top grin, finger guns at the ready. "Now go next door to the Glacier Brewhouse for a cocktail with Kyle."

"*Kyle*? I'm pretending to be a Canadian yoga instructor, for a guy named *Kyle*," I mutter. Still, she's already pushing me out the door.

Glacier Brewhouse is where locals sip on craft Alaskan microbrews and cocktails, casually observing tourists while critiquing them, as if it were an Olympic event. I adjust the red beret and slide the clip out of my red hair, letting my curls cascade around my shoulders. I channel my inner *Summer*—standing tall, mostly nodding, and fighting the urge to slouch.

The date with Kyle—a rich guy new to Alaska because no one drops serious cash on a dating service if they're not loaded—starts out *fine.* I walk in, and a tall guy waves at me from the corner. He's wearing one of those "I'm here to be taken seriously" suits. I make my way to the table.

"Hi, I'm Au—*Summer,*" I say, sitting down and shaking his hand. He launches into some complicated financial planning spiel, and I actively dissociate. I nod randomly, wondering how long I need to sit here before I can call it a night.

Kyle leans forward, intrigued. "So, tell me more about your yoga philosophy."

I freeze. "Oh. Yeah. Uh..." I wave a vague hand. "I do... a lot of, um, moose-in-repose pose?"

He blinks. "Is that a real thing, or did you invent it?"

I nod sagely. "I create all sorts of Alaskan poses. The moose pose is all about inner stillness. Like when a moose stares you down on the road, facing off with a car with no fear, the confidence of winter tundra and summer city living."

Kyle makes a thoughtful noise. "Wow. Deep."

Oh my God, it worked.

I smile, a surge of victory filling me. This is going to be fine. At least, that's what I tell myself.

Just as I congratulate myself for managing to not be a total embarrassment in front of Kyle, a familiar figure slips past, brushing too close.

I feel the heat of her presence before I see her—the sexy, smug, *absolutely-too-hot* bartender from last night. Slate. She smirks directly at me as she passes, her leather pants practically making a *sound* as they stretch over her thighs.

I lift my cocktail, the colorful concoction looking more like a work of art than a drink, and give her my best "Don't say anything" look. She stares back at me, her grin wide enough to make me wonder if she can smell my panic.

"A friend of yours, or a yoga student?" Kyle asks, glancing between me and Slate's *goddess-like* figure.

"Uh..." I start, but Slate's already opening her mouth before I can think of a suitable lie.

"Well, well," Slate drawls, folding her arms over her toned, tattooed arms and leaning on the table uninvited but *definitely* providing a much-needed distraction. "If it isn't Miss Coors Lite drinker herself."

I internally combust. Outwardly, I sip my cocktail aggressively, as if the drink will somehow absorb my awkwardness. "Who drinks that cheap stuff?" I mutter, almost too quietly, but enough for her to hear.

Kyle glances between us, clearly bewildered. "How do you two know each other?"

Slate's grin turns wicked. "Oh, we've just met."

I consider faking my own death. A quick dive into the nearest decorative plant might be more graceful. "She's joking. She's an old friend," I manage, trying to keep my voice steady.

Slate raises an eyebrow, utterly unconvinced. "Yet, I feel like we just met yesterday."

Kyle's eyebrows knit together. "Wait. What's going on, Summer?"

I gulp. "She's just joking. Slate, this is Kyle. Kyle, Slate. She's a *great* storyteller and works over at Ronnie's Sushi."

Slate outright laughs, and I swear I can feel my life *sliding off the rails* at full speed. Kyle, bless his clueless heart, nods like this makes total sense.

I shoot Slate a desperate "Please, for the love of all things holy, let me survive this date" look. She winks and rubs her lips on the edge of her glass seductively.

My brain short-circuits.

Kyle, the oblivious charmer, offers, "A date with two beautiful ladies. The night just keeps getting better. I'll get you a drink, too. Anchorage

Cosmo, okay?" He gives Slate an enthusiastic thumbs-up before heading to the bar.

Slate turns to me, her eyes dancing with mischief. "So, tell me, *Summer*, are you an escort?"

I choke on my drink. And that's when my phone vibrates in my pocket.

Darius's text flashes across the screen. "I heard you're killing it as Summer. Also, you have to be at the temp agency by eight a.m. Don't be late, or I'll make your first gig something with spreadsheets and guys with calculators in their pockets."

Well, now my chaotic life choices have officially caught up with me. I suppress a groan and sip my drink like it's water, not a fancy, overpriced cocktail.

Slate keeps smirking, her eyes never leaving me. I, *Summer*, am doing my best not to burst into flames.

"Please," I say, waving my hand vaguely, "Do not say anything about my name or, uh, being an escort. I'm on this date as a favor to a friend."

"Okay, but," she says, leaning in a bit, "I want your number. And to show you why you're wasting your time dating businessmen." She gives me that *sinister* wink that makes my stomach flip.

"I am *not* interested," I reply firmly, taking another sip of my now-vexing drink—some sort of fancy Alaskan blueberry-infused concoction with a burnt dried orange slice garnish. It's ridiculous. But it looks beautiful.

"Right," I continue, mentally preparing my escape plan. The date has officially gone long enough, and Slate is one *sexy* walking disaster waiting to blow my cover wide open.

Kyle slides between us, placing a drink in front of Slate. She sips it, then licks her lips in a way that makes me think I might spontaneously combust into a heap of awkwardness. I wonder if she also specializes in converting bisexual girls to Team Lesbian because she *looks* ready to devour me, body and soul.

I need an exit strategy. And I need it *now*.

"Hey, Kyle," I say casually, touching his arm. He beams, looking like he's finally won the dating lottery. "Yeah?"

"You know who would *love* hearing more about your portfolio?" I gesture toward Slate, who raises an eyebrow, clearly *catching on* that she's about to be used like a voucher in a dating prize grab.

Kyle looks over, shrugs, and nods approvingly as if offering Slate as a "real estate *investment* opportunity" is normal. "Sure, why not?"

Slate, in her effortlessly cool way, turns her attention to Kyle and includes me like it's a cozy little chat between old friends.

"I'm enjoying our conversation..." Kyle says, his voice trailing off as Slate, with impeccable timing, starts asking him solid questions—probably skills honed during her time serving sushi rolls, not cocktails. I smile and sit back, relieved that the situation is slowly sliding out of my control.

But five minutes later, I've had enough.

"Right?" I say, hopping up from my chair. "And Slate is totally into real estate investment. She's got a few properties, right?"

"Oh, absolutely," Slate says smoothly, her voice dripping with fake enthusiasm. "And Summer,"—she looked at me pointedly—"you promised to text me about that property opportunity we discussed, right?" She holds out her phone, waiting for me to enter my *real* phone number.

I smile, and my insides *cringe*. "Of course, friend," I lie, typing in Lisa's number, *not mine*. "But, um, Kyle is way more into it." Another lie. "You two would totally hit it off." The biggest lie of all.

Slate gives me a sly smile and winks. "Glad we're on the same page."

I'm already moving. "Oh, you know," I say breezily, "Being a yoga teacher is all about waking early, so I should run." I clap her on the shoulder like we're lifelong pals.

"Enjoy!" I finish, pivoting and heading straight for the door.

Before either of them can respond, I'm weaving through the crowd, dodging barstools, tipsy patrons, and that embarrassing moment when you know you've just committed the *most* dramatic exit of all time.

"Hey, Aurora! Summer!" Slate calls after me, her voice rich with amusement—and a hint of *seductive* annoyance peppered with a threat.

I do not look back.

I do not falter.

I do not acknowledge the sound of my real name being used and pray that Kyle isn't going to be super-mad and complain to Lisa's dating agency.

Pushing through the door into the cold, crisp Alaskan night, I take a deep breath and pull out my phone. I transfer funds into my checking account—goodbye, dangerously low balance—and swipe open my alarm app. 6:30 a.m. on Monday.

I've got my first day of work at the temp agency ahead. Because, despite tonight's chaos, one thing is clear—I'm *absolutely* slaying this whole adulthood thing.

Probably.

Maybe.

Okay, at least I'm trying.

I pull the itchy beret off and stuff it in my pocket. With my phone in one hand, I strut toward my car. Behind me? One confused investment bro and one aggressively sexual lesbian. Ahead of me? A new day. A normal day. And definitely, one where I won't have to lie about being a Canadian yoga instructor *ever again*.

Right?

Chapter 6

Unexpectedly Steamy Job Interview

"*Aurora!* About time you got here! Ready to dazzle the boss?" Darius's voice practically bounces off the walls as he leans against the office door, his fingers drumming with way too much excitement for a Monday morning.

I swallow hard, feeling my nerves whip into a frenzy like an Alaskan blizzard in the middle of July.

I glance down at my mismatched shoes—one blue, one black. Darn, my foggy-morning brain. I blame this shoe fiasco on Lisa and her *forced* date last night. No, seriously, the *one* time I could've given my shoes a second look, I got roped into helping Lisa with her matchmaking nonsense. Story of my life.

Darius catches my glance and doesn't miss a beat. "I told her you're so amazing that even with those mismatched shoes, she'll still impress." His playful smirk makes me want to curl up into a ball and never leave this hallway.

I laugh, finger guns blazing, shrugging innocently as if I meant to do this all along.

"Darius, what exactly did you tell your boss about me? Because, honestly, I'm a little scared of what you said to hype me up."

"Nothing but the truth, girlfriend." Darius links his arm through mine, and we sashay down the hallway like a fabulous power duo. He starts humming Katy Perry's "Fight Song" like it's the theme music to my life, and, honestly? It *kinda* feels like it.

As we approach the office, my heart does a stupid little flip when I spot her through the glass. It's the stranger who rescued me at Ronnie's.

She's standing there in all her messy-haired, chiseled-jawed, effortlessly-cool glory. Her white shirt is unbuttoned just enough to reveal a hint of something under it—and she's rocking red canvas shoes like she's been doing it her entire life. My heart *skips*.

And then I remember her scent and smile, and a flicker of lust tickles me–I almost giggle.

I gasp involuntarily, completely forgetting how to breathe. *This is bad.*

Before I can scramble for words, the door swings open, and out walks the stylish Latino guy that I saw at Ronnie's with her. He's chuckling about something, and the hot, badass business woman's voice floats after him. "I'd hardly call your balls a special delivery," she offers with a stiff laugh.

Darius—never one to miss an opportunity for a snarky comment—whispers, eyes locked on the guy. "Alexis, I'd call his balls an *extra-special delivery*," he says, his glib remark making my cheeks go from pale to flaming red.

Alexis catches sight of me, her smile widens, and the corner of her eyes crinkle, making my heart go into overdrive.

I'm caught staring at her, and I have absolutely no control over the blush spreading across my face. "Ah, hi!" I manage, completely failing at looking like a functional human being.

"You're Aurora!" Alexis greets me with a warm, teasing grin. "What brings you here today?"

"Alexis, this is my friend I told you about," Darius jumps in before I can say anything.

"Well, I have a job interview with you, I guess," I mumble, fiddling with the strap of my purse.

Because who needs to be confident and poised when they have mismatched shoes and the nerves of a squirrel on espresso, right?

"You're hired, Princess Ariel," the ridiculously good-looking model with too many abs quips, spinning me like I'm a ballroom dancer's dream. I don't even know what to do with my arms as he twirls me, and for a split second, I'm pretty sure I black out from the sheer ridiculousness of it all.

Ever the professional, Alexis shoots him a withering look before quickly opening the office door. "Get out of here, Richard," she says, a hint of exasperation in her voice. "Sorry, that's my partner."

"Partner?" I blurt before Alexis can respond.

With a wink, Richard adds, "The guy she just can't seem to best," just as Alexis shoots him another *death glare* and practically pushes him out of the office.

I stumble slightly as I process that delightful tidbit of information. "Are you sure this is a good time?" I ask, now feeling like I might actually combust from embarrassment and adrenaline.

Alexis's grin stretches wider. "Perfect timing, actually. Please, have a seat." She gestures toward the chair with a fluid, effortless motion like everything about her is designed to make me feel both nervous and at ease at the same time. She tilts her head slightly. "I didn't know you were an accountant?"

I blink hard. "An accountant?" I repeat, giving Darius the most *unamused* look I can muster.

Darius just grins and whispers, "You got this, girl!" Then, he practically skips out of the office, leaving me alone with Alexis.

I sit down, adjusting my skirt like I know what I'm doing, but my hands shake slightly. I clear my throat to avoid sounding like a total disaster. "I had no idea you were the manager at this agency," I say, trying to break the ice. "Darius doesn't talk about work much, but he seems to enjoy it here."

"Yeah, I'm a bit young, right? It's a family business. My dad started it, and I'm running things for him. Don't let my hero, handyman vibe fool you. I'm a very serious boss," she says in a serious tone, then cracks a smile.

I nod, more at ease, and repeat the line I practiced in the car. "Darius thinks I would be a good fit here. I'm really hoping to become a part of the team."

Alexis raises an eyebrow, which is now making me more self-aware. "Glad that Darius likes how I run the show around here. He's a great employee. The business is doing well and always looking for more team members."

"Running the show, huh?" I reply, attempting to sound cool even though I feel like melting into the chair. "You definitely look like you've got everything under control."

She shrugs, her confidence practically radiating off her. "I don't like to brag, but... yeah. I do."

Her voice is smooth and controlled—just the right amount of confidence to make my heart trip over itself. I shift in my seat, trying to focus on anything but the warmth spreading across my cheeks. "I bet you're the kind of boss who gets exactly what she wants."

Alexis clears her throat and doesn't respond. She pulled out a printed sheet that must be my resume, which Darius had created. Then, she leans back in her chair slightly, letting the silence hang between us like she's waiting for me to fill it. *God, this woman's power is unreal.*

I'm about to speak, but my mind blanks. Darius was wrong—I'm not prepared for this at all. I'm wearing mismatched shoes, nervous as hell, and now I've got this ridiculously attractive woman looking at me like she wants to know everything about me.

"So, *Aurora*," Alexis says, breaking the silence with a hint of playfulness. "What made you want to join us?"

My brain stutters. *What made me want to join?* Right, okay, I have to answer this like I'm a professional, not a flustered mess.

"Uh, well..." I start, pausing to gather myself. "I like challenges? I'm good at them? And, uh... the opportunity seemed like something I couldn't pass up." I cringe internally.

Alexis's eyes flicker with interest as she watches me stumble over my words. Then, her lips curve into a knowing smile, and I swear the room gets slightly warmer.

"I see," she says softly, leaning forward slightly and making my pulse race again. "Well, I'm sure you'll do great."

Alexis grins, flipping open a folder. "So, Aurora Thompson, tell me about your experience with office temp work."

"Oh, I'm an expert." I clasp my hands, hoping confidence will mask my absolute lack of experience. "I've done... so much temping."

Alexis quirks an eyebrow. "Yeah?"

"Yep." I nod way too enthusiastically. "I mean, I was just tempting...erm... I mean temping, the other day. And, technically, all my past jobs were temporary. Because I didn't stay with them for long."

Alexis stares at me for a beat, then laughs—a full, genuine laugh that makes my stomach flip. "You're honest. I appreciate that."

She flips a page in her folder. "Alright. Let's see what we've got here... Darius wrote, 'Accounting whiz, financial genius, human ca lculator.'" She lifts an eyebrow. "That true?"

I let out a strangled laugh. "Oh, for sure. I once calculated exactly how many dates it would take for me to afford a new pair of winter boots. I made a spreadsheet and everything. I do extra work taking on last minute dates for a dating agency that is a part-time gig. Turns out I didn't need the spreadsheet or formula, because I got dumped before dessert."

Alexis chuckles. "Creative budgeting. I respect it. What about your weaknesses?"

"You'd probably never guess, but I've got a bad picker," I say, biting my bottom lip with honesty.

"A bad picker?"

"It's genetic," I explain. "My mom picked a deadbeat dad, and now if I walk into a room of people, I'll immediately fall for the person who's in between jobs and lives in their mom's basement."

Alexis laughs and says, "I was expecting you to say spreadsheets or something like that."

Spreadsheets. That's not my problem, and I love a good spreadsheet to organize. I'm not an official accountant, but I can enter numbers into a spreadsheet. Darius sold me as a math prodigy, and I won't disappoint him. I'm a winning math-lete competitor. I nod with confidence I do not have. "Oh, absolutely. Love spreadsheets. Rows, columns... so organized. So... titillating." My cheeks redden even more with my jumbled response.

Alexis lifts a brow. "Great. Because we've got a client's massive payroll reconciliation to tackle. I'd love to see your skills on that project."

I swallow hard. "Oh. Yay." I am the one who can hardly balance my bank account and is in charge of payroll.

Alexis presses her lips together like she's trying to suppress another laugh. "You're not what I expected, but I like the unexpected."

For a moment, the air shifts. Her smile softens, and I suddenly become hyper-aware of our closeness. There's a flicker in her eyes, something warm, amused, intrigued.

I force myself to look at anything other than her sultry brown eyes. "Sooo, does that mean I'm hired?"

Alexis pretends to think it over, tapping her pen against her chin. "How do you feel about office chaos? The occasional emergency coffee run? And your friend Darius dramatically quitting every other Friday?"

"I can handle that," I say as professionally as I can, starting to wonder how I am going to survive working for a sexy woman I've been fantasizing about at night since we met.

Alexis slides her short, manicured thumb down a legal pad, poised after her next question. "What's your skill level with Excel and Microsoft Office software?"

"Expert level. I started business classes at University of Anchorage when I was in high school so I've used the newest version of excel, creating charts, inserting graphs, and all of that," I explain, ready to demonstrate.

Gripping the pen in her large fingers, Alexis scribbles my answer. I imagine Alexis, still in her tailored suit, above me, pinning my wrists with her firm grip. I would like to ask about her skill level on a few things.

"Where do you see yourself in ten years?" she asks.

"In ten years, I'll be running my own successful business, and probably married," I add with a giggle. "Sorry, I might be oversharing since I've been making my vision board, but hashtag visionboardgoals, right."

Alexis nods appropriately and says, "I'm a believer in writing down goals and manifesting. That's how it's done."

I add, "Of course, I need a J-O-B to pay my bills right now and then maybe I can afford my university classes. I'm starting business school. Really, I have business skills and an open schedule since it's summer, so I'm perfect for this position." The last line is the only other line I practiced for this interview, so I smiled that I got in both my lines.

She nods once I finish. "We need someone reliable and hardworking. From what Darius tells me, you fit the bill."

Relief washes over me. "I'll work hard. I promise."

Alexis smiles warmly. "Welcome aboard, Aurora. We'll start your training today, if you'd like."

"Thank you so much," I say, unable to contain my excitement. "I'm ready to start."

Alexis stands and offers her hand. "Any questions?" she asks as I grasp her hand and feel a spark of electricity course through me.

And suddenly, the world doesn't feel so terrifying. Maybe I'm a bit of a mess, but that's okay. Perhaps that's enough for Alexis to notice me or at least be intrigued by my chaotic energy.

Or maybe I'm just wishful thinking. Either way, I'm not leaving without giving it my all.

I flash Alexis a sheepish grin. "I'll do my best."

She doesn't answer immediately. She silently watches me like she's waiting for me to show her what *Aurora* is all about. And, for the first time in a while, I feel like maybe—just maybe—I've got this.

Alexis's smile deepens. "Consider yourself hired. I'll have Darius get you set up with payroll, and we'll get you started."

Bang! Bang! The door rattles from the firm knock, and Alexis's partner swings it open before Alexis responds.

"You left this in my car," he winks at me and then turns to face Alexis. "And I refilled it at Kaladi's Coffee downstairs for you." He hands the mug to Alexis and gives her a playful punch on the arm.

"Thanks. I'll buy you coffee tomorrow," Alexis says, taking a sip and raising the cup in appreciation.

"You'll need the caffeine to keep up with me."

Their banter and warm vibes are as sweet as the vanilla I smell in her steaming coffee. It makes me wish I had a partner.

Alexis shakes her head. "I'm only four years older than you."

Watching them tease each other is both heartwarming and a little painful. I can't help but yearn for a partner who surprises me with coffee, still wants to come home with me, and can't wait to visit me at work. And then, a pang of guilt hits me—why did I ever let myself fantasize about Alexis—my new, utterly off-limits boss?

"Errm. Sorry. Aurora," Alexis says as her partner saunters out with a wave.

"I know you're busy," Richard says over his shoulder to Alexis. "Aurora, please excuse my rude interruption."

"Nice to meet you, again," my glossed lips respond automatically.

The whiff of bitter espresso and sharp vanilla notes hang in the air from the coffee, and the click of the door shutting brings my attention back to Alexis and our interview.

"Any questions for me?" Alexis asks.

What's it gonna take for you to switch sides and date me? I glance again at her red shoes, my fingers itching to touch her and make a more intimate connection. Biting my lower lip, I shake my head and smile.

"Thank you," I smile to confirm my interest, and my hand tingles with her touch as I give her my medium-firm handshake.

As I walk out of her office, I can't help but feel a sense of disbelief. Not only did I land the job, but Alexis, the person that I couldn't stop thinking about, is my new boss. It's a lot to take in, but for the first time in a while, things are finally looking up.

I laugh, still dazed, as I stop abruptly at my friend's desk. "Darius, thanks for setting this up."

"No problem at all. Let's celebrate. Do you want a coffee from downstairs? Drinks are on me. New Co-worker!" Darius offers, giving me a playful nudge.

"Sure, thanks," I say, ready to get my caffeine on and start my first day.

Chapter 7

Aurora Thompson, Girl Boss in Training

The air in the Alaska Temp Agency buzzes with the frantic click-clack of keyboards and the hum of overworked computer fans. The training room feels less like an office and more like a high-stakes game show—Who Wants to Be Employed?—with everyone speed-typing like their rent depends on it.

Spoiler—mine does.

The scent of stale coffee mixes with that oddly metallic tang of new electronics. Outside, imposing mountains gleam under the blinding Alaskan sun, mocking the fact that I'm stuck inside doing online orientation modules on "email tone" and "ethic policies."

Darius slides into the chair beside me like he owns the building.

"Boom," he announces, tossing his pink silk-lined coat over the back of the chair. "Capitalism has arrived—and she's moisturized."

I stare at him, blinking. "You wear *that,* and I'm the one who got the sign-on bonus?"

His outfit sells his flamboyant manager vibes, with the checkered blazer, pink silk bow tie, and high-waisted trousers tailored within an inch of their life. Here I am, in a black skirt that kept trying to climb up my thighs. My emerald blouse is safety-pinned at the chest because there's too much gap between the buttons to be work-appropriate.

"My outfit says, 'Please don't regret hiring me.' Yours is saying, 'I'm the next CEO, watch me slay.'"

Darius twirls in his chair and laughs like a Disney villain. "Oh honey, you look great. Very... *young intern in a Hallmark movie about to win over her intimidating, but hot, boss and move back to her small town to open a bookstore.*"

"Helpful," I mutter, trying to smooth down the wispy red flyaways behind my ears. I cross my ankles and shift in my seat, like if I fold myself up small enough, no one will notice how long and awkward my legs look. I am all limbs and no grace, some weird human ruler taking up too much space.

The truth is, I *am* trying to impress someone—Alexis. My new boss. Possibly my new mentor, in her sharp suits and statement shoes, if I play my cards right.

I haven't seen her yet this morning. Not that I'm watching the hallway like a hawk or anything.

"So," Darius drawls, pulling me back to earth, "how's my favorite newly employed bestie adjusting to corporate life?"

I give a little shimmy smile. "Pretty good. I already spent half my bonus on rent, groceries and new shoes, and now I'm trying to prove I'm not a total fraud to the woman who may or may not hold the future of my career in her hands."

Darius raises his brows. "Wait—bonus? We're doing those now? Since when do temps get benefits *and* bonuses?"

I flush. "I didn't ask for it. Alexis just... gave it to me. Said something about recognizing hustle."

"Girl," Darius whispers with full dramatic flair, "she sees you—and all that untapped, dazzling potential."

I snort. "Please. She probably skimmed that resume *you* made and thought she was hiring a licensed CPA. Then I showed up, babbled through the interview, and she realized I was just desperate enough not to ghost orientation."

"No," he says, bumping my shoulder. "She's playing chess. Everyone else is playing checkers. She knows talent when she sees it."

I look down at my perfectly alphabetized stack of training forms. "I just don't want to let her down."

"You won't," Darius says, softer and more serious. "You belong here. And for the record? Alexis doesn't hand things out to just anyone. She probably has a whole spreadsheet tracking ROI on your potential."

That makes my heart do an embarrassing little flutter. I picture her in her glass-walled office, quirky heels on the desk, sipping coffee from some sleek ceramic mug while making billion-dollar deals and casually conquering the world.

Does she drink cold brew? Maybe that cinnamon oat milk thing I tried once and pretended to like? Wait—no, she drinks vanilla Americano's, I'd guess. Her partner brought it in yesterday. Right. Serious caffeine and vanilla. Smooth, aggressive, sweet, entirely out of my league.

"Earth to Aurora," Darius says, waving a hand in front of my face. "You just blacked out for a full ten seconds."

"I was thinking," I say quickly, "about productivity. And caffeine."

My phone buzzes. I glance down and wince.

"Speak of the guilt-trip," I mutter. "It's my mom."

Darius leans over and stage-whispers, "You can take personal calls as long as you're not within earshot of the boss or working for a client. Just don't start trauma-dumping in the break room like Melody did yesterday."

I take a breath and answer. "Hey, Mom."

"Aurora! Finally, I thought you'd forgotten about your poor, neglected mother. The one who *birthed* you."

Yup. There it is. Full-on dramatic flair with a twist of passive aggression.

"I left you a voicemail this morning," I say, trying to keep my voice light. "Wanted to tell you I got the job."

"Oh, *darling*, you wouldn't believe my day. The cat threw up, and my neighbor—Bob—locked himself out again, and then the gas company—"

I tune out. After five minutes of narration about everything *except* my news, I gently interrupt her.

"Anyway, Mom, I've gotta go. New job and all."

"Alright, alright," she sighs. "Don't forget to call your loving mother once in a while."

"Of course. Bye, Mom."

As the call ends, something old and prickly twists in my chest. I shove it down. Unlike Melody, my trauma stays buried.

Darius looks at me with all-knowing eyes and raises a brow. "Was that... the guilt train pulling into the station?"

"First-class ticket," I say, forcing a smile. "Let's just say nothing new is happening with my mom."

"Oh honey," Darius says, "Don't worry about her drama. I'm happy you are here and you'll get proper experience to put on your resume so next time you won't even have to lie. "

I squeeze my cold hands together as his kind words flash me back to months ago when our high school's winter break ended last year.

It's freezing. The kind of cold that bites through my coat and settles in my spine. Snowflakes drift down like they've got nowhere urgent to be—pretty, soft liars. I'm shivering in front of the school's locked glass doors, arms crossed tight, debating if losing a toe is worth waiting one more minute.

My phone's dead. My ride? Even bleaker.

Mom was supposed to pick me up after the Debate Club.

She doesn't.

Instead, a miracle rolls into the parking lot, tires crunching snow—Darius's mom in her slightly dented silver Jeep, window already rolled down, heat blasting like an angelic furnace.

"Aurora, sweetie!" she calls, leaning over the passenger seat. "Get in before you turn into a popsicle!"

I don't hesitate. I yank the door open and slide into the backseat beside Darius. He's still wearing his debate medal and a smug little smile. Without a word, he shoves a half-empty cup of gas station hot chocolate into my hands.

"She forgot, didn't she?" he asks gently.

"She probably got busy," I mumble, sipping. It warms my tongue, and I hold on like it's life support. "She works at the school, y'know? She has, like, a million kids to think about."

He doesn't say anything. He doesn't have to. His mom clucks her tongue like a concerned auntie with a sixth sense.

"I hear you're already taking classes at the university?" she says, glancing at me in the rearview mirror. "That's incredible. A high school senior already in college? You're a genius, Aurora. Your mom must be bursting with pride."

I smile. It's tight. Polite. Practiced.

I don't correct her.

The Jeep smells like cinnamon gum and old pine air fresheners, and I let myself sink into it, let the heat thaw my fingers, let the warmth of people who notice me settle in my bones.

When we pull up to my house, the porch light flickers like it's unsure whether I deserve illumination. I mutter thanks, climb out, and crunch through icy gravel to the front door.

Inside, the TV blares. Real Housewives drama echoing through the living room. Mom's sprawled on the couch, a crinkly bag of nachos in her lap, remote in one hand, phone in the other.

She doesn't even glance up.

"Mom," I say, standing in the entryway, coat still zipped, backpack still on. My fingers tremble as I pull the letter from my pocket. "I got the scholarship. The one I wrote the essay for—remember?"

She squints at the screen and doesn't pause it.

"That's... embarrassing," she mutters, barely loud enough for me to hear over the fake drama on TV. "People'll think you only got it because I work at the school. You don't need college, Aurora. I didn't go, and I turned out fine."

I stand in my thrift store coat with my big-deal scholarship letter crinkling in my hand, my heart sinking.

She doesn't ask to see it.

Doesn't hug me.

Doesn't even say "congrats."

I swallow the lump in my throat and nod like I agree, like she's right, like I'm not unraveling in silence.

Later, in my room, I lie on my unmade bed, phone charging on the floor, and text Darius:

"Your mom's fab. Also, thank her for the hot chocolate. I got the scholarship."

He replies with eight sparkle emojis and a TikTok of a raccoon stealing a bagel.

I laugh. It's quiet, small. But it's real.

I should've stayed in that Jeep. Should've let Mrs. Martinez adopt me and renamed myself Aurora Martinez.

Darius's voice pulls me out of my emotional sinkhole. "You okay?" he asks, brows knit. Concern replaces the usual sparkle in his eyes. "You've got that faraway look, like someone just brought up cafeteria pizza and trauma."

I huff a laugh, blinking fast. "Something like that."

He leans closer. "You know I'd never let anyone bully you. Not then, not now. I'd fight a teenager. With rings on."

"I know," I say, giving him a grateful smile. "I'm lucky to have you—and Lisa, of course. I wouldn't have survived high school without my glam squad."

"Oh please," he says, hand to chest like I wounded him. "You were like a feral fox we had to slowly domesticate with patience, flair, and Lisa's tragically chaotic dating advice."

I snort. "Still can't believe she works at a dating agency and is helping with developing a new dating app for Alaska. She doesn't know how to copy and paste in Microsoft Word. And she once set me up with a guy that was so short he looked like someone I was babysitting."

"That was an iconic disaster," he sighs, deeply nostalgic. "But! Enough about Lisa's crimes against romance. I'm going to get you set up with the perfect temp job. Something where you shine, maybe wear a side braid, give off major business bitch energy."

I finger-gun him. "My career destiny is in your hands. Just don't make me work at fast food or at a botox clinic."

"I would *never.* Now doing the payroll for a fast food restaurant... maybe."

I laugh again, but my fingers stray to the slight crease between my brows—the one that always appears when I think too hard about my mom.

"You get that wrinkle when she crosses your mind," Darius says softly, catching it like always. "You are moved out and you don't need her, Ro. She's toxic."

"But she's my mom," I mumble, like it's some sacred, binding excuse. "She's... all I've got."

He reaches for my hand across the shared desk space, squeezing gently. "Family isn't about blood. It's about who actually shows up. And she hasn't."

I nod, swallowing hard. "Just thinking about the past makes me extra glad to be out of there."

"Then don't look back," he says, straightening up like he's about to conduct a symphony. "Today is a fresh chapter. We're talking full-time, fun, and fabulous. Get those forms done, and I'll work my matchmaking magic to find you the perfect job match."

"I think Alexis already has something in mind," I say, fiddling with my pen.

He perks up. "The Boss mentioned a job? What's the gig?"

"Accounting."

He wrinkles his nose. "Ugh. Death by spreadsheets."

"You told her I was good at spreadsheets," I shoot back, mock-offended. "And hello, business major here. Numbers are my love language."

Darius fake-gags. "Fine. Accounting it is."

He's mid-sip of his latte when his phone lights up. His smile flickers quickly across his face before he locks it again.

I arch a brow. "Lisa?"

"Nah."

No group text? Hmm. Maybe a new boyfriend? I suppress a grin. Darius deserves good things. We both do.

I dive back into the training modules with a renewed purpose. The online orientation swears it'll take two to five days to complete. I decide I'd do it in one afternoon out of sheer determination to be the best employee and working as a temp as soon as possible.

Click. Privacy policy. Click. Office dress code. Click. Workplace safety video narrated by a cartoon bear.

My fingers blur across the keyboard. I'm working. I'm earning. I'm proving that I belong here. I'm not just some temp mistake who lucked into a sign-on bonus. That I'm worth someone taking a chance on me—even Alexis.

Especially Alexis.

She's a powerhouse, and somehow, she saw something in me. Maybe she sees more than I do. Perhaps she believes in me... which is terrifying because I don't know if I believe in me yet.

And office romance? I'm a little star-struck by her boss bitch energy, but that's all it was because she has a hot boyfriend, *and* she's my boss.

This is about a job and nothing more, not romance, and most definitely not the l-word. People say they *love you* all the time with no meaning. My mom only said it as punctuation. *Love you, bye. Love you, now go get the remote. Love you, but don't embarrass me again.* It never meant much. Not in the moments that mattered.

So when people talk about love—whether it's romantic or just emotional support—I don't buy it. Not unless they *show* it. Words are cheap. My mom said, "I love you," all the time, but she never showed up when it actually mattered.

But maybe... maybe this job is a step toward figuring out what real support looks like.

Not that I'm totally lost. I've got ride-or-die support. Darius, who once saved me from a makeup emergency in the cafeteria line with his glitter survival kit, and Lisa, who keeps setting me up on her little gigs of tragic dates, but hey—she's trying. Effort counts.

"Thank you again," I say quietly, glancing at him. "For getting me this job. For everything, really."

Darius takes one last sip of his coffee and scans the buzzing training room like a benevolent queen. Everyone is in today for a new mandatory training about client confidentiality–I already finished it online.

"Honestly? You'd probably still be waiting outside high school if I hadn't rescued you," he whispers so none of the other twenty employees in the room will hear him.

I grin. "True."

"I'm serious," he says. "You're not going back. Not to her, not to that past version of you who didn't think she was worthy of anything good."

I nod, eyes flicking toward the hallway again. There's a rhythmic *click-click-click* of heels on the tile. My heart leaps.

Please be Alexis.

Please don't let my blouse be gapping.

Please let me look like I belong here.

I straighten my stack of forms for the sixth time. Because if I can't control how fast my pulse goes when Alexis walks by, I can at least control the stack of paperwork.

My phone vibrates.

"Did you say something about working a temp job? That sounds terrible! I told you living on your own would be harder than you thought, but you wouldn't listen to your dear old mom."

Chapter 8

Temp Job, Permanent Sass

My hand shakes, trying to silence, then turn off my phone completely. The buzzing ruins all the confidence I built.

Mom. Seriously, *seriously*? Getting a job, living on my own, and making a plan to start university is good. Like, capital-G *GOOD*. But all she could focus on was the temp agency, the negative nature of it all. Next, she'll remind me of how I'm probably going to end up back on her couch, eating frozen dinners and regretting every life choice I've ever made.

My carefully constructed wall of "I've got this!" crumbles like a glacier calving into the Bering Sea. *It's not fair.* I'm trying. I'm *really* trying. This job with Alexis, winning the scholarship to help with some of the tuition, saving up for the rest of the university costs – it's everything I'm hustling for. But my Mom's voice worms its way in, all critical and undermining. Suddenly, I'm an awkward middle schooler again, tripping over my own feet and saying all the wrong things.

I'm not in the training room anymore. I'd mumbled something about needing air. Now, I'm huddled in the tiny, windowless supply closet, surrounded by enough paperclips and manila folders to build a fort of despair. Tears well up, hot and stinging. Not the dramatic, movie-worthy kind, but the silent, shoulder-shaking ones that come when you feel like you're out of options.

A soft knock on the door makes me jump. I sniffle, trying to sound casual. "Occupied!" My voice cracks on the last word, betraying my Oscar-worthy performance.

The door creaks open anyway, and Alexis is standing there, silhouetted against the office light. My breath hitches. *Of all people.*

"Aurora? You okay?" Her usual confident tone is softer, laced with a genuine note of concern that throws me off balance.

I scrub at my eyes with the back of my hand, probably smearing mascara everywhere. "Yeah, fine. Just... admiring your extensive collection of label makers." My attempt at a joke falls flatter than a cement pancake.

She doesn't buy my story for a second. Alexis leans against the doorframe, her arms crossed, her sharp gaze surprisingly gentle. "You don't sound fine."

I sigh, the fight draining out of me. What's the point of pretending? She probably sees right through my usual sparkly façade anyway. "It was my mom," I mumble, looking down at my mismatched socks. "Just... you know. Mom stuff."

"Not the supportive kind, I gather?" Alexis's tone is understanding, almost... knowing?

I manage a weak, watery laugh. "Supportive in theory. Critical in practice. Apparently, being a temp isn't a 'real job,' even if it's paying my bills and not involving me dressing up as a giant hotdog."

A small smile plays on Alexis's lips. "Hotdog gigs have their own merits, I'm sure."

"Oh, trust me, they don't," I say, my voice still thick with unshed tears. "It's just... I got this scholarship, which is huge for me, and all she could talk about was how I'm probably going to fail at this temp thing and end up a disappointment. Again." The last word comes out as a choked sob, surprising even myself.

The emotion hits me in a wave. Suddenly, I can't hold it in anymore. The tears start falling for real now, fat, clumsy drops hitting the dusty floor. I turn away, mortified. Alexis, my intimidating, effortlessly cool boss, is witnessing my complete and utter unraveling in a supply closet. This is not how I envisioned impressing her this afternoon.

"Hey," Alexis says softly, stepping fully into the small space. The scent of her perfume – something crisp and sophisticated – fills the air. She doesn't touch me, but her presence is a quiet comfort. "It's okay."

"No, it's not," I say, my voice muffled by my hands. "I'm supposed to be this optimistic hustler, right? The one who can turn any disaster into a funny story. But sometimes... sometimes I just feel like I'm not enough. I'll never find my place and fit in. Like she's right."

There's a beat of silence. Then Alexis speaks, her voice low and surprisingly vulnerable. "Everyone feels like that sometimes, Aurora. Even the people who look like they have it all figured out."

I finally look up, my eyes blurry. "You?" It's hard to imagine someone as put-together as Alexis ever doubting herself.

She gives a small, almost self-deprecating shrug. "Trust me. The pressure to have it all together, to meet expectations... it's a universal language."

Her honesty catches me off guard. It's like seeing a glimpse behind the perfectly tailored suit and confident smile. "But... you're Alexis Anders," I say, still a little teary. "You *do* have it all figured out."

She shakes her head slightly. "Not always. My dad... he has very specific ideas about how this agency should be run. And sometimes, no matter how hard I work, it feels like I'm constantly trying to prove myself." Her gaze softens, meeting mine with an unexpected warmth. "Just like you are."

The shared vulnerability hangs in the air between us. It's a moment of unexpected connection, a crack in the professional façade that allows a sliver of something real to shine through.

"So," Alexis says after a moment, a hint of her usual playful tone returning, "label makers can wait. How about we get you some coffee or a muffin? My treat."

I sniffle again, a small smile finally breaking through. "Only if you promise not to tell anyone I had a meltdown in the office supply closet."

She grins a genuine, unguarded smile that makes my heart do a little flutter. "My lips are sealed."

As we step out of the supply closet, the Alaska sunshine streaming through the office windows suddenly seems a little brighter. The weight on my chest hasn't completely vanished, but it feels a little lighter. Maybe, just maybe, I'm not carrying it all alone. And maybe, Alexis isn't just my boss after all. Maybe, we could be friends.

At the end of my shift, my brain is only half-committed to the training modules. The rest is busy daydreaming about Alexis and side-eyeing Darius flirting with some new guy.

Honestly? I envy him. Darius says what he thinks, handles drama like a pro, and never apologizes for being fabulous. Meanwhile, I once apologized to a Starbucks barista for ordering off-menu. Twice.

He laughs and tucks away his phone.

"Your sass is unmatched," I whisper, shaking my head.

"Darling, I'm not here for matches. I'm the whole fire." He lowers his voice dramatically. "But really, how does it feel to be officially employed? Future Boss Bitch."

I shrug. "Honestly? Kind of amazing. I've got a job, a little money in my account, and this whole 'functioning adult' thing is starting to feel slightly less impossible and almost manageable."

Darius's phone buzzes. He peeks and smirks. "Another contender for my social calendar. They just keep coming to be roasted today."

"Be gentle," I say.

"Never," he says, texting away as he checks his email for the last time.

I log off and start tucking away the messy paperwork.

"Guess what? Alexis texted me. Your assignment starts tomorrow. Downtown government office. It's chill. You'll probably just sit there and look competent."

"Yes! Okay. Now, what does one wear to look both competent and hireable for a full-time position I may or may not beg them to offer me permanently?"

Darius lights up. "Office fashion montage time."

"No shopping!" I wave my hands. "Remember? I have exactly one pair of new shoes."

I cross my legs to show off my shiny, flat, black Mary Janes.

He gasps. "Those are cute! Classic. Now we build around them. Come over tonight. My mom's got business clothes for days and she's still high off watching *The Devil Wears Prada* again."

"You sure she won't mind?"

"She'll love it. You're her favorite adopted daughter, but don't tell Lisa I said that. Mom said you made that dress you borrowed for graduation look like couture."

"Okay," I say, smiling. "But I'm not letting you put me in pearls."

"We'll compromise. Sweater set and a power bun."

"I guess I'm lucky your mom is tall. My limbs are already long enough—I look like a redheaded stork in heels."

Darius steps back and surveys me like a tailor. "What you see as stork, I see as statuesque. Amazonian, even. We're going for 'future CEO,' not 'nervous intern hiding behind the water cooler.'"

"You're really good at this," I admit.

"I know," he says, unbothered. "Let's make them see what I already know—you're worth it."

I blink, my heart stuttering, not because of the compliment but because someone meant it.

"You're the best, Darius," I whisper.

He wraps me in a tight hug. "You too, girl. I'm always here. Always."

Chapter 9

Oops, I Did It Again

"No one uses copiers anymore," Lisa types in our Glam Squad group chat. "The only reason to have a copy room is for making out with coworkers or as a hideout for scrolling social media."

She adds a winking emoji for emphasis because, of course, she does.

I swipe *Mute* on my phone and shove it into my pocket, resisting the urge to roll my eyes. This is my first real job—well, a temp job—but still. Someone has to maintain at least the illusion of professionalism around here.

Technically, I'm a Deferred Compensation Specialist, which sounds very important but mostly means glorified paper-pusher. I shuffle retirement files, print out pension forms, and offer a sympathetic nod whenever someone panics about their 401(k). It's not glamorous, but it's a paycheck—and right now, I'd alphabetize fish guts at a cannery if it meant I could afford rent.

At least this first temp assignment is blissfully low-stress. Filing and data entry are nothing compared to the anxiety of watching your bank account dwindle. At the same time, college costs loom in the distance like a financial horror monster in my closet, waiting.

My phone buzzes again. A text from Jamie:

"Need assistance in the copy room"

Right. The copy room.

The infamous Copy/Fax Room is the stuff of workplace legend. Every office has one. It's quiet. Windowless. Soundproof. It smells vaguely like plastic and toner. If there's a steamy office romance unfolding, odds are, it starts here. And the thought of a clandestine moment in that tucked-away room sends a jolt of hot electricity through my spine.

Still, I play it cool. I grab a random file and casually stroll through the office like another underpaid government employee on an extremely *normal* errand.

The office hums with soft chaos—phones ringing, printers beeping, someone in the next row over launching into a passionate rant about which Costco location has the best free samples—spoiler: it's the southside one. The air smells like over-brewed coffee, plastic binders, and low-key panic. It's comforting in a weirdly bleak way.

I glance around my cubicle before leaving. It's an organizational masterpiece, inherited from the previous employee who, I'm told, was a legend in their own right—until a medical emergency knocked them out of commission. Their misfortune became my opportunity. Every file is labeled. Every sticky note is color-coded. It's like being gifted a pre-organized life. Stress-free. Barely supervised. A dream gig.

My manager—whose name might as well be "Guy Who Occasionally Drops Folders on My Desk Without Making Eye Contact"—barely remembers I exist. That's fine. Keeps the pressure low.

And then there's Jamie.

My current workplace crush-slash-situationship-slash... honestly? I don't even know.

We hit it off fast. She helped me figure out the lunchroom microwave settings on my first day. By that evening, we were watching Netflix at her condo, which overlooked the bay like a movie set. I've lived in Anchorage my whole life. Still, I've never been inside one of *those* homes—the kind with floor-to-ceiling windows, modern art, and zero evidence of financial stress.

Jamie doesn't just live in that world. She floats through it.

She's tall and lean, with the kind of nonchalant beauty that could land her in an indie fashion campaign. Her dark brown hair is cropped short and messy but somehow still perfect. She has that unbothered air that only people with wealthy parents and good bone structure can pull off. Probably skateboards. Probably sips iced lattes year-round. Probably doesn't own a single piece of fast fashion.

I reach the copy room, trying to tamp down the anticipation fluttering in my chest.

The door is propped open. Jamie leans casually against the counter, one hand resting on the copier like she invented it. She's wearing a navy button-down tucked into high-waisted slacks and a leather jacket slung over one shoulder—office casual meets accidental runway.

"Excuse me, Miss Office Worker," she says as I step inside, her voice low and laced with amusement. Her brown eyes glint with mischief. "I hear you have top-tier collating skills. I'm in desperate need of your professional expertise."

I raise a brow, playing along. "Professional expertise doesn't come cheap. What kind of assistance are we talking about?"

Jamie pushes off the copier and closes the door behind me with a soft click. Her fingers brush my hip on the way, light and teasing.

"I need someone to... properly pound in these staples," she says with mock seriousness, stepping into my space. "It's a two-person job. Very delicate. Very... hands-on."

I try to hold back a grin. "Are you seriously using office supply innuendos right now?"

"I'm a woman of many talents," she says, her voice dropping half an octave. Her fingers trail along my arm. "And you love my office jokes. Admit it."

I laugh, caught off-guard by how easily she disarms me. "I'm working," I say, though the breathiness in my voice completely betrays me.

"Oh, yeah?" Jamie murmurs, gently pinning one of my wrists to the countertop while her other hand slides up my side, settling right in that hollow just above my hip. "I thought this was a team project. You know, for employee morale."

I bite my lip, glancing toward the copier like it might save me. But it only hums its useless agreement. "And what exactly is in this for me?"

"Oh, I don't know," she says, grinning. "Maybe some personalized motivation? A little physical appreciation for all your hard work?"

Her mouth finds mine, soft and slow at first—testing. Her lips are warm and confident, tasting like mint and danger. She kisses like she knows I'll cave, and she's right. I do. I lean in, deepening the kiss, my hands sliding into her jacket, pulling her closer. Her body presses against mine, all lean muscle and sharp intent.

The copier whirs to life beneath us, and I nearly laugh—somewhere in the mash-up, a button got bumped. Papers spill out like confetti.

She pulls back slightly, breathless, eyes locked on mine. "God, you taste good," she says, licking her bottom lip. "Do you always make out like you've got a point to prove?"

"Only when I'm being evaluated on performance," I shoot back, trying not to visibly melt.

Jamie smirks, snags her newly stapled papers off the counter, and smooths her shirt like nothing happened. "So... after-work playtime this weekend? You free?"

I straighten my blouse and lift a brow, trying to collect what's left of my dignity. "I'll check my availability."

She shoots me one last smug grin before sauntering like a woman who just closed a deal. The door swings shut behind her with a satisfying whisper.

I exhale slowly, heart pounding, and pick up a pink pack of small sticky notes for appearances. Can't let anyone think I came in here just to get kissed senseless.

Not that they'd be wrong.

Darius's name flashes across my screen, followed by a text that's peak chaos energy:

"Are you alive or currently in copier-related peril? Have you horny girls forgotten this is a group chat?!"

I snort and type back, "Alive. Definitely in peril."

Before I can hit send, Lisa's message pops up like clockwork:

"Says the thirstiest guy we know!"

Darius ignores her, naturally, and fires back a personal message.

"I love office romance... Tell me everything."

"Romance—NO. Casual hot-and-heavy hookups—YES," I shoot back.

"More on this later. I'm working.No phones at work. Just finished my first solid week of employment and I am the picture of professionalism."

"Sleeping with coworkers = worse than phone use. FYI," he replies, with the breezy judgment of someone sipping a cold brew in silk pajamas.

"Jamie isn't a real coworker. She's an intern. Don't worry—it's fine," I write, then pause.

That's what I keep telling myself. It's fine. It's just fun. Just hot copy room chaos and zero strings. Definitely not me catching feelings or pretending like this temp job isn't the first time I've felt capable in forever.

I lean back in my squeaky government-issued swivel chair and contemplate texting Jamie to "help" with another mysterious stapling emergency. Maybe she's exactly the distraction I need from the slow, terrifying realization that I actually like working here.

Before I can spiral any deeper, my phone buzzes again—Lisa.

"I did a background check on Jamie. Clutch your pearls. I found her engagement announcement for the end of summer."

I frown. Excuse me, what?

My thumbs freeze mid-text as a photo loads. There she is—Jamie Gunderson in a Pinterest-perfect engagement shoot, beaming next to some tall, smug, yacht-club-type guy who probably owns multiple pairs of boat shoes. They're wrapped around each other like a couple straight off the front page of *White Linen Weddings Quarterly.* The caption reads:

"Jamie Gunnderson & Mark White—Summer Wedding at Alyeska Resort."

My jaw drops. I zoom in. Nope, not a doppelgänger. That is 1000% Jamie. Same flirty smile, the same expensive hair highlights, and the same black nail polish I thought was edgy. It's not so edgy when you're cheating on your fiancé during your government internship.

"OMG I'm the OTHER woman...the office secretary...ewww!" I text back in horror.

Lisa responds instantly with a skull emoji and:

"You better dump her before she cheats on you with her mailman too."

I want to argue. I really do. But she's right. Again.

Usually, I'd be annoyed that Lisa's running digital background checks on my hookups like she's the FBI, but today? I owe her a drink. Maybe two. Honestly, I should probably start Googling my dates. I've officially reached the "learning the hard way" phase of adulthood.

Also—what kind of psycho cheats *during* their engagement? Was I just... convenient? A temporary fling to spice up her bachelorette era?

I mean, sure, I knew this was casual. But still. I feel slimy.

I drop my forehead to my desk with a dramatic thunk.

This was supposed to be a fling. Now, it's a deleted LinkedIn post that is a click away from becoming a scandal. And the cherry on top? I've disappointed the two people I care most about impressing: Darius, who pulled strings to get me in here, and Alexis... the walking, talking contradiction of tattoos, confidence, and business blazers I might be crushing on.

Before I can mentally rehearse my apology tour, the clunky desk phone—yes, the actual landline phone I forgot even worked—starts ringing. The screen flashes "HR." My stomach drops so fast that I think I leave my soul behind near the filing cabinet.

Nope. Nope, nope, nope.

I consider letting it ring until it spontaneously combusts, but some self-preservation instinct takes over.

I pick up the receiver with a shaky hand.

"This is Aurora in the Deferred Comp Office," I say, doing my best impression of someone who knows what she's doing. Spoiler: I do not.

"Hi, Aurora. This is Beth from HR. How are you today?"

Beth sounds like she moonlights as an ice sculpture in the lobby. My heart jackknifes.

"Great!" I chirp, my voice several octaves too high. "Super great. Productive. Filing things. So many folders."

"We've been informed about an inappropriate relationship between you and an intern," she says, all business. "While your temp status exempts you from our full employee policies, I spoke with Jamie to evaluate your fit for a permanent position. Unfortunately, her report led us to decide not to extend an offer."

My body freezes, and my breath catches in my throat.

Permanent position?

I was about to be hired *permanently*?

Like regular paychecks? Health insurance? Tuition reimbursement?! A shiny, structured, grown-up job that would've made college financially possible?

Beth continues, completely unbothered.

"Your contract ends today. Your computer access has been terminated. Please return your keycard and parking pass before leaving the building. Thank you for your service."

Click.

She hangs up.

I stare at the phone like it just slapped me. Did I just get fired for... kissing someone in the copy room? Someone who was cheating on their fiancé *and* sabotaging my job behind my back?

I should be mad at Jamie, but I'm mostly numb. And beneath that numbness is a slow-burning panic.

I text Darius, fingers trembling.

"So... remember the copy room tryst I said wasn't a big deal? I might've... sort of... gotten fired. Is Alexis going to be pissed?"

His reply comes fast:

"They didn't tell us anything. Actually sent a note saying you were great and 'would use again.' No worries. Also—you never told me anything. I will deny all knowledge."

I let out a shaky breath. Okay. So technically, I'm not fired-fired. Just... prematurely dismissed with a weird HR scolding. But still. I'd been doing *so* well. For once in my life, I liked my job. I liked the work. I liked how capable I felt.

I liked how Alexis looked at me. I wasn't just some temp, filling space.

And now? I feel like a giant disappointment.

I start packing up my desk, stuffing Post-its and highlighters into my canvas tote like I'm leaving a crime scene. My phone buzzes again—Lisa.

"Karaoke night. We'll find you a new copy room buddy."

I roll my eyes but smile. Lisa thinks karaoke can cure anything. Honestly, she's not totally wrong. Maybe a night of scream-singing Avril Lavigne is precisely what I need to stop feeling like human garbage.

"See you tonight," I text back, adding a disco emoji for flair I do not feel.

As I reach for my coffee cup, my phone buzzes again—Darius.

Dots. Pause. Dots again.

Then, finally, he texts, "Busy tonight. I'll try to make it. "

Wait, what?

Darius never skips karaoke night. He *created* karaoke night. It's our weekly therapy-slash-happy-hour ritual. And now he's bailing?

My stomach flips. What if he's mad at me? What if I embarrassed him in front of Alexis? What if my whole mess jeopardized his rep at the agency?

I bite my lip. Maybe he's just busy. Or maybe... he's disappointed in me.

Worse—what if Alexis finds out? Not just about Jamie and the hallway kissing and the awkward HR exit, but that I crashed and burned in the easiest temp role known to mankind?

The thought of her dark eyes narrowing in frustration and her confident stride slowing in disappointment makes my chest ache. Alexis believed in me. She gave me this chance.

I clutch my tote, suddenly feeling twelve years old again. That same queasy fear of screwing up something good before I even know how to hold onto it.

Then—out of nowhere—I remember that weird, flirty phone call Darius had last week. Maybe he's not mad. Perhaps he's just… distracted. By a secret boyfriend. Or girlfriend. Or whoever gets him to skip karaoke.

I shake my head and let out a breath that's half relief, half despair. God, I need a drink.

And a new job.

And maybe a tattoo that says "No Copy Room Hookups Ever Again" in cursive across my ribs.

But first—karaoke.

Because if I'm going to spiral, I might as well do it to the soundtrack of Destiny's Child, my fake ID, and an aggressively large mango margarita.

Chapter 10

Karaoke Bar

"I'm stuck!"

I spin at Lisa's cry, nearly falling into the stall door. She's tangled in my low-cut, black lace top, arms flailing like a trapped inflatable tube man.

"Hold still! You're gonna rip it." I yank the shirt down over her face, muffling her protests. "We are *so* sober right now," I deadpan, shimmying into her jade halter top that exposes my back, while she wriggles and wrestles her boobs into the top.

"Mmmmfft!"

"I *said* hold still." I tug and rearrange limbs until we're finally swapped and dressed—albeit barely. I notice that Lisa's cleavage is about one bounce away from a wardrobe malfunction.

We were crammed into the stall at O'Malley's midway through karaoke night and way past our beer limit. Somewhere between our third game of foosball and that weird conversation with a tourist about "how true Alaskans wrestle moose," we decided outfit swapping was essential.

Half-dressed and drunk with power, Lisa declares, *"Your green eyes will pop in my top. Also, I want your cleavage—shhh, don't tell Aurora."*

"Girl," I said, "*I* am Aurora."

"Details."

The bathroom door creaks open, and we freeze like raccoons caught raiding the trash. Lisa's elbow jabs into my ribs as we silently scream in unison.

Click-click-click.

The sound of high heels stabbing the tile like stilettos of war. Then—*boom*—a fog of synthetic perfume hits us. It's Zara Yellow Velvet. I swear I hear my nose groaning in agony. Oh wait, that's my lip. I slap a hand over my face, hiding any noise and stifling the sneeze that would absolutely blow our cover.

"Omg, *he kissed me like he was trying to win a contest!*" says Whiny Girl #1, bursting into the room in a cloud of glitter and regret.

"Okay but like, *was it a kissing contest?* Because maybe you won. I mean... you got a drink *and* a free makeout. That's BOGO," says her friend—who I now mentally dub Stinky Perfume Girl.

Whiny Girl snorts. "He tasted like cherry vape and desperation. Honestly, my boyfriend back home should thank me for showing restraint. I could have any man I want in here."

Stinky cackles. "Pfft. YOLO. Your boyfriend's on the slope for like, *three weeks.* You think he's sleeping alone?"

"Oh my God, *I hope not.* I told him to have fun so *I* could have fun, and now I'm like, 'Have *fun*, duh.'" She pauses to aggressively adjust her boobs, jamming the large girls back into a black bra that is entirely visible through her light colored top.

Lisa, eyes watering from the perfume, bites her fist to keep from audibly losing it. I lean toward the stall crack, whispering, "Do we look like this?"

Lisa barely manages, "Never. We're sophisticated. This is *champagne drunk*, not *Twilight Fanfiction drunk.*"

Right. Totally different. We're half-naked, in a bar bathroom, mid-top-swap like tipsy drag racers—but yes. Classy.

"I'm gonna find a man with a *big truck and a platinum credit card,*" Stinky declares. "Preferably someone with emotional issues and a Costco membership."

"I want *someone emotionally unavailable but financially very available,*" Whiny Girl agrees, nodding solemnly. "Like... *Daddy issues but with a Discover card.*"

They pause at the mirror, striking identical duck-lipped poses and spritzing more Zara death mist into the air. I legit gag.

Then, like chaotic swans, they teeter out—heels clacking like tiny angry hooves. Their laughter fades behind the slam of the door.

We tumble from the stall like circus clowns, gasping and choking on glitter and lies.

Lisa collapses against the sink, wheezing, "Costco membership—*I'm done.*"

I lean against the paper towel dispenser, tears streaming from laughter and chemical warfare. "I want *someone emotionally unavailable but with dental insurance!*"

We meet eyes in the mirror, two disasters in swapped tops and smeared eyeliner, and burst into full-body cackles.

Classy. Definitely.

"Let's go destroy Max and Chez at foosball," Lisa says, pushing her nipple back inside my top that looked PG-13 when I was wearing it but now looks downright erotic on her petite frame with all the curves of a swimsuit model.

"That's a threat *and* a promise." I fluff my hair, eyeing myself in the mirror. The halter makes my eyes pop, and my hair looks fiery. Lisa was right—this top *is* magic.

We rejoin Max and Chez—aka the tourists who called us "Sunny" and "Stacy" and think we're the twins from *Coyote Ugly*. Honestly, they're too focused on boobs to notice we switched clothes *or* names.

"Sunny! Another pitcher?" Chez says, handing Lisa a beer.

I raise a brow. "Guess I'm Stacy now. Or is that my cleavage's name?"

Lisa smirks. "You've been promoted."

We wreck them at foosball in under four minutes. I sip beer with the satisfaction of a woman who scored twice—in the game and in the outfit lottery.

"Karaoke time! Sunny and Stacy to the stage!" the DJ announces.

Lisa beams. "It's Suicide Karaoke, baby."

"You *did not*," I say, even as she drags me toward the stage.

"Oh, I did."

The music starts—Cyndi Lauper. *Girls Just Wanna Have Fun*. I groan. Lisa squeals. I down the rest of my beer like it's liquid courage and grab the mic.

We belt it out like two drunk banshees on a mission. Lisa pulls two girls from the crowd for backup vocals. I spot Max and Chez leaving—with the perfume twins. Whiny Girl is practically climbing Max like a jungle gym.

I elbow Lisa. "Guess he thinks she's Stacy now."

She snorts. "Wait till he finds out the new Stacy is married!."

As we finish the last chorus, the crowd roars, and I see her—Alexis, gliding through the bar like a bossy goddess in business casual. She lifts a hand and gives me a subtle wave.

My heart *hiccups*. "Oh no."

Lisa sees it. "Oh *yes*."

"Stop. She's my boss."

Lisa's eyes sparkle. "You've got it bad."

"She's in a committed relationship."

Lisa grins. "*So were those perfume twins' boyfriends.*"

We hop off the stage and practically bump into Alexis, who's suddenly right there—tall, calm, the opposite of our chaos. She's all smooth lines and tremendous confidence. A total vibe killer... if the vibe wasn't already confusing and hot.

"Alexis! What brings you to this den of glitter and bad decisions?" I ask, leaning into her for a hug because, apparently, beer makes me brave.

She smiles. "Darius invited me. Said we were celebrating your first successful week."

"Ah yes. Nothing says 'congrats on surviving the copier' like karaoke and outfit-swapping."

Her gaze lingers on my halter top for a beat too long. "That's a strong fashion choice."

"I stole it," I admit.

Lisa slides in smoothly. "Hi. Alexis. I've heard *so* much about you."

Alexis shakes her hand. "Hopefully only the professional stuff."

Lisa snorts. "Define professional."

I bury my face in my drink.

"Join us for a drink?" I ask, gesturing to the bar, praying for a distraction.

Alexis raises a brow. "As long as I'm not singing."

At the bar, she orders shots like a seasoned manager throwing a quarterly morale booster.

"To temp jobs and terrible karaoke," she says.

"To cleavage and chaos," Lisa adds, clinking glasses.

We drink. I watch Alexis. She watches me. Lisa watches *both* of us and smirks into her beer.

"So, what's next? Another song or rematch at the foosball table?" Alexis asks, all polished curiosity.

Lisa and I answer in unison: "*Livin' on a Prayer!*"

Alexis laughs. "I'm surrounded by lunatics."

"Welcome to Anchorage nightlife," I say. "Population: Unhinged."

Just as we turn to go, I spot Darius slipping out the back door. My brow furrows.

"Everything alright?" Alexis asks, noticing.

"Yeah," I say too fast. "Just... Darius being mysterious."

She hums. "He's good at that."

We hit the stage again, and Lisa belts out Bon Jovi like there's a record agent in the crowded bar. I scan the crowd. Alexis stands at the bar, holding her phone like a concert lighter, cheering us on. I flush, heart hammering from something that has nothing to do with high notes.

Darius returns mid-song, a smug smile on his face. He's definitely hiding something. But tonight? I don't care. Not yet.

Back at the bar, Alexis leans in close. "You've got guts, Aurora. That confidence? Use it. In karaoke and in life."

"Noted. I'll start by not quitting tomorrow."

"I'd prefer that," she says, clinking glasses with me again.

Lisa raises her drink. "To the fearless!"

"To the flirtatious," Darius adds, appearing out of nowhere with a pitcher and a stack of cups like magic.

And just like that, everything feels right. The mess, the music, the mischief. My first week might've been a disaster, but maybe—just maybe—I'm exactly where I need to be.

Chapter 11

Work Secrets & Closet Encounters

Darius and I are bound by the sacred oath of queer gossip and shared trauma. We've survived bad dates and worse outfits, and at that time, we accidentally double-matched on Tinder. He's my ride-or-die. Except today, he's giving off suspicious "I'm hiding a secret lover" energy.

I'm supposed to be helping him file paperwork at the temp agency. Still, I'm currently employed as a professional desk leaner, watching Darius type on his phone like his thumbs are trying to win gold in the Text Olympics. His lips twitch like he's hiding a joke—and maybe a body.

"Okay, who are you texting with that face?" I prod, flopping halfway across his desk like an adorable, nosy throw pillow. "That is not your 'Just updating the spreadsheet' expression."

He doesn't even look up. "Can a man not send a thoughtful meme without being interrogated?"

"Not when his meme face looks like he just got proposed to via emoji."

Still no response. I try a more serious tone—aka my fake dramatic whisper. "Is it Lisa? Did she join a pyramid scheme again? Wait—is it a boytoy? Are you in love with someone? Are you running away to Vegas? Did you elope with a barista?!"

That gets his attention. He jerks his head up and slaps his phone face-down on the desk like evidence. "Me? In love? Aurora, be serious."

Oh, now he's deflecting. Classic Darius move.

Before I can launch my full investigation, the office door flies open like a tornado made of tax forms, slamming so hard the blinds rattle. Darius bolts upright so fast he knocks over his iced coffee—liquid panic in his eyes.

"What the hell—" I start, but he practically tackles me with a hissed, "Closet. Now."

"Are you serious?" I whisper-shriek, resisting like a toddler at bedtime. "Who's out there? Is it the IRS? A ex-lover?"

"No time! Hide!"

And then I'm in the supply closet. Just—whoosh. Door shut. Left alone with printer paper and betrayal.

It smells like lemon cleaner and toner—the opposite of danger. But knowing Darius, either a serial killer or an ex, is in the lobby. I should stay here for the moment.

I lean against the shelf and try not to overthink things. This is impossible because I have the brain of a raccoon hopped up on espresso. Naturally, I spiral.

Is this about his mystery texts? Did I just get shoved into a closet so Darius could sneak in a secret boyfriend? If so, it's rude. I would've offered to distract the other people in the office.

I pull out my phone, type myself a reminder to refill my birth control, and then almost choke on my own spit because, wow, I really haven't had sex in... a while. Not that it matters. I don't do love. I do "mutually agreed upon low-stakes vibes with snacks."

And then I hear it.

Through the thin office wall.

Darius's voice. Low. Soft. "I love you, too."

I freeze. My mouth goes dry.

Who is he talking to?

I lean back against the wall, stunned. Not by the words. But by the certainty in his voice.

Love. Like it's real. Like it's *not* terrifying.

Love is messy. Love is unpredictable. Love is the thing people say they feel three weeks into dating when they're just bored.

And yet. The way Darius smiled at that text? It didn't look boring. It looked terrifyingly real.

I relocate the Windex to the bottom shelf with the solemnity of someone cleaning up their emotional baggage. Then, I alphabetized the pen boxes, straightened the paper clips like soldiers preparing for war, and glanced at the door for the seventeenth time. It's been at least ten minutes—has Darius forgotten he shoved me in here like a rogue raccoon?

Then, when I peek out—boom. Alexis is standing there. All dark curls, crisp lines, and calm authority. Like a Greek statue brought to life. Her lips twitch.

"Coming out of the closet?" she murmurs.

I blink. "Been there, done that, kept the emotional trauma."

Darius chokes on his coffee behind her. *Traitor.*

Alexis lifts a brow, not missing a beat. "Didn't look like you were suffering from emotional trauma too much last night."

My mind goes perfectly, inconveniently blank.

Oh. Oh, we're doing *that* kind of banter today.

"What can I say? I thrive under karaoke pressure."

"Mm." She doesn't smile, but her eyes gleam like she's enjoying watching me squirm.

Before I can say something genuinely embarrassing—like confessing my undying love for her voice—Darius steps in. "Alexis, should I schedule a meeting with Grant Fairbanks at Alaska Cruise Travel and Tours?"

Completely shifting gears, Alexis handed him a file like she wasn't publicly flirting with me. "I think I landed them. Don't say anything yet—I want to announce it at the anniversary party next month."

Darius whistles. "Cruise and Tours is huge. That's next-level."

"I like next-level," Alexis says smoothly, then grabs her jacket. "I'm grabbing coffee with Richard. I think he's already outside waiting. Don't burn the place down."

She exits, leaving me in a daze.

Darius practically tackles me. "Oh my God. She was totally flirting with you."

"She was just being... professional," I mumble. "Professionally flirty. Boss banter."

"You are in denial," he sings, spinning away before I can retaliate. "Ooh, Lisa texted."

My phone dings, too.

Lisa: "Emergency. Signed you both up for a singles mingle BBQ this weekend. It'll be sexy. And meat-based. You're welcome."

"Absolutely not," I mutter.

"I already RSVP'd," Darius says, like a man who's accepted his fate.

But I snap back to the real mystery. "Wait. You never told me—what was with the weird closet thing? Who were you hiding me from?"

Darius freezes mid-step. "Oh... just covering for someone."

I narrow my eyes. "Who?"

But he's already backing toward the coffee machine. "Caffeine emergency. Filing awaits. Later!"

"Darius!" I call after him, but he's gone.

I exhale sharply, eyes locked on the door where Darius vanished like a magician mid-act. Alexis—my boss, my mentor, my potential HR violation—just possibly flirted with me. My heart is pounding so loud it could land a role on *Euphoria*.

Then there's *that* word I overheard.

Love.

I replay it in my head like a broken record. Darius said *I love you.* Not *that I like you* or *that I'm obsessed with your playlist*—no, it was the real deal. Love. And I have no idea who he said it to.

I should leave it alone. Mind my business. Respect his privacy. But of course, I won't. Because if Darius—serial dater, king of casual, emotionally allergic Darius—is out here dropping L-bombs, something's up. And if my best friend is hiding something from *me*, it's either serious... or messy. Possibly both.

And that makes it *my* business.

Still, love? I don't get it. It's like cryptocurrency or skincare serums—everyone swears it changed their life, and I'm just over here, broke and breaking out. It feels fake. Dangerous. Temporary.

I like my relationships like this temp job—short-term, low stakes, and easy to walk away from.

No surprises. No heartbreak. No real risk.

So why does Alexis make me feel like I'm standing at the edge of a cliff and want to jump? Why do I keep replaying how she looked at me—cool, amused, like I'm worth something? Like she sees me?

Does she care? Or is she just good at managing people?

Am I imagining this whole thing? ... God, am *I* an HR violation?

I wrap my arms around myself and stare at the exit, thoughts tangling into knots.

Something is going on with Darius.

And I have an itch that something, *maybe*, is sorta happening between me and Alexis.

Chapter 12

Complicated Friendships

Strolling back to my apartment in the cool evening instead of hopping on the bus, my mind races with thoughts of office drama and Darius's mysterious behavior. I need a distraction, and I know exactly who can provide it. I shoot a text to Lisa, hoping she's available for some light-hearted girl talk.

"I know it's a Monday, but drinks tonight? I need to unwind."

Her reply comes almost instantly. "I'm already drinking. Our usual place in thirty. K?"

I change into a casual dress, letting my red hair fall loose from the tight professional bun it's been trapped in all day. Heading to our favorite bar, I mentally prepare for some much-needed laughter.

Lisa's already there, waving energetically. She's dressed in a bright yellow sundress, looking like a ray of sunshine. "Hey, A! What's up?" she chirps as I slide into the seat next to her.

"Oh, you know, the usual office work. Darius is acting super weird, and I'm pretty sure my boss, Alexis, is part of it. Maybe it's just the workplace vibes since I'm still new there, but I just feel... weird."

Lisa raises an eyebrow, smirking. "Weird? That's new for you! I mean, Alexis is super-hot—totally your type."

"My new type is available and drama-free," I say, lifting my glass.

"Whoa. Are you breaking up with me?" she teases, pretending to gasp. "I thought those practice dates would be fun! You aren't mad at me, are you?"

I shake my head, laughing. "It's just... everything. Trying to pay bills, get a real job, deal with my mother guilt-tripping me for moving out, save up for fall tuition... I'm all over the place."

"You are rocking it, girl! Don't stress so much—Darius and I have your back, always. Now, spill the tea on this workplace drama. Another copy room incident?" Her eyes sparkle with excitement.

I recount Friday's events, from being shoved into a closet by Darius to Alexis's potential flirting. Lisa listens, her eyes widening with every detail.

"So, workplace drama, huh?" she asks, leaning in.

"Yep. And Darius totally has a secret boytoy, right?" I raise an eyebrow, waving my hands dramatically. "Do you think it's the FedEx guy? Or another employee at the temp agency? What if it's a *woman*?"

Lisa cocks her head, rolling her eyes.

"I hate being on the outside of inside jokes. Darius is my best friend."

She starts to open her mouth.

"After you, of course!" I hastily add, holding up my hands in mock surrender.

She leans back, shaking out her hair with a thoughtful expression. "Maybe it's not about a boytoy. Remember when Darius started that rumor he was a vampire just to see how fast it would spread through school?"

I sigh, swirling my drink. "With Darius, anything's possible. I wouldn't be surprised if he's been bitten and is hiding a secret life."

Lisa bursts out laughing. "A vampire? In this economy? More like he's just too busy to share details about his love life!"

We spend the next hour chatting and laughing, the office drama slowly fading into the background. Lisa's infectious energy lifts my spirits, and I feel lighter when we part ways. She's probably right about me overthinking the office vibe. She is Darius's cousin, after all—she knows him best. Darius loves to be a peacock, strutting around and having fun. I'm sure whatever it is, it's harmless.

Back at my tiny apartment, I curl up on the couch, scrolling through my phone. Darius's cryptic behavior still nags at me, but there's something else I need to focus on. I open the email with my next assignment's details:

> Location: Downtown Anchorage
> Job Position: Admin & Data Entry
> Length: 2-5 days until the assigned tasks are completed
> Supervisor/Contact: Neil

Data entry sounds easy enough, and I've created a lot of Excel documents before. How hard could it be? Sure, I've only completed a few business classes. I may have exaggerated my skills a bit during the interview with Alexis, but who doesn't embellish a little? I take a deep breath, trying to quell the anxiety bubbling up inside me.

I glance around my still-bright, small studio—I really need to buy blackout curtains. The faint hum of the fridge in the kitchenette is the only sound breaking the silence. My eyes land on a stack of unopened bills on the coffee table, mocking me. One envelope, with "Past Due" stamped in red, sits on top, a reminder of how close I am to plummeting down the financial abyss. I've paid my cellphone and rent, but my other bills are piling up, and I desperately need a paycheck. My bank account is barely above zero, and the thought of rent being overdue again makes my stomach twist.

Tomorrow's my first day at a new job, and I must make a good impression. No after-hours outings or even glancing at an intern.

Setting out my outfit for the next day, I silently thank Darius' mom for loaning me professional clothes. I choose a smart yet comfortable ensemble that says, "I'm a professional, and I mean business." I lay out a crisp white blouse, a delicate gold necklace, tailored black pants, and my trusty Mary Jane flats. Professional, but not too stuffy.

I double-check my bag, ensuring I have everything I need—laptop, charger, notepad, pens, and a granola bar for emergency sustenance. Zipping up my bag, I catch my reflection in the mirror. "You've got this, Aurora," I whisper, trying to convince myself. "You can handle a little data entry."

Drifting off to sleep, my mind dances between thoughts of Darius's secret, Alexis's smirk, my new job, and the ever-present shadow of my mom's expectations—or, rather, her lack of expectations. Her voice echoes, reminding me that women aren't made for business. You don't need a business degree. You need a competent partner to pay your bills.

I flip over, shoving the pillow over my face to block the midnight sun. This time will be different. I'll show her I can succeed. I am smart and will make enough money to finish my business degree and be a respected, successful business woman like Alexis!

Pushing the pillow tighter over my face to block out the midnight sun, I drift off to sleep but decide that tomorrow, I'll show everyone—and prove to myself—that I can handle this. I will slay this next job done, make money, and finally start putting my life together.

And if Alexis gives me a hint of that teasing little smirk again? Well, I'll deal with that later.

Chapter 13

Taco Time & It's Not Even Tuesday

The morning sun filters through my tiny apartment's cheap, too-thin curtains, slicing through my dreams with laser precision. Instead of blocking Alaska's unrelenting, searing daylight, my flattened and folded pillow suffocates me. I groan, toss it aside, and blink blearily at my phone. No new messages from Darius.

Suspicious. I expected from my self-appointed life coach, my daily fashion advisor, and my new manager something... a pre-work pep talk, a funny coffee meme about surviving the workday, or at least a local clothing sale. *But today?* Radio silence.

Darius is hiding something for sure.

I don't have time to spiral about that right now because I have a job–a paycheck–to focus on. Today's mission: Impress Neil, my new temp job supervisor, and pretend I'm a professional and know all the fluff in which my resume says I'm an expert.

After a rushed gourmet breakfast of instant oatmeal—heavily modified with stolen sugar packets from yesterday's cafe run—I pull on my carefully curated "I am a professional businesswoman" outfit. A crisp white blouse, tailored black pants that are semi-clean, and flats that say, 'I'm competent and will absolutely not accidentally get a file or appendage stuck in a shredder today.'

I give myself a last once-over in the mirror and point at my reflection. "No flirting. No disasters. No getting fired before lunch. Make us proud!"

With that pep talk, I grab my bag and step outside into the retina-searing Alaskan morning. The air is brisk, scented with pine, and the distant, unmistakable whiff of someone frying reindeer sausage. Across the street, a float plane roars to life, lifting off into the clear blue sky. Tourists in overpriced fleece jackets gawk at it, snapping photos.

I could drive, but gas is expensive, and my nerves need an outlet. I opted to walk and take the bus. Arriving at the bus stop, I rehearse my game plan—I arrive early, nod intelligently, avoid talking too much, and above all, do not let anyone discover I am wildly unqualified to work in any business setting. University starts in two months, and I need money as soon as possible.

The ride downtown is uneventful, filled with the usual groggy commuters drinking coffee and students glued to their phones. As we roll past a group of joggers, I check my reflection in the window. Professional. Capable. Not at all panicked. My sweaty palms and racing heart disagree with my assessment.

Glancing out the window, I watch the cityscape blur past, my thoughts a jumble of anticipation and anxiety. I arrive at the office building overlooking the bay. This sleek, modern structure is too sleek and polished against the rugged Alaskan backdrop, which only needs a log cabin and moose to be the perfect Alaska postcard. Taking a deep breath, I step inside the glass and steel monstrosity, ready to tackle whatever lies ahead.

I am immediately assaulted by the aggressively overpowering chilly air conditioning. The professional-looking receptionist beams at me like she's been waiting all morning and waves me into Neil's office.

Nodding and noting her nameplate, Beth, I'm already following my game plan, and it's working.

Neil greets me with a warm smile. He looks like the average middle-aged exec, with a gray business suit and a direct, confident demeanor, which makes me swallow hard.

Come on, Aurora. You got this. You've fooled Beth already.

"You must be Aurora. Welcome! You're a lifesaver. Our accountant is on maternity leave, and we are way behind. It's basic, straightforward accounting work."

I bite my lip to stop from saying something inappropriate, like, "Did you get her pregnant? Can I make coffee instead of doing accounting this week? Does this building heat up like a greenhouse in the summer?" And those are only the thoughts that flashed in my mind a millisecond after his enthusiastic greeting.

Advanced accounting work? I thought this was a simple data entry job. I smile and nod, sticking to the plan.

"Your temp agency is so well known, so of course I called for someone to fill-in," Neil adds casually, flipping through a stack of papers.

My heart goes into a face-to-face bear encounter panic mode.

My confident and dangerously distracting boss is sending me on an assignment with a new client. My face reddens at the thought of Alexis. My plan may not work in this pressure cooker accounting situation.

I force a bigger smile. "Oh! That's...nice!" With Neil's hours of silence, which was in normal human time one second, my pulse quickens, and I add, "Thanks, Neil. I'm excited to be here."

He walks down the hall with me, pointing me to the accounting office, which is filled with files and a computer with three screens. Who needs three screens? *Do I need three screens?*

I can hardly inhale with the heaviness sitting on my chest. Oh my gosh, this is what a heart attack feels like!

"I'll show you the rest of the office then let you dive right in," he says.

"Absolutely," I say, echoing his professional tone.

His professional demeanor breaks as he removes his readers to laugh. "Great attitude."

Handing me a badge, he says. "Let's get you a stack of files to start today. Good luck!"

Luck. That's not a good sign.

"Oh, your time is so valuable. I can have Beth show me around," I offer, wondering if everything I do will be reported directly back to Alexis. Will I get fired before the day is done?

Before he answers, I spy an escape.

"I'm going to duck into the bathroom for a moment," I say, sneaking into the ladies' room as we pass by.

I clutch my bag and look at myself in the mirror, trying to channel the energy of someone who knows what they're doing. Ha! The joke's on me. This "straightforward work" Neil mentioned feels like advanced calculus in a foreign language. My fingers twitch, itching to Google "variance analysis" without him noticing. I duck into the nearest bathroom stall, my heart hammering against my ribs like a trapped hummingbird.

My thumb hovers over Alexis's contact in my texts. What would a *boss bitch* do? She would probably not admit she's in over her head ten minutes into a new assignment. But then again, I'm Aurora Thompson, a professional chaos coordinator. Maybe a little honesty is the most chaotic move of all.

Pulling out my phone, I fire off a desperate text to the only person who might understand my current level of "existential accounting dread."

I type fast, so I'll send it before I regret it. "Alexis, SOS from downtown. This accounting work? I'm drowning in numbers I don't recognize. Feeling like I'm way out of my depth."

A beat passes, and then her reply pops up surprisingly fast.

Alexis texts, "Aurora. Remember your orientation? You grasped the system faster than anyone we've had. Darius might have embellished your experience, because he's an over-the-top person, but your underlying skills are there. You're smart and you learn quickly. Trust that. Don't panic. Break down the tasks and ask Neil specific questions when you need help. You're more capable than you think."

Her words are a surprising lifeline in this sea of unfamiliar ledgers. She acknowledges Darius's... embellishment... but still sees something in me. A small spark of confidence flickers to life.

Alexis thinks I can do this. Maybe, just maybe, she's right. Time to put on my brave face and try not to bankrupt this company before lunchtime. I exhale and step out to Neil, who is waiting for me.

He nods, handing me a folder. "Here's the start of the paperwork. I guess I can let Beth show you the break room. We just need you to input invoices into the system and cross-check them with the client accounts. Should be pretty straightforward work for you."

I open the folder to pages and pages of numbers. So many numbers. They blur together, mocking me. I swallow hard and smile. "No problem!"

Neil smiles warmly back, utterly oblivious to the internal meltdown happening behind my eyes. "Great! If you have any questions, you know where to find me."

Questions? Oh, I will have *so* many.

But I hold back on my usual blurting and follow my game plan, nodding at him again and shuffling back to the accounting office and behind my desk near the window and way too close to his office.

I boot up the computer and stare at the unfamiliar software, willing my brain to absorb and learn information through sheer force of will.

Thirty-eight minutes later, I successfully logged in, opened the invoice spreadsheet, and inputted exactly...three numbers.

This is fine. I am fine.

My phone buzzes. A text from Lisa. "How's the new job? Did you set the office on fire yet or find the copy room?"

I glare at the screen. "Rude. Also, no. I'm following a winning game plan that doesn't involve copy rooms or texting during work."

"Boooring! I can't text Darius, he's still socially MIA. Proud of you. Don't get arrested but if you do...I've always got bail money for you!"

I snort, pocket my phone, and refocus on my screen.

Okay, Aurora. Time to figure out what the hell an invoice reconciliation is.

By lunchtime, I've made progress. Not *good* progress, necessarily, but progress. The invoices are entered, though I have a sinking feeling that I've put at least a few numbers in the wrong place. Neil hasn't come running to call me a fraud and fire me, so I'll consider it a win.

Just as I'm about to escape for lunch, a familiar voice drifts from behind me. I'm staying at my desk, hoping to make a good impression as a diligent, studious employee. Also, downtown Anchorage's lunch prices during tourist season are no joke.

I spin in my chair to the person in my doorway, with my stomach protesting with the betrayal of skipped lunch. Neil stands in the doorway, leaning casually against the frame, arms crossed, an easy smile on his face.

"How's it going?" he asks, stepping inside like he owns the air I breathe. Which, technically, he does. Boss privileges.

I paste on a chipper smile, way more enthusiastic than I feel. "Good! Just getting everything done."

Neil nods, but instead of heading back to his big corner office, he steps further in—dangerously close to my desk—then closes the door behind him.

My stomach tightens. Closed-door conversations rarely end well for temps who can't tell the debit from the credit column.

"Did you need help with something?" I ask, forcing a light tone, though my heart is already in fight or flight mode. He's going to fire me.

He exhales, his entire business-executive cool shifting to something... *warmer.* Chummier. Suspiciously, friendly.

"Errm, no," he says, lowering himself into the chair across from me. "Obviously, meeting you like this is a little awkward, with us messaging and all."

I freeze. I have never messaged this man in my life.

Neil leans in slightly, his tone softening. "How about I take you out to a Mexican place after work?" He winks—he actually winks—then flashes me a playful smile, like this is a rom-com setup where I swoon and say something breathy like, 'I'd love that, Sir,' and the day ends with me doing a Julia Roberts shopping spree, *Pretty Woman*-style. Darius would love that!

Except this is real life, and what actually happens is my brain short-circuits, my pulse does an embarrassing gallop, and heat floods my entire body.

What. The. Hell?!

I blink at him, struggling to process how we jumped from 'How's it going?' to 'Do you want to date your boss?' My internal systems flash a big, neon *ERROR*.

His expression remains perfectly casual, as if it were normal for executives and their accountants to date during lunch hour.

I stall. "Sorry, my mind's hyper focused on work right now. Let me think about it." I force a polite smile that, hopefully, does not scream panic.

Neil gives me a long, unreadable look. "Alright. Let me know."

He lingers. *Why is he lingering?!* I stand abruptly and nod at the door, the universal signal for 'Meeting Over, Please Exit.' It looks like I can fake a professional-type person, after all.

"I should grab more files from Beth," I say, the verbal equivalent of slapping a 'Go Away' sign on my forehead.

He frowns slightly, tilts his head, and then rises with the grace of a man who is absolutely not used to being dismissed, especially from a temp. He ambles out but tosses a final glance back at me.

I panic. This is a disaster. If Neil complains to Alexis, I could be out of a job, and then what? Ramen and regret are not options in my university meal plan. My brain, unsure what to do, makes me default to my usual friendly gesture of double finger guns.

Neil's brows shoot up, and he nods, grinning.

Why?! Why did I do that?!

He waves, then disappears down the hall.

Oh no. *Oh no, no, no.*

Finger guns are ambiguous, right? What if he thinks I meant 'Hells to the yes,' instead of 'I am socially and professionally malfunctioning, please never ask me out again'?

Why is everyone so obsessed with dating and romance and not actual work at work?

My stomach churns. I grab my phone and bolt to the nearest bathroom.

The tiny stall feels like a joke. I'm practically slouching to keep from bumping my head on the doorframe. I'm tall, but this? This only adds to my next-level awkwardness. *I don't belong in this stall or at this professional job.*

Sitting fully clothed on the toilet, I text Lisa. "Odd thing just happened. Are you doing MORE than using my pics for a testing profile on your Hook and Reel Dating website?"

Lisa responded in less than a millisecond. "I get bored at work and sometimes flirt. Maybe I occasionally send messages from your profile. It's my job, though. I want the guys in our dating service to feel wanted. There's no harm in sending a few nice messages, right?"

"Wait. What exactly did you send a guy named Neil?" I text back, my stomach already in a knot. Lisa's flirting skills are on par with a neon sign blinking 'look at me' in a quiet library. It's not subtle or pretty.

"I'll check. Hold on." She texts.

How many guys is she—or am I—texting from my dating profile? It must be a lot if she can't remember what she texted Neil. A heavy sense of dread settles in my gut. I frantically try loading the dating app, logging in with the urgency usually reserved for escaping burning buildings.

The app loads, and there's my picture, front and center, "BangingAurora" is my username, and that's the *least* suggestive part of the profile.

"Noooooo! What the hell, Lisa," I muttered while scrolling through the public profile she created for beta testing. I agreed but assumed she would give me a pseudonym and use some standard pictures.

There, in my pictures, is a picture of her breasts—*covered,* thank God–but encased in tortilla shells. The caption?

"Taco Tuesday, anyone?"

I slap a hand over my mouth to smother a shriek.

No. No, no, no, no, no.

Neil thinks I flirt and wear taco bras.

My whole body goes nuclear with secondhand embarrassment.

"I just wished him a good day and liked his profile—so no big deal." She texts back.

A knock on the stall door startles me into silence.

"Are you okay in there?" Beth asks, overly concerned.

Oh God, I cannot admit what is going on. It's bad enough that I have no clue what I'm doing. Now, I'm hitting on my supervisor through a dating site.

"Fine," I croak.

Pause.

"Are you sure?"

I scramble for an excuse. "Uh. Period?"

Her response softens into understanding, "Oh, honey. Here." A tampon slides under the stall door.

I stare at it. I have never used a tampon, let alone had a tampon handed to me in a moment of emotional distress. "Thanks," I say, meaning it as I appreciate her support.

"Go ahead and take a two-hour lunch. Tackling those numbers is hard enough. I'll cover for you."

"Thanks," I mumble, ready to absolutely destroy Lisa.

I text her one last time. "No more using my profile to flirt and take down that taco tits pic, asap. It's hard to be a professional with that online."

Lisa answers, "Omg, really?! Fine, but promise you'll still fill-in when dates fall through. I need a short notice girl for hot dates."

Shaking my head, I text back, "Okay, but no more flirting using my profile and really—remove that taco picture."

"It has so many likes. Is Italian cool? I can hold pasta over my chest? It's not really your boobs."

"YOU ARE NO LONGER MY FRIEND."

"That's because I'm family! But like... are you sure about the taco pic?"

I groan into my hands. "LISA!!!!!!!"

How am I going to work with Neil all week, knowing he *thinks* he's seen me in a taco bra, and I flirted with him?

My game plan didn't cover this kind of disaster. I squeeze the tampon, and it's surprisingly stress-relieving. I guess a tampon is useful in high-stress situations!

Chapter 14

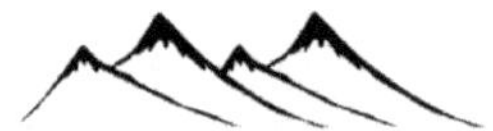

Slaying Spreadsheets & Avoiding Workplace Scandals

Friday morning, my alarm blares, dragging me out of a restless sleep. I slap at my phone, missing twice, before finally silencing it. I lie still for a few blissful seconds, and then it hits me—*Friday.* It is my last day pretending to be an accounting professional— I survived!

Somehow, against all odds, I've made it through two weeks without causing an accounting catastrophe. Stretching with my joints popping in protest, I roll out of bed, wobbling slightly. My apartment is still a mess of unfolded laundry, and my stack of university notices and unpaid bills remain scattered across my table. But today, the mess on the table is less terrifying because I'm getting paid as of five o'clock.

I rummage through my fridge, settling on last night's leftover mac and cheese, eaten cold and straight from the container. Breakfast of champions.

Dressing for my last day is infinitely easier than my first, as my outfit shouts, "ready to celebrate surviving my first professional office job." A Navy v-neck blouse, black skirt, flats for practicality, and silver bangles for flair make me smile at my professional facade in the mirror.

"Fake it till you make it," I murmured at my reflection before giving myself a silly finger-gun and then my confident professional nod, which I've perfected this week.

The morning commute is refreshingly uneventful. No near-death experiences on the crosswalk, no accidental eye contact with any lost tourists looking for directions. The sun's golden light spills over the Chugach Mountains in that surreal way that only an Anchorage summer can pull off.

Beth waves me down inside the office before I reach my desk. "Aurora! Ready to conquer your last day?"

I manage what I hope is an effortless grin. "Born ready."

"You bring such energy to the office. I'm going to miss you," she says.

I finger-gun her because I'm terrible at taking compliments. Somehow, I can make any compliment–even her friendly one–into an awkward exchange.

She laughs. "You've done a great job this week. Honestly, you've pretty much cleared our backlog of invoices. I heard Neil telling Alexis how amazing you are." She leans in and whispers, "Even I struggle with that accounting system sometimes. You are like a superhero temp."

Wait—what? I pause mid-step, blinking. Alexis knows? I hope only my good work and professionalism have been reported on and not any reference to my fake profile or taco bra.

I blush and smile back at Beth. "Really?" I ask, trying not to sound too eager. "I'm not really a superstar. I watched a few YouTube tutorials. And I used the help button. A lot."

She grins. "Whatever works, right?" She leans in, conspiratorial. "Would you mind if we requested you next time we need a temp? I mean one of your weeks is equivalent to three months of me trying to enter invoices in."

My stomach does a weird little flip at her compliment on my skills. "Wow. Uh, yeah! I mean, I'd love that."

"Great! I'll let Neil know."

Neil, who I am still actively avoiding because of The Incident, but I may have to reconsider being a frosty ice queen to him if he's reporting good things to Alexis.

My heart thumps louder, and a blush spreads. I mumble a thank you and duck into the accounting office before I ruin my professional interaction by being myself.

The day passes in a whirlwind of numbers, spreadsheets, and minor panic attacks where I'm second-guessing my data entry skills. But I triple-check everything, and by the time the clock inches toward five, I feel a deep sense of satisfaction settle over me.

I did it. I survived this assignment and didn't set the office on fire, financially or literally. It's payday. *Finally, I'm* one more week closer to having enough for my university expenses. Maybe I won't have to skip a university meal plan to live off instant noodles.

Neil strolls by just before quitting time, pausing at my desk.

I brace myself, my heart rate tripling. I'm ready to ignore him or grab a file from Beth, which has been my go-to all week for avoiding him.

He clears his throat. "Well, Thompson," he says, hands on his hips. "You did good work here."

My eyes widened. Compliments and no attempt to ask me out?

I muster what I hope is a professional smile. "Thanks, Neil. I appreciate the opportunity and your professionalism."

He gives me a slight nod before heading back to his office. I let out a slow breath, shoulders dropping. Crisis averted.

As I shut down my computer and gather my things, my phone buzzes with a text from Lisa.

"TGIF! You did it, Queen. Drinks are on me!"

Grinning, I grab my bag and wave to Beth as I step outside their office, escaping before the accounting system notifies them I'm a fraud, or I trip down the stairs. Through the windows, the mountains stand tall in the distance, watching over the city and me.

It's time to celebrate.

Soaking in my victory, I strut out of the office building. I didn't get fired for being inappropriate. I wasn't arrested for causing an accounting scandal—that's what I call *growth*.

Stepping outside, the crisp Alaskan air rushes to greet me, fresh and biting against my skin. The Alaska sun lingers in the sky, refusing to set on my momentous day. I fish my phone out of my bag to check the time and see if Lisa's waiting, but—

"1 New Message: Alexis."

Oh.

Oh!

My stomach does that ridiculous fluttery thing that is unprofessional and unnecessary. I tap the notification, acting casual even though there's no one around to witness my nervous giggle and dead stop on the sidewalk.

"Neil gave a glowing report. Good job. I'm adding a bonus to your direct deposit paycheck this week. Keep it up."

I blink. Then reread it.

A bonus *and* Alexis noticed my amazing, *very professional-like* work.

I need good news, and more than that, I need a dose of kudos from my employer and potential business mentor. *#GirlBossGoals*

A delighted squeak escapes before I can stop it. I slap a hand over my mouth and glance around as if someone might've heard me humiliating myself in the middle of the sidewalk.

Getting *extra money* and the text suddenly makes going to college this fall seem a little less terrifying and even more attainable. But, if we're being honest, that's not even the best part.

The best part? *I have Alexis as my boss.*

She's a good boss and the epitome of a badass woman slaying the business world. I glance at the text. And she's invested in her employees. I'm sure she checks on all her new employees as a professional courtesy.

I start to respond, but a professional doesn't need to thank her boss for paying her, right? I tell myself, "Don't read into it."

But it is a Friday night, and she *did* text me personally. It's not some boring auto-generated corporate email. Not some payroll person whose name I'll never remember. No, no. Alexis herself took time out of her CEO day to text *me.*

She has *hundreds* of employees. *Hundreds.* And yet, she's texting *me.*

I must be at least *a little* special to her, right?

I shake my head and start walking, but I can't help letting my giddy energy spill out with a giggle and extra hip shake. Some guy walking his husky gives me a weird look. I don't care. I'm rocking being a businesswoman. I am impressing my boss, confident, and getting paid. This is officially the *best* day of my life.

Well. Top five.

I type back, trying to sound chill. "Thank you! That's amazing! I appreciate it!"

Immediately, I regret my flair and the excessive amount of exclamation marks. I should've thrown in a *wink emoji.* Or a casual, "*What's a girl gotta do to get a raise around here?*"

No. No, that's *too* much. *Keep it together, Aurora.* I take a slow breath to calm my nerves.

Her reply pops up faster than expected. "You earned it. Hope to get you another placement soon. Darius will give you next week's schedule. See you later."

See me later?

My phone pings again before I can spiral into a whole dissertation on *What Alexis's Text Really Means: A Critical Analysis* and *How a professional should respond*.

"Drinks? we still on?"

I shoot back a thumbs-up emoji and start walking to meet up with Lisa. Hopefully, Darius will be there to give me the scoop on exactly what Neil reported back to Alexis. I did rock the invoices, and Beth liked me.

My first week started with disaster. Miscommunications, Neil's awkward innuendo, Lisa's drama, and my imposter syndrome screaming at me *YOU DON'T BELONG HERE.* But by the second week, I finished it strong.

And I get to cap it all off with Darius, Lisa, and a celebratory drink.

And, if I let myself daydream a little, maybe—just *maybe*—my boss is thinking about me becoming her best employee or even a friend–a workplace person she can text and hang out with. How cool would it be to hang out with Alexis and be treated like a businesswoman friend? We could gossip about workplaces and shop for shoes together.

As if Alexis is reading my thoughts, she sends one more text, "BTW someone is catfishing with your picture. You may want to google yourself, and get the fake profile taken down."

Chapter 15

Wrong Turn, Right Payday

"We already discussed this all last week. How was I supposed to know you'd meet Neil in person? You are the unluckiest person I've ever met!" Lisa giggles through the phone, as I'm crazy driving—at least it's crazy since Lisa's involved—dating service's BBQ instead of sleeping in this weekend.

She's lucky I like her so much. A deep sigh escapes me, frustration pricking my skin. "I guess it was sort of random, but Alaska is one huge small town. Promise me you will no longer use my profile to flirt with guys anymore."

She sighs loudly. "Yes. I promise." Changing the subject with a quieter tone, "What's really bugging you? I know it's more than a sexy taco pic."

"My mom, as always," I mutter, swerving to avoid a pothole. "I'm supposed to be catching up on my bills and getting ready for University of Anchorage this fall. But this morning my mom wiped out my bank account and won't return my calls."

"Turn Right," my GPS commands. I pull the wheel onto an even smaller dirt road that will take me to an amazing secret lakeside camping site or a serial killer's remote cabin.

"No way! She knows you are saving for university this fall. Maybe it was a mistake, like the bank teller took her withdrawal from the wrong account?"

"I wish," I mumble, irritated. "Are you at this Singles Mingle event? It looks sketchy as hell," I blurted, looking at the ominous woods enclosing the car and darkening the sky above. I realize I'm being cranky, taking out my frustration at my university tuition money being stolen on her. I did promise to attend her weekend dating thing, and she is giving me cash for showing up.

"You should've carpooled with Darius. It'll be fun! And I can't go because I work there," she explains.

"I would've carpooled but you know how busy your cousin has been lately," I remark, blinking the road dust from my eyes.

"Darius will be there as the token gay guy for diversity, you know. And I need you, too. It's still like two guys for every woman in Alaska. I can't have this BBQ event become a big sausage fest!"

"Lisa, you're terrible! I thought at least *we* could hang out today," I complained, wishing I knew she wasn't coming before I started driving.

"Free drinks. Fun single people–you'll love it–but I want to hear a full report all about how everyone behaves or misbehaves. Um'kay?"

I grumble and add, "Sorry, it's not you or the BBQ. I'm just mad at my mom and the whole situation she has put me in."

"Your mom is *terrible*. I never imagine that she'd steal from you intentionally, that's downright narcissistic bitch behavior," she says. The phone reception is already making it hard to hear every word. She adds, "What can I do... Do you need a loan or a hitman?"

"Thanks," I say ruefully. "I'll get it back. I forgot she was even a signer on my bank account. I guess it's my own fault for not getting her off of it when I turned eighteen."

She responds, but through the bad reception, all I hear is "let loose" and "put the F-U in fun today."

I grip the steering wheel, my eyes darting between the road and my phone screen for directions to the HARD Single Mingle that Lisa signed me up for. My phone flashes with yet another offline notification. The gravel crunches under my tires, the late Alaskan sunlight casting long shadows over the winding dirt road. The state bird of Alaska—the relentless mosquito—swarms around my car, forcing me to leave the windows up despite the afternoon heat. I turn on my wipers to clear the thin layer of road dust and to maybe discourage the bugs.

"Aurora, I can hardly hear you. If you are still complaining about that taco tit picture, it's no big deal. Build a bridge, girl. And put your phone down. You're worse than a teenager," she says, which comes through clearly.

"I don't need to build a bridge because I'm already over it. And I *am* a teenager!" I blurt, completely failing to prove I'm mature.

Glancing at the dirt cloud my Subaru is stirring up, I turn off the vents. *I'm not choking on road dust.*

"Fine! I need to be on moose watch anyway. With my luck, I'd hit a moose—or Bigfoot."

"Love...sweetie," she says, "Take pics... You are...."

That is all I hear before the call drops.

"Great," I say, braking slowly for another pothole on the gravel road.

I plaster on a smile and try to focus on the silver linings—at least she offered me a loan *and* is paying me to show up at this thing. Plus, I'll finally get to see Darius, who's been dodging me like it's his full-time job. If he hadn't sent my schedule in a late-night work email on Friday, I'd be tempted to stalk his socials or "accidentally" swing by the office just to confirm he's still breathing.

I ease my foot off the gas pedal, adjust my crop top, and take a deep breath, the tension in my shoulders easing slightly. Driving through the forest's quiet along the narrowing dirt road, climbing higher into the mountains, feels surprisingly calming. The air is crisp and fresh, filled with the scent of pine and untouched Alaskan wilderness. I really should get out to the mountains more often—I live in one of the most beautiful places in the world. I don't need money or a date to enjoy a good hike—or, at the very least, a scenic drive.

I chuckle, looking at my heels. I would *need* hiking boots, though, and maybe a compass and map. The idea of hiking is probably better than *actually* hiking the Alaskan mountains.

My phone dings, bringing me out of my driving meditation. I glance at my phone screen. "I'm running late. I'll catch up with you there."

I frown. Darius better not ditch me at this event. Looking around at the remote forest, this is definitely not his scene. "He'll be here," I say to myself, more confidently than I feel.

Finally, I see a banner leading to the Chugach Community Campground area on my left, *Freedom Group Mingle.*

We are past the "freedom" holiday, the Fourth of July, but the banner and balloons are eye-catching. I see a crowd by the shoreline and under the covered eating area. I expected a more professional sign and catering, but at least I found the event—I'm no longer lost in the woods.

"Well, there's Bigfoot," I mutter, looking at a burly, hairy Alaskan man sitting by the fire pit. The blue, diamond-sparkling lake is a breathtaking backdrop, almost making that harrowing ride worth it.

Parking my Subaru in the gravel lot, I frown at the thin layer of dust now coating my once-clean car. The place is packed—trucks, four-wheel drives, and an absurd number of guys in flannel. I scan the crowd of about fifty people. There's something... off. No sign of Darius's blue BMW, which is strange considering his car is easy to spot because it's always shinier than a reality TV star's veneers.

Darius must be running later than me. And Lisa was right about this easily becoming a sausage party since there are primarily guys here.

With a sigh, I slick on another layer of lip gloss and check my reflection.

Hair? Fluffed. *Crop top?* Smooth. *Sunglasses?* On. *Cowboy hat?* A bold choice, but I'm owning it. It's a wilderness, s'mores-making singles mingle—outdoorsy cute is my vibe.

Looking at the dusty, buggy, and hairy view, Darius will take one look and run. The man once refused to go glamping because, quote, "Nature is best appreciated through a window with a mimosa." He's probably late because he is agonizing over which designer jeans he's willing to let touch the outside world.

I shoot him a text. "I'm here. See you soon!"

A quick crowd scan confirms that people are dressed casually—lots of T-shirts and shorts. I sent another text to him, "Very casual 'fits. No slacks or button-ups."

Moving through the sea of chatter and the mouthwatering smell of grilled meat, I raise an eyebrow at the variety of attendees. Middle-aged couples, elderly folks, a smattering of people my age… This is surprisingly inclusive for a HARD (Hook and Reel Dating) event.

Good on them! Lisa had made it sound like her Hook and Reel singles were all buttoned-up corporate types looking for love between PowerPoint slides.

"Allie!"

My stomach twists at the familiar voice. *No. Freaking. Way.*

I turn, and sure enough, it's Thomas—the walking red flag who dined and dashed on me. In hindsight, he looks better sober, which is a massive red flag. No heavy alcohol odor, jeans, polo, wavy hair that doesn't look like it's been slept in. The polo has some odd awareness-type pin on it. His smile is broad, like we're besties.

It was as if he didn't vanish mid-date faster than my self-esteem after lunch with my mother.

"Aurora," I automatically corrected him, immediately wishing I hadn't reminded him of my actual name.

"Oh yeah. I'm Thomas. Remember?" he says like I don't already know. He gestures to the covered picnic tables. "You want some fresh meat off the grill? It's about to start."

I glance around, looking for Darius or, failing that, a way to disappear into the woods. "Have you seen my friend Darius?"

But Thomas is already busy greeting someone else, leaving me stranded at the picnic tables. *Fantastic.*

As I inch closer to the BBQ grill, something starts to feel... off. People aren't just being friendly. They're being *too* overly friendly. There's a weird vibe, like, *culty-weird*.

Is this a secret outdoor, swinger-orgy event? *Damn, Lisa!*

I stare at my useless cell phone, the screen showing no bars and no sign of reception.

A beaming man behind the grill—wearing the same purple pin with a triangle inside a circle pin as Thomas—waves me over.

I return his smile hesitantly and ask. "Where's the beer?" Because, at this point, I feel like I will need it.

His smile tightens, and his expression changes to amusement. "They don't serve alcohol here."

I blink. "At a BBQ social?"

He nods, still smiling. "This is a *sober* event."

My brain stalls. "A–What now?"

The grill guy taps his pin to draw my attention to it. Before he elaborates, Thomas reappears, clapping a hand on my shoulder. "This is a gathering for our Freedom Group, a sobriety support network."

I stare at him blankly while my brain tries to make sense of his words, my lips parting. "You mean to tell me I accidentally crashed an AA BBQ?"

Grill Guy—bless his enthusiastic heart—beams. "Thomas is my sponsor—sober for eight years now. Freedom from addiction."

My mouth drops open. My brain is buffering. Thomas—the same man who got blackout drunk and left me with an outrageous sushi bill—is an AA sponsor?

Thomas fixes me with an unreadable look, his jaw tightening. "You could join us, Allie."

Oh, hell no.

I take a careful step back. "Wow. Okay. So this is *definitely* not where I'm supposed to be."

"Or," he says smoothly on cue, "exactly where you're meant to be."

I throw my hands up. "Yeah, see, no offense, but I *like* alcohol. I'm a big fan of margaritas. Also, I was looking for my friend's event, not an intervention."

Before anyone can pray for me, my phone buzzes. *Darius*. Thank the universe for a random cell signal and the much-needed distraction.

I answer in record time. "Darius, where are you?"

"Where am I?" He sounds delighted. "Where *are you*?"

I lower my voice. "I'm at an AA BBQ."

Silence.

Then, Darius *howls* with laughter. "You are at what?"

"I thought it was the Singles Mingle, okay?" I hiss, glancing around. "There are *Bibles* coming out, Darius. I need an extraction, *fast*."

"Oh my god." He's wheezing now. "I'm at the *actual* Singles Mingle event, drinking a free cocktail, and watching hot people flirt."

I let out an exaggerated groan. "Where?"

"At the Chugach lodge. How did you—wait, never mind, Lisa is such an airhead with giving directions. Get over here before I get too bored trying to get these guys to become switch hitters."

My phone pings with a location that is well within city limits. I glance around at the *Freedom Group* as a thought occurs to me. "Hold that thought. I'll see you soon."

Marching back to Thomas, I plant a hand on my hip. "You owe me two hundred dollars for ditching me at the sushi place. I'll take a Venmo payment now."

"Fine. Here." He barely hesitates before pulling out his phone, typing in the info, and handing it to me to enter my information.

I don't return his phone until I see the transfer goes through. I need the money. He should pay for lying and dashing out on me anyway. Then, I deleted my info off his phone. "Don't try to contact me."

I stride back to my Subaru with confidence, my cowboy hat tilted from the swagger of my victory. Of course, another romantic misadventure follows—even pretending to date turns into a disaster. I'm completely lost in the woods, the car covered in road dust, and mosquitoes start to swarm. On the bright side, my university savings account is looking healthier.

Not a total loss.

Chapter 16

Résumé Reality Check

A text pops up from my mom: *"You owed me & I got notified of the deposit."*

I stare at my phone, the words blurring as I try to stay professional at work despite the annoying message. It's been three days since I asked her what was going on, and this is her response?

The text makes no sense. I didn't borrow any money from her. Even if I did, she should've asked before taking anything from my account—or at least called me back over the weekend instead of leaving me in silence.

Her text isn't just frustrating. It's cryptic—offering zero explanation for why she's drained my entire checking account.

I rub my temple and swivel in my office chair at Alaska Professional Temp Agency. The rhythmic creak of the chair fills the otherwise silent reception area. I take slow, deep breaths, trying to make sense of it.

Okay. It's not like she hasn't pulled stunts like this before. She's "borrowed" my clothes, my hair products, even pawned my straightener once, claiming I owed her for "all the years of room and board." But she's never outright stolen cash.

I open up my banking app to view my accounts. $0.31 in checking and $300 in my savings from Thomas and Lisa's dating cash. At least my university fund isn't empty.

I shove my phone into my purse, teeth clenched. This isn't a crisis I can solve right now. First, I have to get through today.

It's supposed to be an easy few days working at the temp agency office instead of being sent to be an office temp at a random location. I'm excited to work in the office and catch up with Darius since we never got to chat over the weekend when I met him at the dating event. We only got a chance to laugh about my accidental appearance and an AA event. Then, we spent most of the evening talking about eligible men and perfect nacho toppings between the loud music and continuous margarita fountain.

Besides hanging with my best friend, I hope to sneak a coffee break long enough to breathe in the same space as Alexis so her badass businesswoman vibes will rub off on me. When I have my business degree and I'm running a company, I want to command respect and own a room, like she does.

But of course, Darius has mysteriously disappeared on errands, leaving me alone in the temp agency this morning with nothing but my slow-brewing anxiety and a playlist of hold music. There's a note that my task details are in my email, so after brewing a new pot of coffee and stalling, I'm hoping to see Darius. I'm finally settling behind a desk to log on.

I refreshed my email and am looking for my next work assignment.

Ding.

"Subject: *URGENT: Immediate Task Assignment*"

My stomach twists. Alexis? Urgent? That's... not comforting.

I open the email, and my pulse skyrockets.

Attached is a list. And not just any list—a terrifying, soul-crushing, someone-must've-accidentally-sent-this-to-me list.

1. Data Entry: Inputting financial transactions into the company's accounting software.

2. Invoice Processing: Reviewing, verifying, and processing invoices for payments.

3. Bank Reconciliation: Comparing and matching the company's internal records with bank statements.

4. Accounts Payable Management: Entering bills and expenses, scheduling payments, and managing vendor accounts.

5. Accounts Receivable Management: Issuing invoices to clients, tracking payments received, and following up on overdue accounts.

6. Expense Reports: Reviewing and processing employee expense reports.

7. Audit Preparation: Gathering and organizing documents required for internal or external audits for the fiscal year.

8. Ledger Maintenance: Maintaining and reconciling general ledger accounts.

9. Variance Analysis: Identifying and explaining variances between actual and budgeted financial performance.

You are assigned to the Alaska Temp Agency office this week. We have the same accounting software that you successfully used last week. Relevant files are attached. Let me know if you have any questions. – Alexis.

My hands tremble as I stare at the screen.

What. The. Absolute. Hell.

I barely survived my last temp assignment and only did because I am skilled at learning from YouTube videos.

This is a CFO-level accounting list that is as long as my trouser inseam. At almost six feet tall, that's saying something. How am I supposed to tackle all of this?

I don't know what half of these things mean. I was hoping for a chill day, maybe some light filing. But this? This is a professional-level accounting nightmare. This isn't an assignment—it's my business career death sentence.

And Alexis gave it to me. Alexis, my ridiculously attractive, terrifyingly competent boss, who, for some inexplicable reason, believes I can do the things on this list.

Wait.

Did she figure it out? This list may be her way of seeing up close and personal if I am cut out to be an office temp and work in a professional office. *Does she know I am faking my way through this job?* Is she testing me? Setting me up to fail?

I print the email, and my heartbeat is an erratic drumline. The printer hums, a slow mechanical betrayal as it spits out the evidence of my impending doom.

I fan myself with the paper, swallowing hard.

Okay, Aurora. Think. You survived last week's accounting and dating disaster. You survived your mom's emotional and financial terrorism. You even survived a margarita-fueled singles event that started with an AA meeting. You can handle this.

Right?

I drop my forehead onto the desk.

"No. No, I absolutely cannot."

"Aurora?"

I bolt upright so fast I nearly tip the chair over, and my heel snags, causing me to dive headfirst into the filing cabinets. Alexis moves from the doorway to catch my arm and steady me.

Oh my gosh–I look drunk. Can today get any worse?

She just gives me that warm smile, immediately setting off my blush mechanism. I straighten and nod thanks, stepping away from my very hot boss. Wait, am I at work, or is this an elaborate leftover weekend margarita-fueled dream?

She chuckles, leaning back in the doorway, one perfectly shaped eyebrow raised like she wasn't catching me talking to myself. She is holding a coffee cup in her hand, steam curling from the lid. I find myself staring at her too long, and her fitted dark green blazer that should be illegal in an office setting because it makes her look *dangerously* good.

"Hi." My voice cracks, and I clear my throat. "I- uh- hi."

Smooth. *Real* smooth.

She steps inside, placing the coffee on the desk in front of me. "For you."

I blink. She brought me a coffee? Like–*for me*?

My body heats up and does an immediate, involuntary *crush alert*, with a clench in the pit of my stomach followed by an embarrassing feeling of hot wetness as I struggle to rein it in.

"Oh. Wow. Thanks." I pick up the cup, trying to look casual as I sip.

Black. No sugar. No cream. Very-getting shit-done, professional, *Alexis-style* coffee.

I inhale slowly and do not die on the spot.

"Everything okay?" She nods at the printed list in my hands. "You got my email with your work assignments for the next few weeks?"

I stare at her, debating my choices. I could fake confidence, smile, nod, and inevitably cause a financial catastrophe.

Or cry.

Or, admit I have no idea what I'm doing and hope she doesn't fire me immediately.

I go with a modified D, Panic, make a weird joke, and hope she thinks I'm charming instead of incompetent.

"Yeah, uh, cool list! I *love* an accounting challenge. Nothing like a little variance analysis to, you know, really spice up a Monday."

Alexis's lips twitch like she's holding back a laugh.

I grip the paper tighter. "Totally doable. I might need to, uh, brush up on a few things. But I'm on it."

Alexis leans against my desk, arms folded. "If you have questions, ask. I've been handling most of the accounting."

Her voice is calm. Open. Not at all like someone plotting my downfall.

I hesitate. "So... this isn't a test?"

Her brow furrows. "A test?"

"Like, you don't secretly know I suck at accounting and want to expose me as a fraud?"

Silence. Then—she laughs. Not a polite chuckle—a full, head-tilted-back laugh.

I blink, momentarily stunned.

When she regains composure, she shakes her head. "Aurora, if I thought you weren't capable, I wouldn't have given you this assignment."

I open my mouth, then shut it.

"But..." I gesture wildly at the list. "This is, like, CFO or CEO-level work."

She shrugs. "It is. And I'm the CEO who thinks you can do it better than I can. You nailed the accounting software last week. Figured you could handle more."

A slow, sinking realization hits me. Alexis actually believes in me. She isn't trying to humiliate me—she thinks I can do this like an honest-to-God, real businesswoman.

And I have absolutely no idea how to live up to that expectation.

I swallow hard. "Right. Yeah. Of course."

Alexis pushes off the desk, flashing a confident smile before heading to her office. "You got this, Aurora. I trust you and let me know if you need anything."

The door clicks shut behind her.

I sit there, stunned, staring at the absurdly professional to-do list.

Then I take a deep breath, sip my too-professional black coffee, and mutter, "Well, guess I'm learning finance today."

I shake my head and think of my mom's last text. No way am I letting her ruin my day. I survived her constant undermining—I'll survive this.

But still... I wish Darius were here to talk me off this ledge.

I grip the list like it's a lifeline and decide to talk to Alexis. She's reasonable. She'll understand this is too much for me.

I take a breath. "Alexis, can I talk to you for a second?" My voice wobbles slightly.

She looks up from her computer and motions to the chair across her desk with a warm smile. "Sure, Aurora. Come in."

I lower myself into the chair, clasping my hands in my lap to keep from visibly trembling. "I wanted to mention..." I clear my throat. "I'm a little worried—"

Alexis interrupts, leaning back like she didn't dump a Denali-sized task list on me. "Honestly, I've been muddling through the accounting, and we desperately need someone who knows what they're doing. You absolutely crushed it last week. I knew you'd be up to the task of helping me."

"Crushed it," I echo weakly. "That's... one way to put it."

She grins, eyes twinkling. "Afraid you'll make me look bad?"

I blink. My jaw might be on the floor. That is the most incorrect assumption in the history of assumptions.

Before I can correct her, she leans forward conspiratorially. "I hope so! Look, I can schmooze clients and run the office, but numbers? Total mystery. My parents stepped back this year to test me, and if I can get the books in order before the gala, it'll prove I'm ready to be CEO."

The sheer confidence in me makes my stomach flip. Has she... met me?

"This is... a lot," I manage, glancing at the dizzying task list.

"I believe in you, Aurora. Just start tackling the list, see how much you can get done."

I chew my lip. "But what if I mess up? I can't afford to lose this job."

Alexis leans forward, elbows on the desk. "Aurora, Neil gave you a glowing report. Said you handled everything like a pro. He even hinted at buying out your temp contract."

My thoughts trip over themselves. "Neil wanted to hire me?"

Was this before or after he tried to flirt his way into a 'casual' dinner? And more importantly—how does Alexis know? There's no way she heard that from anyone but Neil. I am not ready to unpack that.

"He did," she confirms. "And look, if you want to leave, I won't stop you." She pauses, then smirks. "But I'm hoping I can lure you into staying—with a raise. And I have something already for your next temp assignment."

I sit up straighter. "Really?"

"Really." She grins. "So here's the deal—after you help get us caught up on our accounting system, I've got a job lined up that you can decide on. A local cruise line. Data entry, vendor accounts, nothing scary. But it doesn't start until next week. This week, I need your magic here."

"Another temp job away from the office?" My heart sinks slightly. But also... more money. Stability. A raise.

I force a bright, eager nod. "I mean—yes! Thank you, Alexis. I won't let you down."

"I know you won't." She stands, walks around the desk, and rests a reassuring hand on my shoulder. "And who knows? Keep impressing us, and we can talk about making you a permanent staff member instead of temping."

Permanent? My eyes widened. "That would be... amazing."

She nods. "No pressure. Just keep doing what you're doing."

I clutch my newly upgraded career hopes to my chest and head back to my desk, feeling equal parts exhilarated and terrified.

As soon as I go back to my desk and sit down, Darius materializes in my office, eyebrows raised in concern. "Hey, Aurora. You okay?"

I sigh dramatically. "Not really. Alexis assigned me this huge accounting project, and I have no clue what I'm doing."

Darius winces. "Yeah, about that... First, I need to apologize. I *may* have overly embellished your business experience to get you hired."

My mouth drops open, because Alexis, and I, know it was more than embellishment. "Slightly?"

He gives me his most charming, unrepentant smile. "Okay, a *lot*. But in my defense, you're actually pulling it off! I'm seriously impressed, girl. You're a numbers badass."

I narrow my eyes. "Darius, I was in the math club. That does not make me an accountant."

"I should also mention," he says, ready to spill more secrets, but his phone lights up, and the moment is lost. He distractedly adds, "Pfft. Numbers, math, accounting—Same difference."

I open my mouth to argue and explain the impossible list, which there's no way I can do, which will definitely lead to Alexis firing me and me having no money for my fall semester. But his phone buzzes. He rechecks the screen, and his expression shifts between nervous and guilty.

"I'm so sorry, Aurora. I have to take this. But we'll talk later, okay? I do need to tell you about something."

My frustration spikes. We *always* need to talk, yet we *never* do, even with me working with him. I nod. "Okay."

As he hurries off, I exhale sharply, shove my earbuds in, and type "basic accounting for small businesses" into the YouTube search, adding in the first task on the list to the search. If my best friend can fabricate my résumé, and I survived doing accounting work at the last temp job, then I can fake my way through a few weeks.

Hours pass. Slowly but surely, I work through my first task. Surprisingly, I understand what I'm doing, and the high of doing some intellectually stimulating work is unreal.

Alexis walks by and peeks into my cubicle. "How's it going, Number Queen?"

I lift my coffee mug with a triumphant grin. "Getting it done."

Her eyes flicker with approval. And is it me, or is one more button on her blouse undone? The curve of her collarbone makes my brain stall for half a second.

"Wow, Aurora. I'm impressed."

Heat creeps up my face. "Thanks."

She smiles. "Knew you'd kill it. We're lucky to have you. *I'm* lucky." She taps her fingers on my desk. "Caramel macchiato, iced, extra whip?"

I squint at her, wondering between this morning's serious coffee and this sweet coffee, which happens to be my usual order. How did she know my coffee order?

"Stalker."

She laughs. "I pay attention."

And okay, maybe that makes my stomach flip *just a little.*

"Don't stress too much about getting everything finished on the to-do list," she adds. "The cruise company job coming up is the real prize. If giving them an expert accounting temp impresses them, I'll get a contract to staff all their summer cruises and tours. It'll be a huge win for the agency—and for me, personally."

And *now* I'm panicking again.

She winks as her phone rings. "Duty calls. We'll continue this later. Coffee's on me, soon-to-be my Employee of the month."

She walks off, and I take a deep breath. This is fine. I *can* do this.

Then my phone rings. My landlord's name flashes on the screen like a judgmental beacon of financial doom.

I answer with a forced cheeriness. "Hey there!"

"Hey, Aurora. Hate to be the bearer of bad news, but your check bounced for this month's rent." His tone is more business than our usual mailbox banter.

"Oh wow. That's—" Not great. "Probably a banking error. I'll sort it out today."

There's a pause, as if he's weighing how much he believes that. "Okay. Just get it to me soon."

"Absolutely! You have a great day now," I chirp, then hang up and groan into my hands.

The phone call reminds me of the financial stress, and I rub a hand over my face. All my businesswoman bravado vanishes.

Step one: don't throw up from financial stress. Step two: figure out how to pay for university when I can't even cover my rent. Step three: pretend everything's fine because spiraling isn't an option.

Before I can dramatically lay my head on my desk in despair, Alexis appears in my doorway like a well-dressed mirage. She steps inside, places a potted plant on my desk, and leans against my chair with the casual confidence of someone who absolutely owns the world.

"You look like you could use a friend to talk to. This is William the Seventh," she says, amusement flickering in her serious, brown eyes.

I blink at the spider plant. "Is this a gift or a bribe to get this work done faster?"

"Both." She looks amused. "You work hard. Consider it a reward."

Darius appears and side-eyes Alexis while winking at me. "Is Alexis giving you one of her babies *and* compliments?"

Alexis shrugs, unbothered. "She earned it."

My fingers graze the slick, chaotic plant–it looks like my morning hair. "Thanks."

Alexis gives me a slow, knowing look. "Try not to work yourself into an early grave, Aurora." Then, with a casual finger gun—my signature finger gun—and a smirk, she's gone.

Darius fans himself dramatically. "That woman is smooth like Alaskan black ice."

I sip my coffee, letting the rich sweetness momentarily dull my stress. "Yeah. And I'm the idiot who thought this job would be boring."

Darius clinks his coffee against mine. "At least you make it look entertaining."

I exhale, glance at the work task list, and think of my to-do list, the weight of everything pressing down. Rent, school, food, survival—it's a lot. But I've handled worse. One task at a time.

I square my shoulders and mutter, "You got this."

Darius adds, "Of course you do, girl. Slay those numbers, math whiz."

And if they are both wrong, and I fail?

I guess, if I fail here, I can always accept Neil's accounting job and hope to avoid discussing tacos or dating.

But first—step one: survive today.

I take another sip of coffee. At least I have caffeine and questionable life choices to keep things interesting.

Chapter 17

Confronting Sandra

After surviving Monday, I pace my tiny apartment, phone in hand, stomach twisting into sailor-grade knots. I've been tackling spreadsheets, budgets, and Alexis's impossible accounting list head-on—so why does confronting my mother feel like the hardest thing in the world?

With a deep breath, I look at my Fall university schedule I hung on the refrigerator. I gently trace the paper, running my fingers down my class schedule.

UNIVERSITY OF ANCHORAGE

Intro to Microeconomics (ECON 101) – Basics of supply and demand, markets, and economic decision-making.
College Algebra (MATH 121) – Required math for business majors, focusing on functions, equations, and financial applications.
Business Foundations (BUS 101) – Introductory business course covering management, marketing, and finance.
English Composition (ENG 111) – A core requirement to build writing and critical thinking skills.
Intro to Accounting (ACCT 201) – Basic accounting principles, financial statements, and bookkeeping

There's no way I'm letting her ruin my plan and my future. I will take these classes, and I will pass them. I will *never* need her help again!

I stab at my phone, dialing. The second ring, she answers, her voice drips through the speaker with saccharine sweetness.

"Hey, sweetie! What's up?"

No pleasantries. Not today.

"We need to talk," I say, voice steadier than I feel. "Why did you take money from my account?"

A pause. The faintest hesitation before she laughs, airy and dismissive. "Really? We already discussed this."

"Mom, you took my rent money! That was for my apartment and my university expenses." My voice shakes, but I push forward, refusing to let her steamroll me into silence.

"Oh, Aurora, don't be so dramatic," she sighs. "Rent isn't that much, and you have a scholarship. *I* needed it. Things have been tight since your father stopped sending child support."

My stomach drops. "What?"

A thick, suffocating silence.

"You told me he was a deadbeat," I say slowly, each word slicing through the growing storm in my chest. "You said he never paid a dime."

"Well, I never asked him to pay, but the government required him to pay," she admits, voice cool and detached, as if she hadn't just shattered a fundamental truth of my life. "But he stopped, and things have been tough."

I sit down hard on the couch, the weight of her words pressing down. "You've been lying to me. My whole life."

"Don't take that tone with me, young lady." Her voice sharpens. "You have no idea what it's like raising a child on your own."

I let out a short, humorless laugh. "No, but I do know what it's like to be kept in the dark. To struggle while you pocketed money that was meant for me."

"Excuse me for trying to keep a roof over our heads," she snaps.

"Our heads?" My laugh comes out sharper this time, cutting. "I don't live there, Mom. You're not paying my rent, I am. And I need *my* money back."

"I can't," she says flatly. "It's gone."

The tears threaten, but I refuse to let them win. "Then you need to figure it out. Because I'm not moving back in with you, and I refuse to let your version of 'love' ruin my future, too."

She mutters something under her breath, and I inhale sharply, forcing my voice to stay even. "I mean it. I need the money by the end of the day."

A long pause. Then, begrudgingly, "Fine. I'll figure something out. Stop by later."

I hang up before she can guilt me into backing down. Relief wars with the dull ache in my chest, but I shove it down.

Not trusting her word, I decided to stop by right now. I need to see the cash in my hand before I believe a damn thing she says. Besides, maybe she didn't spend all of my paycheck, and giving her any extra time means more of my paycheck might be spent.

Before I know it, I'm in my car, tires crunching against the pavement as I pull into the driveway of the tiny, tired house I grew up in.

Empty.

No car in sight. No lights in the windows. Nothing.

I knock, but there's no answer.

She's avoiding me.

The realization slams into my ribs. She never intended to pay me back. She never planned to face me.

I clench my fists, swallowing the burn in my throat. No. I will not cry over this. Not here. Not now.

Fine. If she won't face me, then I have more important things to focus on.

I need to work. I need to make sure I can survive without her.

I drive straight to the Alaska Temp Agency, where Darius is waiting, where Alexis's impossible list is still sitting on my desk.

I need to focus on work. Anything is better than dwelling on how I've been lied to–Mom is sabotaging my university dreams and future. Work is something I can control. And even with the huge, chaotic mess of numbers in front of me, I'm figuring it out. One problem at a time.

And right now, my biggest problem is making sure I can afford to stay far, far away from her twisted idea of love.

Why didn't she tell me my dad was paying child support?

Chapter 18

Hook and Reel Dating, and Sinking, Fast

If there is a hell, it's probably run by Lisa, with a big sign proclaiming, "The Fun Heaven," and the jacuzzis are fire pits filled with awkward first dates.

I stare at the text on my phone for a full minute before responding.

"Emergency. One of my clients got ghosted, and I need a stand-in. Plz."

I text back, "No."

"You need the cash."

I sigh. She's right. "...Fine."

I met her after work. I changed into an easy summer dress, and I put on some lipstick for that added razzle-dazzle. "Oh, thank God. You showed up." She clasps my hands dramatically. "I owe you my favorite houseplant for this."

"You'd have to keep a plant alive first, Lisa," I deadpan.

"Rude," she sniffs. "And for the record, I kept a basil plant alive for three whole weeks."

I arch an eyebrow. "Where is it now?"

Lisa waves a hand. "Irrelevant." Then, she claps her hands together. "Okay, listen up. Your date's inside, and we are already in 'code red' territory because his original date bailed last minute. Which means I need you to be charming, delightful, maybe a little flirty, but not in a way that suggests marriage."

"Lisa," I groan. "I have told you so many times—"

"You need the cash," she interrupts, holding up a crisp hundred-dollar bill like she's summoning a feral animal. "And you already shaved your legs. Don't waste that effort."

I snatch the money from her, grumbling, "You're a menace."

Lisa beams with excitement, waiting outside the over-the-top tourist bar with an enthusiastic taxidermy-decorated interior, *The Grizzly Fork*. "Okay, here's the deal. His name is Brad. He's a dentist. Normal. Tall. Loves hiking. *Totally* your type. It will be so easy."

I squint. "I don't have a type. And this is an older guy, right?"

She waves off my comment with a giggle. "Okay, well, he's someone else's type, and they bailed, so you're up." She shoves a crisp hundred into my hand. "Now get in there, champ. Table six. Be *nice*."

I sigh dramatically, but my wallet *does* need the boost. I push inside, scanning for a Brad-shaped person.

Then I see him.

And... he's already got a woman across from him. She is older but has similar hair color and facial features.

I stopped abruptly, and Lisa plowed into me.

Luckily, I grab a caribou hind quarter that is supposed to be a cute Alaska bar stool, and I pivot. "He brought his mom. I'm leaving."

Lisa's grip lands on my elbow with *unholy* strength. "Nope. You took the cash. You're on the hook."

"Lisa," I whisper through clenched teeth. "You cannot be serious."

"Sometimes guys need a dating service because they are socially awkward. It's really racist of you not to date him," Lisa nods, as if saying that what she had said made total sense.

"*Racist* isn't the right word," I hiss.

"Yeah, whatever. But hear me out—she's paying for dinner and he's super boring whereas I think she used to be a waitress at a casino in Vegas so her stories will be so entertaining. You'll laugh the whole evening."

I glare at her. "I hope a sharknado eats your car while you're in it."

Before I can argue further, Lisa shoves me toward the table. "Here's your date, Brad. Aurora, this is Brad. Have fun, you two," she says with a laugh and a wiggle of her fingers. She finally lets go of the vise grip she had on me, freeing me from my escape route.

I reluctantly sit down at the table.

Brad's face lights up. "Aurora?" He gestures to the older woman beside him. "This is my mom, Beverly."

Beverly, who looks like she's personally vetted every single girl her son has *ever* breathed near, folds her hands. "So, Aurora, tell me—are you good with children?"

I blink. "Uh. I mean. I babysat once?"

Beverly's eyes narrow like she's about to pull out an application. "Do you cook?"

"Did you work in Vegas?" I ask, trying to deflect her questions as I sit and butter a sourdough roll.

Lisa, at the bar, is dying of laughter.

"Do I look like I worked in Vegas?" She's wearing a unisex wool sweater, jeans and boots. This is almost identical to the outfit her son is wearing, except he's added a collared shirt under and horn-rimmed glasses, not as a fashion statement.

I'm going to kill Lisa.

I smile tightly. "Well, I'm *great* at ordering takeout."

Brad chuckles nervously. "Mom, maybe we let Aurora breathe?"

She pats his arm. "I'm just saying, time is ticking." The waiter brings three glasses and a bottle of white wine.

She eyes me over her wine glass. "Do you see yourself settling down in the next few years?"

I snap my gaze back to Lisa.

Lisa gives me a look that says, "Be nice."

I glare back with the look, "I'm setting your house on fire."

Which she misinterprets and nods enthusiastically back to, giving me a thumbs up.

Brad smiles, oblivious. "So, Aurora, tell me—what do you do for fun?"

"I fight to survive every day."

He blinks.

I clear my throat. "Uh. I mean. I'm a survivalist, like the hiking and camping type."

Beverly hums approvingly. "Good. A strong mother for future children. You're tall but your hips are so narrow. You might have to get c-sections."

C-Sections? She's already planning our multiple children.

I glare at Lisa.

Lisa won't even look at me.

Brad, thankfully, looks *one second* from shriveling into dust.

I take a gulp of wine. "Yeah, no. I'm out. Brad, if you want to get drinks or dinner without your mom, please let Lisa know."

"Are you sure? Dinner hasn't arrived and I ordered meatloaf for the table."

"Yeah, Mom has a good eye for meatloaf," Brad says.

I look between them, my brain short-circuiting. "Okay. Yep. I'm out."

I push back from the table, grab my purse, and power-walk toward the exit, flipping Lisa off on my way to the exit.

At the bar, Lisa was shaking with silent laughter, then beelined to the exit, beating me there as I had to navigate an entire taxidermied army of animals to get out the heavy log door.

Already waiting outside, Lisa is *cackling.* "Okay, okay, I might have messed up that one. I'm glad Brad got at least one date from our agency. I don't think we'll be able to match him."

I scowl. "You think?"

Lisa sighs, dramatically clutching her chest. "Aurora, this is just a reminder of what could have happened if you had an overly involved mom. The next one will be normal, I promise."

"Two. Hundred. Dollars for the next date," I say flatly.

Lisa wheezes. "Deal. It'll be a normal date," she promises.

"You've *never* set me up on a normal date. I'm not even sure you know what a normal date *looks* like."

"You confirm that love is only possible in Hallmark movies and I confirm why I should never date again."

Lisa, still giggling, takes me by the hand as we head to our usual spot. "Okay, okay. Maybe that one was *slightly* bad."

I groan.

"But admit it. You're kind of enjoying the chaos, and what else would you've been doing. Eating ramen and watching youtube tutorials on some boring excel sheet formula how-to."

I lift a brow, "That would have been better than Brad and Beverly."

Lisa stretches. "Soooo... I'll let you know if I need you next week."

I glare.

Lisa grins.

I sigh. Then, return her smile and pull her in for a hug. At least this builds up my university savings account, and at least Lisa is enjoying her career.

Chapter 19

Khakis, Chaos, and Cake

The scent hits me first—vanilla, buttercream, and my stomach rumbles with the betrayal of my broke girl hunger. I haven't eaten since last night's dinner of emotional granola, followed by half a bag of chocolate chips.

I shove open the Alaska Temp Agency door and stop dead.

This is not... normal.

Where there should be phones ringing and keyboards suffering under caffeinated rage, there are balloons. Everywhere. They're floating at the ceiling like they've ascended to office heaven, curling ribbons waving gently in the air conditioning like *Congratulations, you survived corporate America.*

In the center of the chaos, a cake. And not some sheet cake from the gas station bakery aisle. No, this one's huge and obnoxious, covered in silver and blue icing like it's going to prom. Across the top, "25 YEARS OF TEMP-TASTIC SUCCESS!" The banner above it matches. Of course, it does.

I blink. "Am I... hallucinating from hunger?"

Then Darius appears beside the cake, one hand perched on his sequined hip like he's guarding the crown jewels. His blazer sparkles so aggressively that I shield my eyes. Honestly, if a plane crashed into this building right now, it'd be *his fault.*

"TGIF, baby! You made it!" His grin is sharp and entirely too proud of itself.

I squint. "I thought I was coming into... I don't know... *work*?"

Darius gasps, full dramatic clutch-the-pearls energy. "Work? On a Friday? Sweetheart, no."

I glance around at the entire office, acting like this is the afterparty for the Met Gala. "You people realize we run a temp agency, not a nightclub, right?"

Darius gasps, pressing a hand to his chest like I insulted his entire bloodline. "Aurora, TGIF. Work is fleeting. Friends are forever."

Lisa nods solemnly, licking frosting off a plastic knife. "Besides, it's Friday. No one works on a Friday."

"What are you doing here?" I look around to see why Lisa is at our workplace and not hers. *Is this some Freaky Friday situation?*

"Free cake and visiting you, of course, I'm here. I told the dating agency I was taking a long coffee break," she says with a wink. "No one's going to miss me except all those thirsty singles you didn't hook up with during your dates."

"Lisa, I'm taking a dating sabbatical. I don't have time to chase relationships, and no one needs to date this hot mess," I say, setting down my purse and giving up on logging onto my computer with the bustling staff around me.

Lisa leans over from the snack table, licking frosting off a plastic knife like she's in a music video. "We should only work Monday through Thursday. Friday's for *relaxing*. I think some offices have a 4 day work week."

"You definitely made that up," I responded. I fold my arms, staring them both down. "Okay, but I actually have invoices to finish. Payroll doesn't file itself. You know—paychecks? Rent? College tuition? That old chestnut?"

Darius flutters his hands like I just suggested murder. "Aurora, please. You're killing the casual Friday vibe. This is not just a party. It's a pre-party."

"To what?" I ask, mostly because I hate myself.

"To the Alaska Temp Agency 25th Anniversary Gala, duh." Darius spreads his arms like he's announcing the birth of a royal baby. "Next weekend. It's *the* event of the decade. They got the cake order date wrong and delivered it today with all the other party stuff. So I proclaimed today, Cake-day and employee team building day. We are easing into the festivities, darling. Mentally. Spiritually. Fashionably."

His gaze drops to my khakis and rumpled button-up. His left eye twitches.

I look down, then back at him. "If you want me to RSVP, I'll need an actual paycheck and a formalwear miracle."

"You're going," Darius says, with the authority of someone who has already color-coded a seating chart.

"I don't even know if I'm invited." I shrug. "I'm new. I'm seasonal. And unless Alexis wants me showing up in my frumpiest cable-knit and Lisa's sparkly heels that pinch my toes but look cute enough to be worth it, I think I'll skip the drama."

Darius freezes mid-frosting swipe. His face contorts like I kicked a puppy. "*Excuse* me?"

"I'm serious. I don't really have anything gala-ready. Buying a new dress is another hundred dollars that could go towards my ridiculously expensive Introduction to Business textbook. Besides, this isn't my scene." I gesture toward the chaos. "You've got cake, and an HR manager doing the Macarena with a balloon animal. Meanwhile, I have thirty-seven unpaid student portal notifications and an anxiety rash."

Lisa hums, not helping. "To be fair, your rash is kind of festive."

"Thank you?" I deadpan.

"Listen," Darius says, stepping into full party-commander mode. "You're not skipping the gala or today's spontaneous office party. I'll help you find something affordable and dramatic. You'll walk in looking like a glamazon goddess. And you'll make every ex who dumped you regret their life choices."

"I've only been dumped once," I point out.

"Then we'll pretend it was *tragic.*" He fans himself with a glittery napkin. "You need this, a fun workday. No invoices. No spreadsheets. Just cake and socializing. It's all to get ready for the big gala in a few weeks, so work-related."

"Again, I'd rather get a paycheck, so I'm going to get back to work," I mutter.

But Darius is already scheming, Lisa is humming the beat to *Dancing Queen*, and someone in the back is inflating a five-foot-tall balloon number two. This "office" has become a full swinging party cult, and I'm the last reluctant follower.

I pull out my laptop and head toward the break room. Navigating through the chattering crowd, I try not to knock anyone over with my long arms as I walk through the office. "I'll be over here inputting invoices," I grumble. "If anyone needs me or if the IRS calls."

Behind me, Lisa yells, "Get her a party hat to celebrate Cake Day!"

Cake day. Because apparently, that's a thing now.

I juggle a massive slice of blue-and-silver frosted sugar brick on a flimsy paper plate while beelining for the quietest corner I can find in this chaotic circus we call the Alaska Temp Agency. I only want one uninterrupted hour to finish my invoice list before it mutates into unpaid overtime.

But life has other plans.

"Aurora."

Cue full-body paralysis.

I don't have to turn around. That low, smooth voice? Controlled like she moonlights as a meditation app. Or an FBI negotiator. Or the woman in my dreams. *Alexis.*

My brain goes full static. I pivot slowly, the cake tilted like it might leap off the plate in protest. There she is, standing like a power-suited mirage, arms crossed, one eyebrow raised like *she* invented casual Fridays and is personally offended I didn't dress for the occasion.

Her burgundy blazer sleeves are rolled up. Her forearms? Obscene. Distractingly sculpted, her tattoo sleeves peeking out. I suddenly forget what numbers are.

"Hey," I croak, trying for chill but landing squarely in squeaky-teen-on-a-crush territory.

She tilts her head, eyes glinting. "You're looking very..." she waves a hand in a slow circle, "...studious. For cake day."

"Yeah, well," I gesture with my cake slice like a sword of productivity, "TGIF. Time to inhale frosting and cry over accounting tables."

She hums. A low, amused sound that should be illegal. "Good. Because the gala's coming up, and I'll need my best team there." She raises an eyebrow at me.

Did she say, best? *BEST?* I physically levitate.

"Oh! Invitations!" I blurt, the volume too high, pointing at the pile of invitations on the table before me. "I was gonna—I mean, I already alphabetized them, obviously, because...systems! And I—uh—if you want me to run point on that? I'm ready. For that."

Smooth. Like a cactus smoothie.

Alexis's eyes flick to the stack of gala invites on the counter, then back to me. There's a sparkle in her gaze. She's holding back a laugh or question.

"You've done plenty this week," she says softly.

And then she touches me.

Fingers light on my forearm, confident and casual. A totally normal, HR-friendly touch. Except my nervous system goes DEFCON 1. Every cell in my body throws a rager. *Touch alert! Sound the alarms!*

"Take it easy and enjoy the mini party before the real one," she adds, her fingers lingering a beat too long. Or maybe that's my brain stretching time like taffy.

I nod so fast that my neck cracks. "Cool, cool, cool. I'll just, uh...return these to the mail bin. With professionalism. And precision."

I pivot, attempting a graceful exit, and instead narrowly avoid flinging cake onto a potted plant.

Deep breaths. Reboot. I reach for the top envelope and run my fingers over the gold-embossed lettering:

Alaska Temp Agency's 25th Anniversary Gala: An evening of elegance, celebration, and esteemed company.

Esteemed company? Unless that includes the feral raccoons from behind the dumpster, I'm not sure I qualify.

And then I see it. The enemy.

Neil's name. Front and center on the top invite. He might have given a good report to Alexis, but he's still a creep. The invite with his name on it is taunting me like a smug high school bully who's both unemployed and still somehow has opinions on my LinkedIn activity.

I scan the room—no one's looking—then execute a flawless mission. Slide. Fold. Toss. Neil's invite vanishes into the trash like daylight in December.

Except—

"Did you just throw something away?" Alexis's voice slices through my moment like a fancy cheese knife.

Busted.

"No." My voice jumps an octave. Darius, already posted near the cake like a snack-loving gargoyle, snorts into his frosting. *Traitor.*

Before Alexis can interrogate me further, the door swings open with perfect dramatic timing.

Richard.

Tall, shiny, and perfectly moisturized. He strolls in like he owns the place, a gym bag slung over one shoulder and a tray of coffees in hand. The air shifts. Even the balloons pause mid-float.

"Babe," he says like he's on an ad for Patagonia Dating. "Got your usual."

My stomach somersaults into a frozen lake.

Alexis's smile blooms—faint but familiar. She steps toward him and accepts the coffee with a soft "thanks." Then he leans in. A cheek kiss. Quick. Comfortable. Intimate.

Like they do this every day. Because they do.

And I—I die.

Inside, I faceplant into a vat of whipped disappointment. Outside, I smile like my soul hasn't been sucker-punched by reality. Darius catches my eye, his expression shifting from "mmm cupcake" to "you okay?" faster than I can fake it.

I lie by smiling and nodding. Inside, I'm a glacier. Cold, detached, entirely fine.

Richard sets a hand on her waist. My brain slaps a Do Not Disturb sign over my feelings and evacuates the building.

Darius claps suddenly, startling everyone and probably saving my last shreds of dignity.

"Alright, party people," he announces, clinking his cupcake against the nearest coffee cup. "Let's redirect this caffeinated energy toward cake. Aurora and I have frosting to faceplant into and we have a lot of cake to eat."

He herds me away like a sheepdog on a mission.

Richard steps in our path. "I brought one for you too," he says to Darius, holding out a drink with a hopeful smile.

Darius's expression shutters faster than a moose spotting headlights. "I don't drink coffee."

Lies. He's literally sipping a caramel latte with two pumps of drama and extra sass every morning.

Alexis raises a brow. I follow her gaze—she's watching Darius with that sharp, assessing stillness she uses when someone's avoiding something. Richard's smile dims, just slightly.

Then Lisa barrels in like the human embodiment of chaos. "I'll get more cake with you guys!"

"What was that?" I hiss at Darius once we reach the cake table.

He grabs a fork and stabs his slice. "Later."

"No, now."

"Lisa's still here."

Lisa is already licking frosting off a spoon and humming to herself. I scoff and close my eyes. I've never noticed until today she eats cake by licking frosting off silverware rather than actually eating it.

Darius leans close. "I need to talk. Privately. It's about..." He glances back at Alexis and Richard.

Lisa slides up like a gossip missile. "What's the tea? I saw tension. Was it romantic tension? Are you finally gonna spill the beans on your workplace romance sitch?"

Darius elbows her with zero subtlety. "Don't you have dates to ruin?"

"I'm off the clock, baby!" She sings. "I called in sick for the rest of the day. Cake-itis."

I chew on my cake, and confusion. Darius is being *weird*. Nervous. Shifty. And he only gets that way around one topic, secrets.

"Later," he says again, eyes on the door.

Lisa and I exchange a loaded look.

"He's gonna tell you," she stage-whispers behind her hand. "I can feel it in my frosting-covered bones."

"I don't know," I mumble. "He's a master of drama and delaying announcements."

"I give it until the end of the cake round two," she grins.

But me? I'm not sure.

I'm barely holding it together between Alexis's touch, her boyfriend's kiss, Darius's secret love triangle, and my identity crisis. Love and relationships are for everyone but me.

I take another bite of cake. *It's fine.* I'll power through. I'll do accounting. I'll finish my task list. I will *not* cry into frosting.

And I'll keep pretending like Alexis's perfectly soft, *not-for-me* smile and light touch don't hurt in ways I'm too broke to explain.

Chapter 20

Cake Day Confessions

Darius and I barricade ourselves in the only quiet space with a door—Alexis's office. The cake is partly to blame, but the office party is veering into chaos. Lisa's attempting to organize a conga line, and someone's making a duct-tape throne for the "Office Queen." The last time I peeked outside, two interns were competing at finishing a crossword first to win a kiss from Lisa.

Professionalism? Absolutely obliterated.

I focus on the task at hand—eating an unreasonable amount of cake, a job I take extremely seriously. My phone dings with a gynecologist appointment reminder, which I dismiss. More pressing matters require my attention.

Like whatever secret Darius is about to spill.

I ease in with an easy question. "Darius, how many pieces of cake have you eaten?" I wave my fork at him, a dollop of frosting clinging to the edge, threatening to launch.

He glances up, guilt written across his face. A smudge of whipped frosting lingers on his bottom lip. "One bite. I'm watching my figure."

"Coward," I mutter, shoving another forkful into my mouth.

Before I can interrogate him further, the door swings open. Alexis strides in, looking effortlessly composed except for the unmistakable smear of frosting on her chin.

"You messy people," I scold, tossing her a napkin and swiping Darius's chin before he can lick the evidence away.

Alexis dabs at her chin, then smirks. "Thanks."

She points a finger at me, her tone deceptively light. "Also, you better not be working in here. That's an order."

I salute her with my fork, taking a dramatic bite. "Mmm. This cake's incredible."

Darius snickers. "You're the only one actually eating. Everyone else is pretending to diet."

"I'm dedicated." I giggle uncontrollably. Then, for some reason, Alexis shutting the door to leave sends me into full-blown, stomach-clutching laughter.

Darius eyes me warily. "Aurora, you good?"

Through my giggles, I blurt, "You know I like Alexis."

Silence.

Darius's expression morphs into something between concern and amusement. "About that..." He leans back in Alexis's chair, steepling his fingers like a supervillain. "I need to tell you—"

The office phone interrupts us. Darius groans, answering it. "Alaska Temp Agency... Uh-huh... Oh no... Got it." He hangs up, his eyes wide with shock. "Emergency. The bakery just called. The cake is pot-infused."

I freeze, fork halfway to my mouth. "WHAT?"

"I repeat: The cake. Is. Drugged."

Having heard the phone, Alexis hears the last thing Darius said as she steps back inside. "Excuse me?"

Darius quickly explains, and she exhales sharply, pinching the bridge of her nose.

We materialize in front of the cake, like Star Trek warp drive or that glowy transporting thing. I'm not sure, but all of it makes me giggle.

"Okay, nobody eats any more cake!" she calls out. "This is a workplace, not a—" She stops, assessing the damage. "How much was eaten?"

Richard glances at the nearly full cake box. "Looks like only a few slices are missing, so that's good... right?"

I glance at the empty plates around me.

Lisa licked some frosting earlier. Darius took a bite. Alexis has frosting on her chin, but did she actually eat any? The realization hits me like an eighteen-wheeler.

It dawns on me like a slap in the face. I am the only one who ate real, substantial amounts of cake.

I open my mouth to confess—but instead, I burp. Loudly.

Silence.

Then, I lose it, laughing so hard I nearly slide off my chair.

Darius winces. "Oh. Oh, no."

Richard frowns. "Aurora, how much did you eat?"

"Oh my god," I whisper, gripping the table. "Darius. I ate so, so, sooooo much."

"Richard asked, not me," he corrects, his eyes widened. "What? Are you serious?"

I giggle, helpless against the rising wave of hysteria. Everything is hilarious, and I have no idea why.

Darius's amusement fades into horror. "Alexis... she's never done pot before."

Alexis's professional veneer cracks for the first time. "Wait, how is that possible? You grew up in Alaska."

I attempt to answer, but my brain has officially left the chat. The room tilts. I sway, gripping Alexis's arm for balance. "You're so solid," I mumble in awe.

Alexis gently steadies me, lips twitching. "And you're high as hell."

Darius claps his hands. "Okay! Crisis mode. Alexis, damage control?"

She sighs, rubbing her temples. "We're sending everyone home for the day. Nobody's suing us if they're off the clock."

Richard nods. "Smart. Should we bring some home for later?"

Alexis glares at him, then softens, exhaling. "My dad is going to kill me. I swear, one mistake and he'll think I'm incapable of running the agency."

A rare flicker of vulnerability. I latch onto it like a lifeline. "Your dad's a fool if he doesn't see how amazing you are," I declare grandly. "You run this place like a boss."

Alexis meets my gaze, something unreadable in her expression. Then she shakes her head, chuckling. "You're out of your mind."

"I'm out of cake, for God's sake," I poetically announce, waving my empty plate.

Darius sighs. "We need to get you home before you start waxing poetry about office furniture."

I blink at Darius's desk. "It's a beautiful desk," I say wistfully.

Alexis snorts. "Alright, let's go before you start reciting poetry to the stapler."

I grin up at her, swaying slightly. "If I write an ode to your stapler, will you take me out to dinner?"

Her lips curve, but she says nothing.

I take that as a yes.

Alexis continues, all smooth professionalism wrapped in authority. "Ms. Thompson, your current state necessitates medical attention."

"I think I'm very high," I announce, then dissolve into a fit of giggles.

Alexis places a steadying hand on my arm, her touch warm and grounding. "You need to be evaluated by a professional."

"No, no, I'm fine," I insist, waving her off—only to immediately drop my plate. It shatters on the floor, the sound echoing like a dramatic drumroll. For some reason, that sets me off into another uncontrollable laughing fit.

Darius whisper-shouts, "Do you want me to take her, Boss?"

Alexis keeps a firm grip on my waist, probably sensing that without it, I might attempt to swim through the broken plate-and-cake debris below. "No, you need to deal with the office and make sure everyone gets home safely."

"You two are soooo cute when you fight," I announce. Then, for reasons that will haunt me later, I lean into Alexis like we're already in a work marriage, best friends.

Alexis stares down at me, amusement flickering beneath her exasperation. Darius watches me with barely contained concern. Seeing them together, something in my foggy brain clicks into place.

I narrow my eyes at Darius, spotting a speck of frosting on his chin. Then I turn to Alexis, inspecting her face for evidence. "Wait. Why did you both have white frosting on your chins?"

Darius's secret detonates in my brain. I gasp dramatically. "Oh my God. You two are secret lovebirds!"

Alexis's mouth opens. Darius bursts into laughter. Richard chokes on his own spit.

Their wildly opposing reactions make me laugh until I nearly tip over. Alexis tightens her hold, exhaling a sharp breath. "Alright. I've got this." She loops an arm around my waist and steers me toward the elevator like an exhausted babysitter who's lost all faith in humanity.

I wave elbow-elbow-wrist-wrist at Darius like a pageant queen. Richard looks like he wants the earth to swallow him whole, so I throw in an extra wave with my finger guns blazing just for him.

The world tilts as Alexis guides me outside, her arm the only thing keeping me upright. Everything is bright. Everything is hilarious. And Alexis smells like vanilla frosting and expensive ambition.

"You need a medical evaluation," she says, her voice measured.

I pat her cheek, my hand feeling strangely disconnected from my body. "You're soooo sweet, Alexisy. Such a good boss. I promise I won't sue. But I really want more cake."

She exhales, the barest hint of a smile betraying her usual control. "Circumstances necessitate expediency."

I sigh dramatically, leaning against her like a structurally unsound rag doll. "Fine. But only if you carry me like a princess."

She doesn't roll her eyes, but doesn't even hesitate. Just sweeps me up into her arms like it's nothing. Like I weigh air. She is a professional through and through, but her grip is steady, her warmth bleeding through my dazed state. "Let's keep this moving."

Somewhere in my giggle-scrambled brain, that registers as the best thing anyone has ever done for me. I rest my head on her shoulder. "Told you I take my job seriously."

And then, because I have no control over my mouth anymore, I mumble, "I like you."

Alexis freezes mid-step.

I peek up at her, my brain sluggishly catching up to what just escaped my mouth. Oh no. Oh no. Abort mission.

Then I giggle, the world spinning as Alexis tightens her grip. A moment passes where I swear I see something flicker in her gaze, something not entirely professional.

I snuggle into her safe arms and sigh.

Best. Workday. *Ever.*

Chapter 21

Gynecology and Giggles

Driving through downtown Anchorage, the late afternoon sun flickers between the buildings, casting shifting shadows across the dashboard. The Chugach Mountains loom in the distance, their snow-capped peaks stubborn against the summer heat. My cheek presses against the cool window as I fight the urge to giggle at absolutely nothing. Thanks to the ill-advised cake incident, my brain is floating somewhere between bliss and confusion.

"Oh!" I blurt out, a rogue thought breaking through the haze. "I have an appointment! With Dr. Winters!"

Alexis glances at me, one brow raised. "Your doctor?"

"Yep! That's why I was going to sneak out of work early today. We can go there." I nod, victorious for remembering.

"You were going to sneak out?" she asks, skeptical. "You could have asked to leave early."

I gasp dramatically. "I don't want to do anything that could get me fired! Like 'asking for time off' in my first few weeks. Besides, it was only a little early, and Darius would've covered for me. My boss is super-hot, and I want to impress her—she's kind of my role model. I mean, I want to be her when I graduate from business school. A badass businesswoman who doesn't take cake from anyone. I'd take a cake from her though."

A pause.

Then, incredibly smoothly, Alexis says, "Thank you."

It takes me a second to process. My brain lags like lousy WiFi. My boss is...her. Alexis. I just called Alexis my role model. And super-hot. And possibly implied I'd consume forbidden baked goods for her approval.

She smirks, but the faintest pink tinge is on her cheeks. "Your doctor's office?"

"Sexishht!" I screech, then dissolve into giggles. "Her gynecology office is in the building next to Alaska Regional. Dr. Winters."

Alexis tightens her grip on the wheel. "Right. Maybe we should reschedule that and go to Emergency."

"No, no, no." I wave my hand, nearly smacking the dashboard. "It's perfect. Getting my lady bits and my—uh—cake situation checked? Two birds, one stoned. Wait—one stoned, two birds. You get it."

She exhales sharply, but the twitch of a smirk betrays her. She shakes her head and holds the door open for me.

Inside the waiting room, the smell of antiseptic and muted dread hangs in the air in the office, with plush furniture and shades of pink coloring everything. I smile at how cute the office is–no rose-colored glasses are needed for my visit here.

I trip over absolutely nothing, and Alexis catches me, her sigh deeply exasperated yet oddly fond.

The receptionist of the gynecology office—a woman with an impenetrable wool sweater and judgmental glasses—barely blinks as I announce, "Hi! I'm Aurora Thompson. I have an appointment with the lady doctor—because women can be doctors, obviously—Dr. Winters."

She eyes Alexis. "Your partner?"

Before I can correct her, Alexis steps forward smoothly. "I'm here to make sure she gets seen and gets home safely. She had an accidental marijuana ingestion."

The receptionist nods like she's seen this exact scenario play out before. "First visit?"

"Yes, but I already trust you," I whisper conspiratorially, leaning over the counter. "I was hoping she'd be like Snow White and summon birds to take my vitals."

Alexis places a firm hand on my shoulder and guides me to a chair before I can say anything else. The moment I sink down, I lean against her shoulder, humming happily as I stare at the cat photos on the wall.

"Soooo," I draw out the word, "ever been to a gynecologist before?"

Alexis clears her throat. "Can't say that I have."

I pat her knee reassuringly. "Don't worry, it's not scary. Well, a little. But Dr. Winters is nice, probably. The reviews say she has collages of kittens on the ceiling."

"Kittens?" Alexis repeats, baffled.

"For when you're, you know..." I gesture vaguely downward. "Something to look at."

Her ears go red as she rubs a hand through her hair.

I grin. My new superpower? Making Alexis blush. And that is the exact superpower I wanted.

"Sorry," I whisper, not sorry at all. "Everything is too funny right now."

The receptionist shoots me a warning glance over her glasses. Alexis shushes me, but I can feel her shaking with suppressed laughter.

Then, a nurse calls my name. I hop up too quickly, and the room tilts dangerously. Alexis grabs my elbow, steadying me before I face plant.

"I'll come with you," she says, voice cool but firm. "For safety."

She's not wrong. Also, her solid yet tender hand is still on my arm, and I have no complaints.

"Fine," I sigh dramatically. "But if Dr. Winters asks, we're here to see the kittens, not my kitty cat."

Alexis presses her lips together, guiding me down the hall, and suddenly, I'm really excited to see those kittens.

Dr. Winters is a petite blonde with sharp blue eyes and zero resemblance to Snow White. "Aurora, I hear you've had an unexpected marijana incident."

"A catering company accidentally delivered a pot-infused dessert to work, and she had two or more servings," Alexis explains, her voice smooth and measured like she's briefing a boardroom and not delivering my medical report.

"This is Alexis," I announce, proudly. "She's my badass boss, hashtag *bossbitchgoals* for me. And you should meet her boyfriend, Richard. He's gay-level hot. You know the type. Like, magazine-cover, unfair-to-the-rest-of-us hot."

Alexis clears her throat. "Sorry, she's a bit confused. I just wanted to make sure she got here safely."

With no cute helper cats in sight, Dr. Winters starts making notes on her iPad. "She's not usually like this?"

Alexis sighs. "No."

I nod solemnly. "There was a delicious workplace accident. Not Alexis' fault–at all. I like cake, alot."

Dr. Winters checks my vitals, and her cool demeanor thaws to almost warm. "Your numbers look fine. It'll take a few hours for the effects to wear off, so I suggest rest and hydration."

"Oh! But I did all the prep and I'm here. Let's do the whole shebang!" I say, yanking at my waistband, my coordination entirely uncooperative.

Alexis stands abruptly. "I'll be outside."

"You're welcome to stay," I sing as Dr. Winters swiftly drapes a warm blanket over me. Even this blanket feels a little short on my long frame. Everything always seems to be designed for someone... smaller.

Alexis makes it one step before I grab her wrist. "No, stay! Moral support! I need those confident vibes for this."

Her face doesn't move, but her eyes flicker with something like alarm. "I—"

"You won't see anything you don't have! I hope!"

Dr. Winters clears her throat. "Aurora, we can reschedule."

"No, I shaved, showered, and filled out all the online forms. I'm ready."

Alexis's jaw clenches. I don't know if she's horrified or impressed, but she doesn't move.

Dr. Winters nods briskly. "Alexis, you can stand at the head of the bed to make sure she doesn't fall off during the exam."

Alexis exhales sharply through her nose as if this is a hostage situation she can't negotiate out of. "Alright then."

Dr. Winters pulls on gloves. "Aurora, are you currently sexually active?"

I burst into laughter. "It's my main form of exercise! Well, it was. I haven't done cardio in over a month, which explains why my thighs aren't thanking me lately."

Alexis makes a strangled noise. I sneak a glance at her. Her face remains unreadable, but the corner of her mouth twitches. The tiniest crack in the stone-cold boss façade.

Dr. Winters jots something down, unfazed. "And are you using protection?"

"Sometimes," I admit. "But it's hard to remember in the heat of the moment. Like when you're making out with a hot intern and suddenly you're in the copy room and—"

"Okay!" Alexis interrupts, standing up so fast that her chair nearly tips. "I think I'll wait outside after all."

As she bolts, I call after her, "Don't forget to look at the kittens. They help you relax!"

By the time my exam ends, I feel a little less loopy. I shuffle out, where Alexis is pacing, hands in her pockets, her controlled exterior back in place.

"All done!" I announce. "No kittens were harmed in the making of this appointment, and the cake is wearing off."

Alexis exhales, glancing at Dr. Winters. "She's okay?"

Dr. Winters nods. "She'll be fine. Just make sure she rests and does not drive or go back to work. I'll call when she's more alert to go over the test results. And, Aurora?"

I blink at her.

"No more cake before medical appointments."

I give her my finger guns. "Understood."

Alexis mutters something under her breath but leads me toward the car, her hand firm against my back. "Let's get you home, Trouble."

Trouble. I like that. You don't give a nickname to someone you don't like, right? But then again, Alexis is a good person. That's all it is. Kindness and professional concerns–nothing more.

As we walk to the car, an older woman in the waiting room smiles at us. "You two are such a lovely couple."

Alexis tenses slightly but doesn't correct her.

I laugh. *Ha! If she only knew how unromantic my life truly is.*

"I didn't realize ensuring my employee's safety would include my first visit to a gynecologist."

"I'm glad I could broaden your horizons," I say with a giggle.

Alexis shakes her head, opens the car door, and nudges me inside. "Seatbelt, Trouble."

Trouble. Maybe she does care slightly more than a coworker or boss. And maybe—just maybe—I wouldn't mind her caring more about me. Even if romance isn't part of the equation.

Chapter 22

Not-So-Accidental Kiss

The drive back is quiet.

But not the awkward kind, more like the relaxing-floating-above-your-body comfortable silence. The air holds a warm heaviness with something—maybe leftover edible weirdness, maybe raw secondhand embarrassment—but it's soft. Safe. Comfortable in the worst, most confusing way.

My head lolls toward the window. Coastal Trail zips by—slow-mo joggers, dogs with flappy tongues, someone biking way too fast for their own good. Everything's slow and fast and floaty.

I bite my lip.

I'm not thinking anything inappropriate, but my acute sense of smell definitely picks up Alexis's perfume—a sexy bergamot that will likely waft into my dreams later. I bite my lip, knowing that if I start giggling again, she'll probably revoke my edible privileges for life.

Alexis taps her fingers on the gear shift, her other hand loose on the wheel.

A giggle escapes my lips.

She doesn't look over when she speaks. "You don't have to be embarrassed, you know."

"Hah!" I say too loudly, and unstick my forehead from the window. "Do you think this is me not embarrassed? Alexis, I told you *about my sex life.*"

"You did."

"And I called you Boss Bitch during all of this."

"Twice."

"Don't make this worse, Boss Bitch!"

She glances over, smirking. "There it is again."

I cover my face with both hands. "Tell me I didn't say that too loudly during the office babbling incident."

"You said it. Enthusiastically. Like, yelled it while mid-burping."

I groan into my hoodie. "If I die tonight, tell my sweet Darius to toss my body into the dumpster with my dignity."

"You might need to write that in your will."

"Oh my God," I mutter, sitting up and waving my hands like an inflatable tube man. "I'm a professional disaster. Who gave me a serious job? Why am I allowed in public?"

"You are fine and behaved like someone that has accidentally ingested pot," she says smoothly. "And it has been entertaining and memorable."

I blink. "Is that a compliment?"

She doesn't answer.

Instead, she lets the silence hang, thick like whipped cream. Her mouth quirks at the edge. Like she's playing a game she's already winning.

I squirm in my seat. "Don't smirk at me like that. It's not fair. You have, like, symmetrical features and cheekbones that could cut glass. Meanwhile, I look like I lost a fight with a pile of laundry."

Alexis raises an eyebrow but says nothing.

Rude.

We pull into the apartment lot, gravel crunching beneath the tires. I'm already halfway to forming a goodbye—probably something stupid like *thanks for enduring my oversharing spree*—when my stomach goes ice-cold.

It's there. On my door. Bright yellow and taped like a slap to the face.

Eviction Notice.

No-no-no. I'm supposed to have until Friday.

I'm out of the car before she finishes parking, sprinting through the weak drizzle. I yank the paper off the door. The ink is already smearing, but I don't need to read it.

I know.

My lungs collapse like an overcooked soufflé. My chest tightens so hard I swear my ribs scream. This was it. This was the "wait for my paycheck" week. This week, I *almost* made rent. There goes my future.

Behind me, the car door slams. "Aurora?"

My hand balls around the paper, crumpling the proof of my failure. "Yup! Mail's here! Love a surprise!"

She walks toward me, stepping slowly and carefully. I'm a wild, unpredictable animal she's trying to feed Cheerios to.

"What is it?"

I shove it in my hoodie like that'll erase the consequences. "Nothing serious. Just my average everyday drama."

"Aurora."

It's not a command. Not a scold. It's soft. Too soft.

That softness breaks me more than yelling ever could.

I cross my arms. "It's fine. I'll figure it out."

"You're being evicted."

"Not technically *yet*." I force a laugh. It sounds like a dying seagull.

She studies me, holding my shoulders. Unblinking. "If money is the solution, then it's not really a problem."

My jaw drops. "Okay, says a *rich person*."

Her brows lift, but she doesn't flinch. "I didn't mean—"

"Yeah, yeah. You meant it like a solution-oriented boss bitch." I backpedal, fingers shaking. "But not everyone has a financial safety net made of solid gold and parents who don't drain their bank accounts like college students drinking Red Bull."

Her brows lift higher, then wrinkle. Not in anger. In something worse—pity.

I hate pity.

I force a smile. "Anyway. Thanks for the ride. And not firing me for… all this."

"You're not getting fired," she says quietly.

"Even after I called you boss bitch again?"

Another one of those almost-smiles. "Especially because you called me boss bitch three more times."

It happens in the silence that follows.

My brain short-circuits, misfires, and spins out like a moose on a frozen driveway. I step forward, meaning to hug her, to thank her.

But the angle's weird. And she tilts her head, my head lifts to look at her, and my cheek grazes hers, and instead—

My lips land on her mouth.

Time.

Stops.

Like…, it actually stops.

My brain stutters. My knees forget how to knee. The kiss lingers for one tiny beat too long. Just enough for electricity to arc between us like static snapping off a wool sweater.

I pull back, gasping.

"I—I meant to hug you!"

Alexis doesn't say anything. Her eyes search mine. Wide. Still.

Oh no.

Abort mission.

"Sorry!" I'm high! Blame the edible!

"I thought—I thought you were leaning in!"

She reaches out, arms gently around my back. Still silent.

I flinch. "This is bad, right? Like, breaking all professional boundaries bad? HR-level bad?"

She doesn't answer. Instead, she pulls me tighter against her and *does* lean into me.

This time, on purpose.

And *she* kisses *me.*

Not a friendly work wife, professional peck. It's not a polite misunderstanding.

No. This one is molten–hotter than my hottest daydreams.

Her lips move against mine with a quiet intensity that flips every neuron in my body into emergency mode. It's a beach bonfire, hot and devastating. One hand brushes my jaw like I'm breakable. The other stays on my back, grounding me like she knows I might float off into the Alaskan ocean's riptide.

And then—

She stops.

Pulls back slowly, breathing unsteady.

I stare. "Did... that just...?"

Her voice—still low, still calm—breaks slightly. "Aurora."

"Don't say my name like that."

"Like what?"

"Like you *meant it.*"

She blinks. And that's worse than any answer.

I step back, heart jackhammering. "This is—this was a mistake. You're my boss. This can't happen. We can't—"

"I didn't—" she says softly.

"Stop! That makes it worse!"

"I wasn't trying to take advantage of you," she says.

"I know!" I look down, unable to meet her eyes. "That's the worst part! You're so nice and weirdly hot, and here I am with my life falling apart, staring at your perfect shoes." I gesture to her soft leather loafers, which probably cost more than my rent.

Finally, I meet her gaze. She stares into my eyes but says nothing.

My mouth moves faster than my brain. "And I already ruined our professional vibe with my cake talking, and now I've ruined your face with my face, and oh god, I'm babbling nonsense, *again*—I have to go."

I spin and flee with the grace of a deranged moose. My keys jangle as I fumble with the door. I slam it shut behind me and press my back to it, gasping.

The eviction notice crunches in my pocket.

My heart gallops like it wants out of my ribcage.

And my lips?

Still tingling.

"Did that *happen*?" I whisper into the dark.

A beat passes. Then...

"Alexis kissed me," I breathe.

Another beat.

"That doesn't mean anything. Doesn't mean she *likes* me. It was probably edible-induced pheromone confusion. Or... boss caring overload. Yeah. Just weird, caring *professional* chemistry."

My phone buzzes. *Darius.*

Oh god. Darius. I accused him of dating Alexis in front of Richard.

I answer the call with a dramatic inhale. "Emergency. Code Flamingo. I did a very bad thing."

His sigh crackles through the speaker. "Like trying to announce an office affair to the whole staff, when the people aren't actually having an affair? Or is it worse than that?"

"Okay, I'm not telling you... worse."

"Aurora!"

I slide to the floor, tangled in my own legs and regret. "I think I did more than accuse Alexis of an affair. I kissed her. And I think she kissed me back. And now I need to disappear into the woods forever. Maybe befriend a wolf pack. Live off berries."

Darius sighs again, long-suffering. "Get a pint of moose tracks ice cream and stay put. I'm coming over."

As I hang up, I whisper to the empty room, "She kissed me like she meant it."

Then, quieter, more scared, I add, "What if she *did*?"

Chapter 23

Blanket Burrito of Broken Friendships

The second I open my eyes, I know two things. One, I'm never touching an edible again. Ever. Not even if a bear hands me one as a peace offering with a little bow tied around it. Two, my life? Fully, tragically, gloriously on fire. *Again.*

Darius *did* come over yesterday while I was in a horizontal coma on the floor. He tucked me into bed and left me soup and crackers, like the best friend I no longer deserve. I remember that he promised to call this weekend.

It's Sunday.

He hasn't.

Saturday disappeared in a blur of reality dating show reruns, fever naps, and Lisa brought me soup and donuts like some chaotic nurse who ignores helping with laundry and dishes and thrives on drama. I rolled over to cry into a maple bar but fell asleep halfway through.

Now I'm burrito-wrapped in my duvet, my phone screen burning my eyeballs like it's punishing me for all my sins. I scroll my inbox with the slow dread of someone opening a report card they know has the word "detention" on it.

There it is. The email.

From: Darius Parker
To: Aurora Thompson

Subject: Monday Assignment

Aurora,
Please see the attached details for your Monday interview at Alaska Travel & Cruise Co.
VERY IMPORTANT!
Have a relaxing weekend.

Best,
Darius

I reread it three times, hunting for any hint of warmth. Or emojis. Or literally anything besides that emotionally distant "Best."

I groan into my pillow like a ghost mourning her own social life.

No, "GIRL, What did you do?"

No "Explain the scandal."

Not even a passive-aggressive GIF.

Just "Best."

I try calling him. Voicemail.

I text him, "D, please. Talk to me. I'm so sorry. I'll let you pick my outfits for a whole week. even the hat you said made me look like an extra from *Annie*."

Nothing.

Darius is ignoring me.

And Alexis... who *knows* what she's thinking. I can't believe she's having me interview to temp for her super-important new client, which makes my stomach clench even tighter.

Ugh, I feel like I might vomit.

I've messed everything up.

And it's not even heartbreak I'm panicking about. This is more important than silly relationship issues. This is my career and future, and I won't even think about the L-word.

I don't do that L-word. Love? That's a fairy tale people tell to keep dating agencies, like Lisa's, in business.

This is worse.

I might've torched my friendships *and* my job. The only two semi-stable things in my life.

And if I lose this job? I'm not just emotionally homeless. I'm literally homeless. With university starting next month and a tuition bill trying to assassinate me in my sleep, I cannot afford to screw this up.

I check the counter. The eviction notice still sits there. Judging me. Looming.

I am one inch away from couch-surfing in Lisa's closet—where she keeps her party dresses and emotional baggage.

I cyber stalk to avoid dealing with my messy life.

This is fine.

Darius? No posts. Not even a reaction to that celebrity breakup that would've sent him into a six-slide rant.

Alexis? Her accounts are locked tighter than the top shelf of a gay bar on Ladies' Night.

Richard? Jackpot. He's posting solo selfies on a beach like a travel influencer mid-divorce.

His caption, "Sometimes you just need to escape."

Escape *what*, Richard?

Alaska? Alexis? The disastrous, mistaken announcement about Darius and Alexis being in a *secret workplace relationship*?! Did you break up with her because of me?!

I squint at the photo. His abs are getting thirsty replies from accounts with usernames like "ProteinPrincess" and "SunsetSlut99."

Ugh.

"Where is he?" I mutter, panic fizzing in my chest like a shaken soda. "I need to figure out what I'm going to do. I can't be homeless or jobless when university starts next month."

My stomach churns. What if I misunderstood everything? What if worse than joking and being confused when I *outed* Darius as straight and Alexis as dating her employee—what if it's not a joke and they are really in a relationship?—they aren't! *There's no way.* I just embarrassed myself and broke their trust and—

Nope. Nope. Abort this spiral of negativity!

I call Darius again. Still no answer.

So I do the only thing left.

I emailed *Alexis.*

From: Aurora Thompson
To: Alexis Anders
Subject: Uh... Hey, Boss Bitch?

Hey, so, um, I hope I didn't completely destroy your Friday with my existence. Also, I might've made things worse with Darius. Now he's missing. I don't know if I made a colossal mistake outing him or if I actually misunderstood everything, which is VERY possible because I am a human disaster. Do you... know anything? Please tell me I didn't ruin everything.

Thanks,
Aurora (Your Least Professional Employee)

I hit send. Then, immediately scream into a pillow.

That is not a professional email.

That's a cry for help wrapped in anxiety and sealed with social ineptitude.

But Alexis isn't a normal boss.

Not after that kiss—wait.

That *hug* I misinterpreted. That perfectly innocent hug where my lips got involved without consulting my brain.

My stomach flips.

Her lips tasted like coffee and mint. Her breath had been warm, sweet, inviting. The way she *looked* at me—like I was something worth noticing. Worth wanting.

I clutch my blanket tighter. "Focus, Aurora."

You've got *real* problems. You need Darius. You need your job. You must not become a cautionary tale on a business student budgeting blog.

I try Lisa again. She picks up, breathless.

"Babe, I'm elbows-deep in a new man. Make it fast."

"Lisa, Darius is MISSING."

A gasp. "Oh my God. Did he run away from his problems like the Pisces he is?"

"I don't know! He won't text. He sent me a cold-as-ice work email like we don't share a secret language and a cursed group chat. No 'girl,' no GIFs, no drama. Just 'Best.' It's a *corporate breakup*, Lisa."

Lisa hums. "That's not right. He'd *at least* send a funny pet meme if he was mad."

"Right?! I think I messed everything up."

She sighs. "Okay. Fine. I'll put Hot Guy Number Four on pause. *Again.*"

"You're a goddess."

"Tell that to my heels. They're bleeding in new shoes." She snaps gum in my ear. "Alright. If Darius isn't answering you or me, we're pulling the nuclear option."

I blink. "What does that mean?"

"His mom."

"Oh God."

"Exactly. That woman's Life360 game is terrifying. She tracks her kids like they're iPads."

"You think she'll tell us?"

"Are you kidding? She's been waiting for this opportunity. Every time I talk to her she's like, *'Tell Darius to call me back, I know he's at that Thai place again, his sodium's too high.'* She's *got* his number and location."

A flicker of hope stirs in my ribcage. "Please. I need him."

"And I need to finish this date, so let's make a deal. I get you Darius intel. You get me a plus-one to your work gala and promise not to rat me out if I sneak in those wine gummies again."

"Done."

"And Aurora?"

"Yeah?"

"You *didn't* ruin everything. You're dramatic, but you're not evil. You're Darius's and my ride-or-die. That hasn't changed."

I pause. "Samesies. Always!"

"Now let me seduce this lumberjack before he gets away. Call you in twenty."

She hangs up, and I breathe.

I don't know what's happening with Alexis. Or Darius. Or my entire spiraling, espresso-stained, emotionally frazzled life.

But I've got Lisa.

And maybe, if the universe's WiFi is still working, I haven't lost everything yet.

I stare at my phone. Waiting. Hoping. Dreading.

And I'm praying I don't end up sleeping on the temp agency's front desk couch next week.

Chapter 24

A Cruise Ship of Misunderstandings

The Anchorage summer sun burns through my windshield like it has a personal vendetta against me. I navigate the clogged morning traffic, one hand clutching the steering wheel, the other gripping my caramel vanilla latte like a lifeline. Today is my moment—my chance to impress Alexis, prove I'm more than a temp, and secure a major client for the agency. No pressure.

"You've got this, Aurora," I mutter, adjusting the air conditioning to high blast because sweat and professionalism do not mix. "Channel your inner Beyonce. Or Michelle Obama. Someone competent." I cannot screw up this week after last week's debacle–and especially with Alexis' faith in me and the looming deadline to pay my university bills.

Usually, I would call Darius to give me a pep talk, but he's been radio silent since Friday. He must have sworn his mom to secrecy and be busy with his mysterious new relationship because I only got another business email as proof of life.

He sent me the details for today's interview with the big cruise client Alexis wants to sign to impress her dad.

I swallow nervously. If I impress them, I'll do more accounting work for the rest of the summer, which would pay for my university and maybe even enough to stay on campus in the dorms. *A girl can dream.*

The Chugach Mountains loom in the distance, watching, judging, radiating a calm wisdom I desperately lack. Meanwhile, the Cook Inlet glimmers in the rearview mirror like it's whispering, *Relax, girl, it's just a job interview.* Easy for you to say, water. You don't have to deal with pretending to be competent.

"Smile and nod, Aurora. You got this," I whisper, and to prove that I don't 'got this,' a bear interrupts my morning pep talk.

One second, I'm cruising along, mentally rehearsing my *I'm a dedicated and responsible professional* speech. The next, a fully grown black bear lumbers into the road, looking like it has nowhere better to be.

"Oh, for the love of—MOVE!" I slam on the brakes, sending my latte flying.

The lid pops off, and before I can react, hot, caramel-scented betrayal spreads across my crisp white blouse.

Why do I even bother owning a white shirt?!

A strangled noise leaves my throat—somewhere between a scream and a sob—as I assess the damage.

The bear does not care. The bear sniffs at the center line like it's the most fascinating odor in existence.

A trucker in the next lane laughs, looks at me, blotting my blouse with a crumpled cafe napkin, and gives me a thumbs-up.

Glad I could brighten *your* day, sir.

By the time the bear decides it's had enough urban exploration, I'm fifteen minutes behind schedule, smell like a Starbucks dumpster, and am approximately two percent away from a full-blown breakdown.

I whip into the Alaskan Cruises and Tours parking lot, tires screeching slightly as I skid to a stop in front of their modern, glass-fronted office. The building stands like a postcard, perfectly framed against the breathtaking backdrop of Cook Inlet. But I've got zero time for scenic admiration.

I reach into the back seat and snatch up a thrifted sweater I haven't even washed yet—whatever, desperate times. I tug it on over my wrinkled shirt to cover my wardrobe malfunction. Somehow, with the white collar peeking out just right, I look business professional.

Then I bolt for the door, praying I don't look as frazzled as I feel.

A warm smile greets me from behind the front desk. "Aurora?" The receptionist, Kathleen, glances at the clock. "You made it."

I nod, summoning every ounce of charm I possess. "Yes, that's me. I'm so sorry I'm late. My car battery died this morning, and I had to get the battery charged from my neighbor. I would've called, but I never use my phone while driving."

No one would believe there was a bear on the city highway—a moose or squirrel, maybe—but not a bear. The on-the-fly lie flows smoothly, and I silently thank my high school drama teacher for the years of improv classes.

The receptionist smiles sympathetically. "Don't worry, dear. These things happen. Mr. Fairbanks is not quite getting ready for your interview. Have a seat, and he'll be out shortly. Do you need a coffee or anything?"

"No," I say, pulling my blazer over the coffee stain on my blouse. "I'm fine. Just *so excited* to be here." I plaster on my best *I-did-not-almost-cry-in-my-car* smile.

"Mr. Fairbanks will be right with you."

Before I can sit and take a moment to recover, a tall man in his fifties steps out of an office. "Aurora, welcome! I'm Grant. I will be interviewing you today."

He shakes my hand, firm but friendly, and leads me into a massive office with floor-to-ceiling windows. Cruise ships glitter in the distance, the whole place radiating *successful businessman with yacht* energy, which makes sense since their company books cruises and Alaska tours.

"Have we met before?" he asks, and I shutter, hoping he doesn't have a dating profile on Hook and Reel's Dating website.

"Um, no I don't think so," I say with a smile.

"Let's get right to it," he says, settling behind his desk. "Alexis speaks highly of you."

My stomach flips. I *knew* Alexis believed in me, and despite losing a day of work last week, I got a ton of the accounting work done. I sit up straighter, ready to be the corporate powerhouse I was born to be. "I'm honored! I love working with Alexis and the temp agency. I believe in making meaningful connections with clients. Since I am a business student, working at different offices really helps me, too." I realize I might be rambling, so I say the line I rehearsed, "Alaska Temp Agency is a great company to work for, and I'm sure you'll love working with Alexis, too."

I bite my lip to stop from talking. *Where did the L-word come from?*

Grant nods, scribbling something down. "Good philosophy. So, tell me about your experience."

Showtime.

I launch into my *Please, Hire Me* speech, weaving my temp jobs and upcoming university business classes into an inspiring tale of adaptability and resourcefulness. I even joked about how working at a tax office taught me the true meaning of despair.

He chuckles—points for me.

Then, mid-nod, he cocks his head. "I feel like I've met you before. Maybe it's your family. Do you live around the Hillside area?"

I do not. My mom grew up there, and Anchorage is more of a small town than a *real* city. As a big city with a small population, I pray he didn't go to school with my mom. Or worse yet, date her. I do not want to be associated with her–especially if he's met my flaky, man-juggling mom. I am a reliable professional. I fall back to my smile and nod. "No, but I went to school in that area. I was born and raised here, so maybe we crossed paths while fishing or at the grocery store."

"How old are you?"

Wait. Is that... *legal*? Pretty sure it's not.

"Uh..." I stall, gripping my chair.

Grant waves a hand. "Oh, don't mind me. I'm surprised to meet you. Alexis said your name but with your qualifications, I thought you'd be older. You're—well, you're young, professional, attractive...*temp.*"

Oh no. Oh *no.*

My internal organs turn into a synchronized swim team of panic.

What did he *just* say? My people-pleasing instincts battle my fight-or-flight response. Do I play nice to keep the job opportunity? Or do I *throw down* because he is giving creep vibes? Plus, he's a CEO, so he should know you can't ask age questions or call someone attractive at an interview. I'm just starting business school, and I know that much.

He leans forward, still smiling. "When's your birthday, dear?"

Abort. ABORT.

Warning bells scream in my head. I glance toward the exit, calculating if I can fake an emergency phone call. But before I can make a decision, he sighs. "Never mind. That's a personal question and not really an interview question."

Relief floods me—until he adds, "I just knew an Aurora once. Love of my life."

What. The. *Hell.* He's super-old, and there's no way he knows me. He lives a posh businessman life, and I'm a broke kid.

My skin crawls since he is old enough to be my father and too old to date me. I force a stiff smile. "That's...nice, Mr. Fairbanks."

"Please, call me Grant," he says, standing. "And I definitely want you. I mean I want you to work here for the summer, of course. I'd love to get to know you more."

The oxygen leaves my body. My stomach plummets and rebounds to my chest, making my heart hammer harder. Alexis' important client—who holds my future employment in his hands and Alexis' chance to impress her dad—*hit on me* during an interview.

I shoot up from my chair. "Thanks for your time! I'll, uh, let Alexis know you are interested in contracting with the company!"

"Oh, no need to rush out," he says. "I'll follow you and jump you in the parking lot..."

I freeze.

He grins and winks, oblivious to the horror dawning on my face.

My *soul* leaves my body.

"*Excuse me*?"

He stands with the confidence that only an old, white CEO who nonchalantly proposed an employee can pull off.

I grab a pen, brandishing it like a weapon. "I am NOT sleeping with you!"

His eyes widened in alarm. "What? No—"

"You disgusting, outdated *creep*! Who says that? *At an interview!*"

I storm toward the door, adrenaline pumping. "You're lucky I don't call the police! Actually, you know what? I *am* calling Alexis to make sure she doesn't send you anymore temps to sexually harass!"

Grant freezes, and I rush out before he can follow me.

Kathleen looks up as I barrel out. "Aurora?"

"Your *boss* is a predator!" I seethe. "Do you *know* what he just said to me?!"

She blinks. "Excuse me?"

"He *offered* to—" I lower my voice. "Jump me. In the *parking lot*."

Kathleen's forehead creases. "Aurora, my husband is offering to *jump-start your car*. You said your battery had issues and I asked him to help you out."

Silence.

Cold, suffocating silence.

My eyes dart to her desk. The nameplate reads *Kathleen Fairbanks*.

Oh. My. *God*.

She smiles, utterly unaware of my spiraling horror. "He's a sweet guy–that's why I love him. Are you okay?"

I nod. Or maybe I have a seizure. Hard to tell.

Oh no. I just screwed up the most critical task Alexis gave me–the interview went horribly. Nothing good ever lasts in my budding career or in my dating life. My bad picker for relationships seems to extend to working relationships, too.

"Come back in if your battery's dead," she adds. "He'll be happy to jump you."

I make a strangled sound and bolt. I *will* be digging a hole in the tundra to disappear forever.

My phone buzzes. A text from Alexis, "How'd your interview go?"

I stare at the screen, shaking. *Oh, Alexis. If only you knew.*

I type back, "Great. I'm driving to the office now. We should talk."

Because, *of course*, my big chance to impress her ended with me falsely accusing a potentially large client of sexual harassment.

"If they want you to start immediately, you can finish the home office's accounting list next month."

I start the car.

It immediately stalls.

Perfect.

Chapter 25

Darius to the Rescue (Maybe?)

My phone blasts to life as if summoned by spite and emotional instability. Celine Dion belts out the ringtone "*Because You Loved Me*" with the drama of a woman who's never faked friendly smiles during dates and never been stranded in a parking lot after thinking an interviewer wanted some side action.

I don't even flinch. "Oh, great. And the soundtrack of my breakdown arrives."

Sandra Thompson–my mother–and the Queen of bad timing. She probably felt a cosmic ripple in the air. She knew I was emotionally wrecked, ready for the final blows before my emotional breakdown.

I slam the *ignore* button like it personally offended me, but not before the screen lights up with my lock screen. Me, Darius, and Lisa—karaoke night—grinning like we know we've got our ride or die, and no one can ruin our night. I choke out a weird, sad snort. We looked so free. I'm so happy. Before I blew up my job, my friendship, and probably my entire future.

Tears come hot and fast. Messy. Unattractive. The kind that mixes with snot, so you're not sure what you're wiping, and it sounds like a pug having an asthma attack.

I can't tell what's worse—accusing Darius of sleeping with the boss last week or tanking the interview with Alexis' most VIP client. Or the part where I might be...fired? Probably. Possibly. Emotionally, I've already given up.

My phone pings again. Voicemail from the woman who birthed me with spite and raised me on guilt.

Deep breath. Tap play.

"Aurora Anne," she snaps like I've personally tarnished the family legacy. "Marjorie from book club called. Her son's hairdresser's girlfriend works at your little agency. Getting high at work? I *knew* working and trying to go to school would be too much for you. This is *not* the young lady I raised, and I do not want people talking about me!"

I slam the stop button right in the middle of her rant and let out this wheezy, hiccuping laugh. Classic Alaska. News up here spreads faster than salmon in spawning season.

I smack both palms against the steering wheel like I can exorcise the embarrassment through brute force. "Well, cool. Guess the whole state thinks I'm a pothead now. Fantastic."

Can I get kicked out of university for being high?

The car's response? Silence.

I twist the key in the ignition, praying. Nothing. Again. Still nothing. The dashboard's deader than my business career.

"Oh come on," I mutter, flipping the headlights on. Nope. Nada. Dead battery or angry car gods.

I slap the wheel again. My palm stings. My dignity is officially in the gutter. I'm stranded in the work parking lot of a place I want to run away from as fast as possible, and quickly becoming emotionally unstable.

And the worst part? Alexis might think I'm a quirky mess, but she thinks I'm a professional and good at office work. But now she'll know I'm professionally incompetent–a mess–too. This might be the last mistake I made as her employee.

I lean back, staring at the endless stretch of blue sky. Alaskan summers are annoyingly gorgeous. Crisp air, glowing birch trees, mountains smugly flexing in the background like they're taunting tourists to try and hike them. I want to appreciate it. I want to feel anything other than deep, pit-shaped dread.

Buzz. New text. Darius. "Hey girl! How'd the big interview go? Coffees later to celebrate? Sorry I missed you this weekend, I was busy but I'll tell you *everything*."

Thank Goodness!

My bottom lip does a weird trembling thing. I *don't* cry at texts. I am not the girl who cries and needs to be rescued.

Except apparently, I am.

He doesn't know. He doesn't know I nuked the interview. He doesn't know I accused the client of sexual harassment *in the first five minutes*. And not in a brave whistleblower way—more like a confused-awkward-threatening-him-with-a-pen-kind-of way. It spiraled fast.

I squeeze my eyes shut and mutter to no one, "Time to fake my death. I'll hike into Denali and become a mysterious hiker lost in the wilderness. I'll become a local legend, haunting hikers, and cursing job interviewers."

My thumbs hover over the screen. Then I type, "Can you meet me in the parking lot? My car's dead. Also... I ruined everything. Again."

A typing bubble appears. Disappears. Reappears. My soul short-circuits.

"Omg. I'll be there in 5 minutes."

The phone drops to the seat. I face-plant onto the steering wheel. "I'm the saddest little mess Anchorage has *ever* seen."

Knock knock.

I sit bolt upright, forehead red, pride obliterated. Expecting Darius, I fling open the door—dramatically.

Except... it's *not* Darius.

It's Kathleen. Holding a half-wrapped sandwich and looking at me like I'm a bird that flew into the glass and forgot how to live.

"Uh... hi?" I croak, wiping at my face with the sleeve of my cardigan that smells faintly of stale kettle corn.

She squints. "You okay? You've been sitting here a while."

"Oh yeah! Totally fine!" My voice shoots up like it's auditioning for a squirrel commercial. "Just, y'know, soaking up the... sunshine. Deep thinking. Meditating. Inner peace."

She glances at the building behind her. "You left fast after the interview and it seems like you had a misunderstanding?"

"All good! Standard interview exit strategy, it's my classic goodbye. But for, like... trauma."

Kathleen doesn't move. Her sandwich sags. I panic.

"Hey... weird question," I blurt. "If someone accidentally—*hypothetically*—accuses Grant of sexual harassment in a meeting... that's... like... not illegal, right?"

Her face. Blank. Then a slow blink. Then, she clutches her sandwich like it might save her.

"I... ummm...Do you need me to get the jumper cables from Grant?" she says. I shake my head while she retreats like I'm a feral animal.

I groan and slam my head against the steering wheel again.

Knock knock.

This time, it's *definitely* Darius. Sashaying across the parking lot in dark jeans and a fitted sweater with a tragic amount of sparkle.

He opens my car door, looks me up and down like a fashion emergency hotline dispatcher, and sighs.

"Girl."

I wince.

"What *did* you do?"

I lift my tear-splotched face, voice raw. "I bombed the interview. Like, bombed it *so hard* they're gonna name a crater after me, and Alexis will tell me to clean out my desk."

He slides into the passenger seat, ignoring the wrappers, the spilled coffee in the cupholder, and the pile of used napkins on the floorboard.

"Start from the beginning. And if you say 'I panicked,' I swear—"

"I panicked."

"Of *course* you did."

"I accused Grant of sexual harassment because I thought he was hitting on me when he was actually talking about his daughter. Then I tried to stab him with a pen to escape. Then I—"

"Stop. Stop talking."

I stop.

Darius tucks my frizzy hair behind my ears and hands me a breath mint. Then turns to me. "You are *not* allowed to die in this parking lot. Not in *those* hideous shoes." He shifts, reaching for my hand, and as his head moves, the light catches a little bruise on his neck – a definite hickey. Okay, so *that's* what "busy" looks like. Good for him. Distracting for me.

"I don't have an apartment anymore. The rent's doubled and I was considering asking for an advance so I could move to the dorms. But I'm getting fired, instead," I blurt out, using another crumpled napkin to wipe my nose.

"Oh hell *no*. You are staying with me and you are not getting fired. And I'm sorry, I missed the memo, you were.. are in crisis. Honestly, my mom said to call, but I got busy," he says, taking my hand and looking straight into my soul. "I'm here now, girl, and you are not getting fired. Not today!"

"Also, my car's dead."

"I'll drive you back and we can deal with this after work. Alexis isn't going to fire you, she thinks you are becoming one of her best employee's–I know, I heard her talking about you to her dad, the guy who signs our paychecks and your bonuses," Darius says.

"Are you sure?"

"She came to our karaoke night and *cheered for your ridiculous singing*. That woman doesn't cheer, ever. That's Alexis-level fangirling."

I clutch the steering wheel like it might morph into a safety raft. "Darius, I kissed her. Like... maybe. On accident."

He gasps so hard I think the clouds flinch.

"You WHAT?"

"On Friday, I thought she was leaning in! But she was probably... hugging! I'm so stupid!"

He fans himself with the portable charger. "Oh my god, this is *delicious*. Keep spiraling. I'm thriving." Then he corrects himself, "You weren't yourself. You were high. Don't worry. If you were going to get fired for that I'd know about it."

I bury my face in my hands. "I ruined it. With her. With the agency. With my university stuff. With you. Everything."

"This is on me. I've been busy lately, and you needed me." Darius scoots closer. Puts a hand on my knee. "Babe. You didn't ruin me. I *love* you. Even if you don't believe in love. I love you when you are tragic and fantastic–and tragically fantastic or fantastically tragic. And Alexis? She's a bad ass boss but she's got a soft heart. She won't throw you out over one mistake."

"It's been about four mistakes now," I sniff. "What if she does?"

"Then open a cupcake bakery. You'll make the coffee, I'll make the cupcakes and then we can drink coffee and eat sweets all day at work. You'll have to write us the business plan and do all the accounting of course. I'll do the marketing and bring the flair."

I hiccup-laugh. "I can do that."

Chapter 26

Rising from the Ashes (Or at Least from the Coffee Stains)

I slump against the familiar, cool metal wall of the office elevator, throwing my hands up as my voice cracks, "A pen, Darius! Who stabs someone with a *pen*?"

Darius, bless his heart, manages to keep a straight face. "Well, the pen is mightier than the sword, or sexual harassment, they say."

I cover my face with both hands and groan loud enough to startle a raven outside. "This isn't funny. I've ruined everything. Alexis is going to fire me. I'll be blacklisted from every temp agency in Alaska. I'll end up living in a wet cardboard box under the Alaska Railroad bridge, feeding Cheetos to a one-eyed fox named Carl."

"I'm the Drama Queen, not you," Darius says, juggling his latte to check his phone. "Look, you made a mistake. A hilarious work mistake, but still *just a mistake.* It's not the end of the world."

"Easy for you to say," I mutter. "You didn't accuse the CEO of a major company, you were supposed to impress, of inappropriate behavior."

Darius shrugs. "No, but I did once spill an entire tray of wine on the governor's wife. And I'm still employed, aren't I?"

Despite myself, I crack a smile. "How do you always know how to make me feel better?"

"It's a gift," he says with a wink. "Now come on, let's get to work before your luck gets us hit by an asteroid."

I manage a weak laugh, the emotional equivalent of a daisy sprouting in a scorched field.

Then my phone buzzes. My entire body stiffens. Darius clocks it instantly.

"That your mom again?"

"Yup." I stare at the screen like it might bite. "Third time this morning."

"You gonna answer?"

I shove the phone back into my pocket like it's radioactive. "Nope. I can only juggle one emotional disaster at a time."

"Your mom is a disaster. You should disown her. My mom would take over being a mom to you–the nagging and tracking you, no problem," he adds with a cocked eyebrow.

"Thanks," I say, adding, "You, my friend, have an important mission."

"Ooh, do I get to be your knight in shining armor or more like an emotional support dive role?" he teases. "Or is this more of a cowboy situation? Flannel? Big truck? I'll need dramatic lighting and a cue card."

"Darius, you are not getting a grammy nomination. I just need you to talk with Alexis and smooth things over," I explain.

He sips his latte. "So just my regular Monday then."

I squint at him. "Why do I get the feeling you're enjoying my suffering?"

"Because I am." He grins, unbothered. "Now the real question. What's the deal with you kissing Alexis during your ER trip?"

Heat floods my face. "Uhhh... so... slight correction."

He narrows his eyes. "Aurora..."

"We didn't go to the ER."

"...Go on."

I chew on my lip. "I.. we went to the gynecologist instead."

Darius makes a strangled sound as we stop at his desk. "You... I can't—WHAT?"

"I don't want to talk about it."

He stops and waits in silence, blocking my path.

I take a long sip of my latte, considering how to best explain, but the whole thing is crazy.

He cocks his eyebrow and slowly shakes his head in the purest form of exasperation. "You dragged your boss—our Boss—who you idolize and are trying to impress—to a gynecology appointment?"

I fold my arms. "It wasn't planned!"

A strangled squeak erupts from Darius as he chokes on his latte.

"I was in a daze and the appointment reminder popped up on my phone," I explain as we glide into the office.

We push through the glass doors of the Alaska Temp Agency and step into air-conditioned civility. I cling to the sound of phones ringing and the faint whirr of printers. Luckily, everyone is too occupied to hear our conversation.

"Oh, I'm sorry, did you misplace your uterus and need adult supervision?!"

"I panicked! And she was driving! We were going to a doctor, and this saved us waiting for hours in the ER to be seen," I explained.

"She sat in the waiting room?"

"I may have forced her to come into the exam room then overshared."

Darius freezes. "Oh my—she knows your menstrual history?!"

"She might have also learned a lot about my sexual history..."

"Girl." He places both hands on his hips. "I am a drama queen, but you? You are a drama magnet."

Despite everything, a laugh bubbles out of me. The absurdity of my life is starting to hit at full force, and Darius's expression only makes it worse. I clutch my stomach, gasping. "I can't— I can't breathe."

Darius sighs dramatically. "Come on, disaster child. Let's get this all fixed before you end up accidentally adopting a coyote instead of a stray dog."

I nod. "I think that could actually happen. I'm not sure what the difference is. They both howl right?" The tension in my chest loosens slightly.

I groan. "Maybe I should go home sick."

"No, you won't." He smirks. "You'd have to walk, and we both know you hate cardio."

"Rude but fair." I cross my arms and pout. He's right, but I refuse to acknowledge it. At least he's forgotten his original question, so I don't have to detail my not-so--terrible-accidental kiss.

Alexis's office door is closed. Which means she's inside. Probably already celebrating landing a new client since I haven't told her.

I do need to tell her everything–including apologizing for the gynecologist and the kiss. My stomach twists.

Darius studies me. "Hey. No running. No hiding. You go in there, you tell Alexis what happened, and you own it. For once, this wasn't all your fault. That guy was being a grade-A creeper. You panicked. We've all been there."

"Have we?" I take a long sip of my latte.

I'm met with silence. Glancing at him, he's reading a message on his phone

I nod, taking a deep breath. "Okay. Yeah. I got this."

He tilts his head, looking at me. "Do you?"

I scowl. "No, but I'll fake it."

"That's my girl." He squeezes my shoulder with his perfectly manicured hand and gestures dramatically toward Alexis's office. "Now, go charm your way out of unemployment."

I swallow hard. "I hope she's in a good mood."

Darius smirks. "Well, if she isn't, you can always take her to a proctologist next."

I groan and shove him as I walk to Alexis' office, bracing for whatever chaos awaits.

I knock twice before stepping in.

Chapter 27

Office Gossip and Other Forms of Cardio

I'm ninety-nine percent sure I'm about to be fired.

Okay, maybe ninety-seven. The other three percent is reserved for the chance Alexis was in a terrible accident and has forgotten the last few days, *and* Alaska Cruises and Tours hasn't yet called her.

Alexis might say, *I wrecked my SUV, but thank God I have you as an employee. I can't remember the last few days, so if you could take all my calls, that'd be great.* Then I'll just ignore any calls from Grant.

I smile at the unlikely scenario and then swallow, ready to face, apologizing for kissing her during a deeply misread emotional moment and then dragging her to a gynecologist appointment like we were gal pals. Oh, and screwing up my interview this morning–*I can't forget about that.*

So yeah. My money's on being fired. Possibly with a complimentary mug that says "Nice Try."

I clutch my latte to shield me as I enter Alexis's office.

Cue internal chaos.

First, Alexis.

Second, Alexis's *legs.*

Third, Alexis's legs *in heels.*

Alexis is bathed in sunlight from the big window as if central casting placed her there. She doesn't look up right away, setting down a shoe box and staring across the room with a surgical focus.

I clear my throat. Loud. Awkward. Incredibly not smooth.

Her eyes lift slowly. Controlled. Calm. Cool.

Kill me.

"Morning," she says, her voice low and smooth. "Did the gynecologist give you a clean bill of health?"

I groan into my hands. "You are not allowed to be funny."

She sits on her desk, leaning on the edge, one shoe off, one shoe dangling from her toes. She crosses her long legs to slip the other shoe on, looking like an ad for a new fragrance, *CEO But Make It Hot.* Her blazer's flung over the back of the chair, and she's in a crisp button-down and black slacks that should be illegal in eighteen states, minimum.

That's when I should have noticed the boxes of shoes and mirror propped against the filing cabinet, and I walked straight into it because I forgot how feet work.

"Nice entrance," she says, eyebrows arched like she's halfway between amused and impressed by my complete lack of grace.

"I like to keep things professional," I blurt, untangling myself from the mirror's base. "And by professional, I mean I bring *a lot* of dramatic tension and humorous distractions to the workplace."

She chuckles—low and warm, the kind that buzzes in my chest like carbonated soda. "Sit."

"I can also stand if this is a short conversation. Like... under a minute. You know, a casual 'you're fired, clean out your locker, thanks for the memories' kind of chat."

Her lips twitch. "You think I'm firing you?"

"Oh, no," I say quickly. "I *know* you're firing me. It's the vibe. You're calm. You're in super-expensive-fancy heels you probably only wear when stomping on someone's dreams. You look amazing, like you're about to ruin someone's life, and I'm the only one here."

She lifts the other shoe, slides it on, and crosses her legs the other way.

"I am trying out heels for this weekend's gala," she says, standing and assessing the slick, badass black stilettos in the mirror. I've never seen her in stilettos. I secretly love how she towers over me since I'm usually the tallest girl in the room.

"I'm not firing you, Aurora."

...Processing. *System Error: Please try again later.*

"Wait, you're not?"

"I'm promoting you."

My brain does a full somersault. "Wait—what? You're serious?"

She walks around the desk and hands me a thick folder. I open it, expecting a cease and desist or restraining order, considering all the pans on her desk. But no—it's paperwork. Actual paperwork with my name on it and the words *Full-Time Permanent Benefits-Included Employee* typed like a headline from a dream I didn't dare let myself have.

"I thought I was still, you know... 'at-will and replaceable with minimal expectations.'"

"You were." Alexis sits, leans back, and gestures at the chair across from her. "But you've impressed me and I don't want to lose you."

My cheeks redden so fast, you'd think I'd been slapped, not complimented. I know because I can see the full embarrassing reaction in her office mirror.

She continues, "Plus, one of our toughest clients signed a long-term contract exclusively with our agency because you charmed the hell out of them in your onsite interview. Your weird blend of chaos and compassion works in your favor–*our* favor."

I blink. "So... I'm not getting a pay cut, fired, or a warning in my file?"

She smirks. "You're a valuable investment."

My heart does this lurchy dance that feels like a parade and a panic attack having a baby.

"And you'll be based out of the main office now," she continues. "You can keep doing accounting projects with me until Alaska Cruise and Tours needs you to start. I want you here. Where I can keep an eye on you."

That last part sounds pointed. Flirty, even. Like there's a secret underline only visible to gay panic. The fly in the champagne is hearing that I'm working for Grant at Alaska Cruise and Tours. *Why did he lie about the interview?*

My mouth flaps like a stranded halibut before I manage, "I'm—thank you. Seriously. I won't let you down. Unless tripping into a filing cabinet counts, because in that case—"

"Aurora." Alexis cuts in gently, a warning in her voice. But I'm already deep in the babble trenches.

"You don't have to wear heels just because you're the CEO–boss—I mean, manager. I actually like your shoes, the flats. They have... personality."

"You're babbling," she says, one brow arching in amusement.

"Right. Shutting up. Total professional. Watch me. Mute. Mysterious. Just—" I mime zipping my lips and throw in a dramatic nod for effect. "Nodding only from here on out."

Alexis tilts her head, gaze steady and unreadable—the kind of calm, collected expression that makes it dangerously hard to focus on anything but the curve of her mouth.

Then, she stands. Slowly. Smoothly. And steps toward me with measured confidence that should be illegal in office lighting.

"Also," she says, "you're not missing the anniversary gala. I want my father, the current CEO–" she taps a picture of her from a long-ago vacation. It shows a younger version of her with shorter hair, softer features, and a slight sunburn with Richard, and an older man who can only be her dad, drinking pina coladas in a jacuzzi– "to see the reason we'll be doubling our profit next year."

"Oh." I pause and nod. The old vacation picture of Richards's slick chest and Alexis' beaming smile between the men she loves adds another wet blanket on what should be my enjoyment, basking in her warm praise.

She smiles. "That was an underwhelming reaction."

"No, I'm thrilled. Like, thrilled enough to cry and possibly ugly dance in public. But also..." I scramble on what to say. *I want to kiss you again, but you're happy and straight.* I settle on a smaller truth, "The gala's a huge, fancy event, and I'm more... flannel grocery store outfit meets Nordstrom clearance rack style."

"You'll be stunning, whatever you wear." She reaches past me to grab her phone, and I'm hyper-aware of how close she is. Her perfume smells like cedarwood, a sweet clementine, and sin. "And *I* want you there."

"You personally want me there or is this a mandatory employee event?"

She meets my eyes.

Her eyes sparkle, and she says, "Yes."

I don't even need to ask her what she's responding to. I'm going to die on the spot, and my cheeks can't get any redder.

"And after the gala," she adds, voice dropping lower, "we should talk."

My heart stutters. "Talk?"

"About our... *situation.*"

Our situation. As in *The Kiss.* As in *The Hug I Misinterpreted That Led To The Kiss That Haunted Me For A Week And A Half. My inappropriate workplace behavior.*

I nod. We actually have a plethora of topics to talk about. "Oh, okay," I squeak. "Yes. Talking. Great. Normal."

She smiles again—*that* smile. The one that practically smolders.

"Don't spiral. It's not bad. I'm just—*focused* right now. My dad's announcing I'm taking over the company at the gala, and I need to make sure everything runs perfectly."

I nod too hard, and my neck makes a weird cracking noise. *Oh, kill me now*—even without talking, I'm awkward. "Totally. No pressure. I'll just... be there. Existing. Your supportive new office employee."

"I'm counting on it."

Cue me backing away and watching myself in the mirror, blinking like a confused forest creature who wandered into a luxury spa. I must leave before I ruin what might actually be a work promotion.

I spin toward the door, desperate for escape, and walk into Darius.

"Were you pressed to the door this whole time?" I whisper, shutting the door as he steps back.

He shushes me dramatically and hisses, "What *situation* are we–or more specifically, *you and Alexis*–talking about, exactly? And why did you look like you were about to kiss her feet in those heels? Were they Louboutins? Don't lie to me, Aurora."

"You're lurking."

"I'm gathering intel. A good employee admin knows everything that's going on in the office and anticipates the Boss' every move."

I shove him gently toward his desk. "She's promoting me. Full-time. Main office. Accounting-slash-temping. And she's about to become the official CEO at the gala."

He squeals like someone won bingo night and drops his latte. "You got *Alexis's* attention, a job, and an invitation to *the* hottest event of the season? Who *are* you, and what dark magic did you invoke?"

"Apparently I'm a valuable investment now."

"Oh, honey. You're a stock that's about to skyrocket. And I'm buying shares–all of them! *Yass, Girl!*"

"Coffee and gossip time, stat," he says.

"Nope. I'm not discussing any office drama until after the gala, when I have my talk with Alexis. Besides, you're the one who should be spilling the tea," I snap back.

"Touché," he says with a wink and sashays away.

Back at my desk, I plop into the chair, staring blankly at the accounting folders I should be organizing. Alexis's voice echoes in my head.

'I don't want to lose you.'

'We need to talk.'

'I want you here.'

'You're an investment.'

For some reason, what stands out most is the picture on her shelf. In my mind's eye, I see every detail of the photo of the teenage Alexis between her dad and a younger but still very dapper Richard. Richard's perfect, *obviously*. He is handsome and charming with no emotional baggage, and they have a long history.

He's also always *around*. They must have a strong relationship if they work out together and share lunch. Laugh in that easy, comfortable way that people comfortable around each other do.

Do not compare yourself to him and your relationships, or lack of relationship, to theirs, I tell myself. *Do not emotionally spiral today. That's scheduled for after work hours.*

Still, I can't help the sharp pang in my chest. Flirtations are easy to misread when your brain's fried and your heart's hopeful.

Alexis might've been flirting.

Or... she might be doing that thing influential people do where they're effortlessly magnetic and make you feel special for ten seconds before returning to their perfect lives with perfect partners.

I poke my calculator. "Do I need to start wearing more professional outfits to work? Does a tailored blazer come with more confidence?"

Darius flops into the chair beside me. "You need a makeover, a gala dress, and a therapist. Not in that order."

Lisa zips in, carrying a cupcake and two office plants. "Gala? Are we talking *gala*? Because I know a guy who rents fake Gucci and real boas."

"Why are you here and holding plants?" I ask.

"Nothing happens in my office before ten, and I'm doing a vibe cleanse."

"No one asked you to do that."

"I noticed on Friday, you guys need these. Besides, no one ever asks me to do anything. If I waited to be asked, I'd never have any fun."

Alexis's door clicks shut, and my eyes flick up again.

She walks down the hall, heels clicking, phone pressed to her ear. She glances my way and smiles. Not a business smile. You're *wanted,* and *I will take you* kind of smile.

My heart throws itself off a cliff.

Then, before I can form a competent thought, she winks at me and strides out the door like some sort of effortlessly hot, executive-level goddess.

And I'm left breathless and braindead. My head is short-circuiting from *so many things* swirling around.

"Oh, yes, girl" Lisa purrs. "You're going to hit that right?"

Darius shakes his head. "She's not talking about it until after the gala."

"Sounds like someone else who's keeping a secret relationship. Am I the only open book these days?"

He tries to smack her, but she dances out of reach.

And right there, in the chaos of our temp agency's beige-walled buzz, I realize I might not be getting fired—but I am 100% getting *wrecked.*

Chapter 28

Makeover Magic

Lisa and—*mostly*—Darius drag me into Anchorage's biggest mall like they're preparing me to storm the runway of a fashion reality show. Before I could even blink, Lisa shoved a too-hot latte into my hands like a bribe. Darius steers me toward a boutique with a gold-lettered *"By Appointment Only"* sign that screams, *You can't afford to breathe in here.*

"This is it, girl," Darius announces, like Oprah giving away cars. He throws his arms wide as if angels are about to descend with sequin halos. "Tonight, you're walking into that gala looking like a mysterious heiress with a secret vendetta."

Lisa pumps her fist. "A fashion-diva ready to accept an award and bitch slap anyone who steps in your spotlight!"

"I don't need to slap anyone," I mutter, slurping my latte like it's my emotional support juice. "I need to look like a slightly more polished version of a broke college dropout faking her way until Fall semester starts."

"You're getting 'sexy, unattainable goddess who is ready to become the CEO,'" Darius corrects, pushing me toward a rack of dresses so sparkly they should come with a seizure warning. "You *will* radiate hot girl mystery and grace, even if you're internally screaming about accounting tasks."

"I'm not the mysterious one holding out," I shoot back, eyeing him sideways. "If we're talking workplace romance, your situationship is more sus than mine."

His eyes glint as he flings a red sequin dress at me like a weapon. "Try this. You're welcome."

He hangs a handful of dresses inside our extra-large dressing room.

Lisa hurls something horrific and shiny into my dressing room. "If you two don't give me real gossip soon, I'll force you both into matching faux-snakeskin. Don't tempt me."

Darius leans on the dressing room frame like he *owns* it. "I'm not telling you anything because I *thrive* on chaos. Now shut up and sparkle."

"Wow," I mumbled, stepping into the dressing room. "Supportive friends are supposed to be *supportive*."

"You *are* being supported," Darius calls. "By the collective power of fashion and our shopping entertainment."

I rifle through the pile of gowns they've hurled at me like fabric grenades, but then—*bam*. I spot it. Hanging at the back like a silent, shimmering goddess, a dark green sequined gown that catches the light like the northern lights gliding across a snowy night. High slit, sweetheart neckline, tiny sequins stitched like secret stars. It's whispering my name. This is *the one*.

I yank it over my head in a flutter of enthusiasm and caffeine.

And instantly regret *everything*.

The sequins dig into my hair like barbed wire and tangle themselves around my bun like they're personally offended by it. My arms flail stuck above my head. I can't see. I'm hot. And—oh *no*—I'm wearing my granny panties.

"Darius!" My voice echoes off the tiny walls. "Emergency! Level: Fashion Catastrophe!"

Outside, he hums a jaunty little show tune. *Jerk.*

"How's it going in there?" he sings.

"Like *Carrie* meets *Project Runway*! I'm being eaten alive by a sparkly whale!"

I wriggle, trying to free my arms, but it only tightens around my ribcage like a clingy ex.

"MINOR SITUATION! NEED MAJOR HELP!"

The curtain *swooshes* open like a reveal on *Drag Race*, and Darius swans in, dramatically clutching his pearls.

"Oh honey... you're giving 'discount Elsa found frozen in a clearance bin.'"

"Don't roast me—*rescue* me!" My choice of gown is as ill-fated as my usual life choices.

He gently starts untangling sequins from my hair while I flap helplessly. My face burns. Not from shame. Okay, a *little* from shame. Mostly because I'm stuck, half-naked, with arms overhead, wearing massive cotton briefs with snowmen on them.

Why? Why today?

Darius doesn't even blink. "Granny panties? In this economy?"

"They're *comfortable*, okay?! And nobody was supposed to *see* them!"

"Bold choice for your big gala glow-up."

I groan. "I should've stayed home. I'm cursed. This dress is cursed. My dating life is cursed."

He laughs and pulls the last sequin loose from my hair. My phone pings on the bench like it *knows* it's about to ruin my life. Again.

I reach for it, but my arms are still partially trapped. Darius scoops it up with a gleam in his eyes.

"Gimme that."

"Nope," he says because he's legally required to be a menace. He reads aloud like we're in English class. "'Confirming. You must attend the gala. Company requirement.'"

He pauses. Then reads the following line slower. "'Looking forward to seeing you there.' Signed: Alexis.'"

My lungs collapse. "It's not a big deal. I forgot to confirm my rsvp."

"For Alexis, this is downright flirty."

"Darius," I warn. "Why does *no one* care that I almost died wrapped in this sparkle green dress of doom?"

Lisa appears in a blinding silver jumpsuit that might get her arrested. She pauses mid-strut, squints at me like I'm roadkill, and sighs.

"Oh, babe."

She steps in, shooing Darius aside, and expertly frees my other arm like she's defusing a bomb.

"You're lucky I have tiny fingers and zero morals," she says, tugging at the zipper. "But we're *never* mentioning those underwear again."

"Agreed."

"Also, you're not wearing that dress. You deserve better. Something bold. Something boss-girl sexy. Something that makes businessmen trip over their briefcases."

"She doesn't carry a briefcase," I mutter. Then I blushed, realizing she wasn't referring to Alexis.

Darius whistles. "We need a gown that makes her shine without the shine."

Freed from sequin prison, I shove the dress onto a hanger like it personally offended me. "Great. Now I need therapy *and* shapewear."

"Try this LBD." Darius dangles a silky black dress that's 85% slip and 15% Victoria's Secret Angel.

I eye it suspiciously. "What designer is LBD?"

Lisa nearly snorts herself into another dimension. "LBD means *Little Black Dress*, babe."

"You don't own one?" Darius looks personally offended. "That's illegal. Every woman needs an LBD. It's Fashion Law."

I wiggle into the dress, and it slides over my skin like cool glacier water, which is slippery and comfy. "I look like a Bond girl who accidentally wandered into a fundraiser."

"You look like you *are* the fundraiser," Darius hums, straightening the hem. "Expensive, mysterious, and possibly dangerous."

I turn to the mirror. *Oh.* Okay. Who is that?

This dress doesn't scream "I cried in the parking lot too many times to count," or "I'm a barista-level employee, not a businesswoman." No, this dress whispers *power.* It whispers *confidence.* It whispers *Alexis will absolutely notice me, especially with perfectly chosen shoes.*

Wait. Shoes. Alexis loves shoes. I need shoes that scream "I read Vogue" and not "I got these from the Ross clearance bin during a half off sale."

Lisa shimmies next to me in a sparkly silver jumpsuit that belongs in either Vegas or space. She strikes a Charlie's Angels pose. I join her without hesitation, finger guns blazing, and we burst into synchronized pouts.

Darius gasps, "*Perfection!*" He snaps a pic with the speed of a gossip blog intern. "Aurora, not you, Lisa. That blacklight-bowling-alley monstrosity is a crime."

Lisa flips him off in style, blowing kisses like she's on a runway. "You don't *get* my vision."

"I *see* your vision," he drawls. "It's giving rave at Chuck E. Cheese."

My phone dings. I snatch it before Darius's nosy fingers swipe it.

Two things pop up, a group text from Alexis with *my* picture and a private message to me.

Alexis. Her response is, "Gala attire suits you, Ms. Thompson. Post-event sake at Ronnie's. 9pm."

Cue internal fireworks.

Cue next, instant panic.

"WHY are you texting Alexis?"

"I'm RSVPing for the gala," Darius singsongs, blinking like an innocent assistant. "She's our boss. Duh."

"Why are *you* managing my life like a nosy assistant in a rom-com?"

"Because clearly you're starring in one," he says, flinging invisible glitter into the air. "Also because your life choices give me hives, and I need to supervise."

My brain stumbles through a bunch of weird puzzle pieces—his weird little smiles, the way he *never* needled me about my whole cake-high freak-out where I accused him of kissing Alexis, and the suspicious quantity of Alexis trivia he casually drops.

A wild, mildly unhinged thought tickles my brain.

He spins me back to the mirror before I say it out loud. "Focus, babe. This is your Cinderella moment. Except you *keep* the shoe and *don't* date the man. Unless the man is a hot woman with an expensive blazer habit."

My breath hitches. Right. I *am* slaying. I am an unstoppable force of shimmery silk and second chances.

I square my shoulders. "Alright. Let's do this."

Lisa waves the leopard-print nightmare she tried to sneak back into circulation. "Or, hear me out—animal print!"

"No," Darius and I say in perfect harmony.

He points at me. "Now, accessories. We need a clutch, jewelry, and shoes hot enough to get you an invite to Alexis's shoe closet."

I twist, watching how the fabric clings to my body like it was tailored for me in Paris by a heartbroken designer who wanted me to shine. "It's a lot of silk."

Darius clutches his pearls. "It's *the* dress."

Lisa fans herself dramatically. "You look like you're about to close a business deal *and* steal someone's girlfriend."

"That's... the goal?" I grin.

Darius grins back. "Shoes. We need strappy, head-turning, aisle-five-of-Nordstrom kind of shoes. And a pedicure. Preferably yesterday."

I protest, but he cuts me off with a perfectly manicured finger. "My treat. Lisa's letting you stay with her for the next few weeks, and I want in on your glow-up arc."

My eyes sting. Dang it. If I start crying, I'll be banned from the mall's fanciest boutique for life.

Instead of melting into a puddle of emotions, I throw them both finger guns. "I hate you both in the most affectionate way."

We cackle wildly as I shuffle backward into the dressing room.

"Let's get her into something more walkable than those gross sandals," Darius shouts through the door. "We're building an empire, not going hiking!"

I peek out as Lisa drags him toward the shoe section. "I don't know if I should be worried or thrilled that this is turning into an all-day retail intervention."

"But it's working!" Lisa yells over her shoulder. "You're glowing like it's your birthday!"

Back in the dressing room, I glance down at the silky black gown, hugging my body like it's rooting for me. My reflection stares back—not panicked, not scared, not trying to outrun the latest disaster.

I'm not the girl who showed up at the temp agency trembling and unemployed.

Not the girl who let her mom's criticism live rent-free in her brain.

Not even the girl who accidentally kissed her boss and pretended it was nothing.

I'm someone figuring stuff out. *Someone choosing herself.*

I'm moving into Lisa's spare room—okay, technically a walk-in closet with wifi—earning paychecks, working toward university, and handling *everything* like a semi-functional adult with a killer dress.

And if Alexis wants to harmlessly flirt over late-night sake?

Well.

She invited me, and she's the boss.

And I've got my first LBD.

So yeah, I might take her up on that.

Especially if I find shoes hot enough to make a woman whose *entire personality includes luxury sneakers* give me a second look.

With one last smirk at my reflection, I reach for my phone and text back, "See you at nine. You're buying the sake and fancy cocktails."

Bring on the gala. Bring on the shoes. Bring on whatever the night wants to throw at me.

I'm ready.

Chapter 29

Spilled Drinks & Gaslighting Cocktails

Walking into this gala feels like stepping into a sparkly minefield. The cocktail hour is already buzzing with Anchorage's most well-known fake-smiling businessman sipping overpriced drinks and pretending they've never sexually harassed anyone or accused anyone of sexual harassment.

So, like, a regular Saturday for them.

I scan for Darius and Lisa—my ride-or-dies. No dice. Who do I spot?

Every. Single. Person. I've been actively avoiding the past weeks. It's *astounding how many enemies I can rack up over the summer.*

First up? My mother. Yes, *her*. Why is she here? Who invited her? Who failed to check invitations at the door? She's at the bar, mid-rant, in a cocktail dress so tight it's basically an honesty declaration. She's trapping some poor stranger in a monologue disguised as small talk, where she only asks a question so she can answer it herself.

Jamie, my former office fling, and then there's Neil, my former temp boss and walking HR violation. He's pretending not to see me while sipping something suspiciously blue. And oh—great. Lisa's here too, perched on a barstool like the chaos gremlin she is, swirling her martini with the kind of smile that means *she's already done damage.*

And right in the middle of it all?

Grant *freakin'* Fairbanks.

The man who interviewed me for a data entry job watched me fumble every question and somehow didn't report me—or press charges when I tried to stab him with his own pen. He locks eyes with me and *smiles.* A slow, knowing, unnerving smile.

"Oh, you've gotta be kidding me," I mutter, ducking my head, wishing I wasn't looking stunning and ready for the spotlight, thanks to Darius' help.

Lisa spots me and waves like we're at a girls' brunch, not in the middle of a social minefield littered with my worst decisions.

Something cold and wet splashes down my sleeve before I can make a beeline to her.

"Whoops."

I yelp, spinning around as Merlot drips down my jacket.

Great. Now, everyone's staring at the tall girl covered in red wine. Being noticeable isn't always a plus.

Slate stands there, holding an empty glass and an unapologetic smirk. She's wearing a catering uniform. "Oops," she says, with zero remorse.

"You!" I shriek.

"Me," she purrs, crossing her tattooed arms and tilting her head like I'm the confused one. "That spill was a complete accident, I swear. Kinda like how you *accidentally* gave me the wrong number, right? I shaved my legs and hoped it was a mistake and that you'd stop by Ronnies to see me."

"I—uh—" I'm already stammering. "That was—well—I meant to—"

Slate's gaze slices through me, and shame creeps up my spine making me sputter. I give up and shrug.

"Mmhm." She eyes me up and down. "At least, the number you gave me was for a girl at a dating agency, so I got a nice connection. I'm still single and Alaska's a pretty small place to be a lesbian. You wanna hookup after this?"

She's joking. *Probably.*

I glance across the room.

My breath catches.

Alexis walks in—utterly breathtaking in a tailored tux that hugs her like it was designed with only her in mind. Unabashedly a badass business woman among men. And there they are—her signature highlighter-yellow Converse, a defiant splash of rebellion against a sea of black stilettos and loafers.

She decided not to wear the sexy new shoes that haunt my dreams, along with her long legs.

Only Alexis could pull yellow sneakers off at a gala with such effortless swagger.

Slate tracks my gaze, then lets out a low whistle. "Ohhh."

My heart stutters.

"Ohhh, no," I whisper.

"You didn't give me your number," Slate says slowly, eyes twinkling, "because you *like her*."

"She's my... That is *not*—that's a bold accusation—" I stammer.

Slate winks. "I respect it."

Then she disappears into the crowd, a wine-staining ghost bored of haunting me, leaving me to burn quietly in my own panic.

And Alexis? She's watching me.

And then—

She winks.

WINKS!

My brain flatlines. My limbs turn to overcooked spaghetti noodles. I suck in a shaky breath, adjust my wine-stained jacket like I'm in control of my life, and march through the crowd like a woman who is not emotionally undressed by a single wink.

Spoiler, I am absolutely not okay.

"Aurora! Hey!"

I whirl around—and there he is. *Neil.*

"Oh no," I whisper, praying for a sinkhole.

He's already halfway toward me, clutching an empty glass like a toddler holding a toy sword—full of confidence, no understanding of consequences. "Hey. Uh. I owe you an apology."

I squint at him. "This should be interesting."

"I didn't realize I was being catfished. Or, like, tested. On the dating site?"

I blink. "What?"

"You know—the Mexican work thing. The fake profile. I thought *you* were the one messaging me and flirting. Then I asked you out at work because I thought you liked me, and then when I showed Alexis the messages and—anyway. Turns out it was a catfish."

I stare. "You showed my boss flirty messages from a fake profile you thought was me."

He nods. "Yup. My bad."

"That's your apology?"

He hesitates. "Yes?"

Before I can explain how *deeply not okay* that is, a hand taps my shoulder.

I turn—and there she is.

Alexis.

Close enough that I catch her perfume—some citrusy, woodsy mix that probably costs more than my rent–if I was paying rent.

"You doing okay?" she asks, low and smooth.

"I'm fine!" My voice cracks like I'm thirteen again. "Super fine. Totally great. *Thriving,* actually."

Alexis lifts one brow. "Good. Because I was hoping to steal you away for a second."

My heart launches into orbit. "Steal? Like, legally? Or—"

"Come on, Trouble." She gestures, but a man appears next to her and whispers, "I need you to check the schedule and podium set-up."

She agrees and turns back to me with a reluctant smile, the kind that knocks the breath right out of me. "We'll talk later.."

"I—yeppers—no, I mean—"

"Relax." She grins. "You're fine. We're fine."

I open my mouth to ask what *she* means, but she holds up a hand.

"We'll talk tonight. I want to be clear about everything. But for now... drink and celebrate."

Before I can respond—before I can *breathe*—she winks again and walks away.

I turn back toward the main room, dazed, and—

Bam. I walk smack into Grant Fairbanks.

Because the gala gods hate me.

"Oh, uh—hi," I blurt, suddenly forgetting how words work. My brain short-circuits into a dial-up internet modem, trying to refresh in this new emergency situation.

Beside him, his wife beams like this is a Christmas party, not the beginning of my social and career demise. "Aurora, we were hoping to see you tonight."

"Really?" I narrow my eyes. "Because that's... um.. unexpected."

Kathleen's smile doesn't budge. "Grant's been talking about you non-stop since the job interview and the snafu."

I blink. "Oh?"

Grant chuckles awkwardly. "I, uh, wanted to apologize."

Lisa appears like a glittery Tasmanian devil, taking in my growing blush, her eyes wide. "Ooooh, is this another copy room scandal? Aurora, you minx."

I toss her a glare. "No. And also, please stop announcing my potential HR violations out loud."

She shrugs, totally unrepentant, sipping from a flute of something suspiciously pink.

Grant clears his throat. "I wasn't professional when we met. I was nervous. Didn't mean to come off as... weird."

"Oh, you're the creep!" Lisa exclaims cheerfully, shaking his hand like they're old friends at brunch.

"Lisa!" I hiss.

"What? I'm being welcoming."

Kathleen smooths her husband's lapel with the casual intimacy of someone who knows all his passwords and tolerates his bad texting etiquette. "He's not a creep, promise. He's my husband. And we'd love to have you work with us."

Okay, now I'm squinting suspiciously. "You're really hiring me... for office work?"

Kathleen nods like I didn't say that with twelve ounces of distrust. "We're planning to work with Alexis's agency this year. But more than that, I'd love to connect with you personally."

I shake my head, and my sleeve drips wine.

She grins. "Coffee next week?"

Grant pipes in, "Let's start fresh. Clean Slate."

I blink at them. Twice. And give a slight, safe nod.

"Why is everyone apologizing to me tonight? What kind of karmic roulette is this?" I whisper to Lisa as they are distracted by the drink tray that somehow misses me.

Lisa hums thoughtfully, eyes scanning the crowd. "You've caused a surprising amount of work drama in a short time. It's honestly impressive."

"Says my emotional support chaos goblin," I mutter.

Kathleen plucks a fancy mini quiche from a passing tray. "You're a smart, professional young woman."

The unexpected compliment stuns me to silence. My face heats like I just ran a sprint in a parka. Compliments? Real ones? About being... capable?

Nope. This is a trap. *Flee.*

I bolt.

I head straight to the coat room.

Gala professional mode, aborted.

This party smells like overpriced perfume, tension, and lousy job offers. Everyone's trying too hard, and there's too much alcohol for any room not hosting a bachelorette party. If I don't get out for air, I'll either cry or throw a shrimp puff at someone's face, and only one of those is socially acceptable. *Hint, it's not either of those options.*

I slow my step, remembering that I'm not the same person who needed a rescue at Ronnie's Sushi Bar. Not the intern who kissed a married coworker in the copy room, went to the gyno with her boss, and nearly got herself banned from every temp agency north of the Yukon. Nope.

Tonight, I'm a professional woman with a job, a growing savings account, and an unshakable mission to start university, become independent, and build a future that doesn't crumble at the first overdraft notice. I sniff and roll my shoulders back, professional mode activated.

This is why it's extra tragic that the first person I nearly plow into pausing during my escape is my mother.

Sandra *freakin'* Thompson.

She's in a rhinestone dress that looks like it mugged a disco ball.

"Oh, honey, you're here." Her voice drips with fake honey and polished condescension, fingers fluttering dramatically over her pearls like she's about to faint from my fashion choices. "And you didn't say hello to me! How embarrassing for you, standing here in that... stained, wet jacket."

Before I can process the emotional drive-by, Lisa catches up to me and whispers, "Sorry. I didn't know Alexis' dad, the CEO, invited your mom. If I had, I would've warned you."

I snap my head toward her. "Why would anyone invite her?"

Lisa nods, grimacing. "Don't hate me, I only just found out chatting up your coworkers. And I don't even think Darius knew."

Before I can ask why Alexis' dad is talking to the woman who birthed me and then emotionally abandoned me, Sandra leans in.

"You don't belong here, Aurora," she hisses, viciously. "This isn't your crowd. These are educated professionals. People with status. Not... scrappy little girls pretending they have their lives together."

I smile like the main character in a courtroom drama right before delivering the final blow. "You mean people who don't steal their kid's university fund for Botox and bougie yoga retreats?"

Sandra's nostrils flare. *Bullseye.*

"I did what was best for you."

"No," I say, ice-cold. "You did what was convenient for you."

We lock eyes.

She's gearing up for another round of gaslighting. Still, before she launches into Act II of her guilt trip, someone announces that the program is starting soon and to move into the ballroom.

Then, her expression shifts. Eyes dart past my shoulder. Her whole smug face freezes.

She looks... haunted.

I follow her line of sight.

Nothing obvious. No flaming ex-boyfriends, no IRS agents with folders.

"Did you spot someone from your secret past life?" I ask sweetly.

Lisa appears next to me and cheerfully adds, "This is Alaska. I've dated half the men in this room. And their brothers. And their dogs."

Sandra glares like we're stains on her designer carpet.

Which is my cue to vanish.

I pivot, cutting through the sea of sequins toward the coat check. I need to ditch this wet coat, whatever weird mother-daughter drama I just walked into, and the odd work drama before that.

Can I fake a migraine and text Alexis my apologies for leaving early?

Out of the loud bar area, I exhale and glance around. Blessed silence.

I reach for my phone to text Darius an all-caps SOS—but a new message pings at the top of the screen.

"Aurora, friendly reminder from Dr. Winters' office to schedule your follow-up. Please call 907-651-9755 to schedule your follow-up for test results and prescription, if needed."

Seriously? *Now?*

I groan internally. "Nope. No medical drama tonight. I'm emotionally maxed out."

I swipe the notification away, close the app, and shove the phone back in my clutch.

Not tonight, mysterious test results. Not when I've got a tuxedo-clad boss, coworkers, a nice drink waiting for me, and a bestie who I see heading into the ballroom while tucking a flask further into her cleavage that may or may not be moonshine.

I straighten up, fix my hair in the mirror, apply a layer of shiny gloss, and set my sights on the dance floor.

I'm here. I'm surviving. I'm slaying in my gala fashion. I'm Aurora *freaking* Thompson.

And tonight?

I need to get rid of my wet jacket and let Lisa and Darius prevent me from getting myself pulled into Alexis's gravitational field again.

Above all, I must avoid socializing with my mother.

Which, now that I think about it, might be the catalyst for most of my current emotional breakdown.

Chapter 30

The "Oh-my-Gay-God" Coatroom Bombshell

I sigh as I escape, shutting the door behind me in the large coat closet.

The bass from the ballroom throbs through the coat room walls, vibrating straight into my ribs like I've swallowed a tiny nightclub. The fur stoles and tailored jackets hanging in this walk-in luxury closet shimmy to the beat, because even the coats are bougie and belong here more than I do.

I'm supposed to be hanging up my coat. That's all I came here to do, but now I feel even more judged by inanimate objects.

Instead, I find myself gripping my damp, but cute, little black ruffle peacoat as if it is a security blanket. It's a Goodwill find, practically begging for its big moment under the chandeliers and twinkle lights. And me? I'm trying not to pass out from gala-induced crisis mode.

These are not my people. These business professionals are high-heeled, manicured, moneyed-up networking machines sipping bubbly and trading business cards like Pokémon. I hustle paycheck to paycheck, clip coupons, and pray every day I don't get found out and fired.

But still—I'm here. At the Alaska Temp Agency's 25th Anniversary Gala. Invited. Wearing lip gloss, a slaying gown, and new shoes. And a borrowed boosting bra that's waging war with my ribcage.

"I belong here," I whisper like it's a magic spell, chin lifting. "I belong here."

My coat finally slips from my hands, ready for the hanger. As I gather my courage, the hairs on the back of my neck stand up. I'm not alone.

I pause in the dimly lit room, then—a sound confirms my suspicions.

A laugh.

A *familiar* laugh.

Darius.

Wait, why is Darius laughing in a coat room?

My head tilts. My brows shoot up in confusion. My entire body freezes, and I pivot toward the back of the closet—right as I hear a muffled *murmur* followed by a low groan that absolutely does not scream "innocent bestie hideout time."

I step forward, moving aside a puff-sleeved parka and someone's fur-trimmed trench.

And then?

I see it.

Them.

Making out.

Full. On. Face-mashing.

My brain doesn't register it immediately. It hits my retinas, but the neurons say, "Nah, surely not."

But oh yes. Darius. My best friend. Currently pinned to the wall like a trophy-winning King Salmon. His hands tangled in Richard's thick, curly hair.

Richard.

As in the suit-wearing, low-voiced man I see almost every morning. Richard, *Alexis's* longtime partner.

Dread and fear flood my mind, but I'm frozen at the sight of my best friend and melting into Richard.

Why hadn't he told me? I knew he was dating someone but... Why hadn't I seen this coming? My heart ached. I'm rooted to the spot. *What the hell?*

My heart races, and a whirlwind of confusion swirls in my chest. It's as if I'm separated by a screen, watching a scene unfold in a movie. But this is real life, and I can't tear my gaze away.

Darius's hand is fisted in Richard's perfectly tailored lapel. Richard's fingers are buried in Darius's hair, the same fingers that I've seen on Alexis' shoulder and wrapped around her morning coffee. And neither of them noticed me, even though I'd just slammed my coat onto the nearest hanger with the grace of a startled moose on ice.

Alexis. My boss. My maybe-crush. My off-limits, gorgeous, confusing, buttoned-up goddess of a boss.

My clutch slips from my hand and hits the floor with a *thud* that makes a couple of jackets tremble.

They don't even notice.

I gawk, slack-jawed, while Darius clutches Richard like he's his favorite thrifted cashmere, and Richard kisses him like we're in a Hallmark movie about two rival CEOs trapped in their burning office's building's elevator on Valentine's Day.

Smoke doesn't billow from the coat rack beside them, but it *should*.

My brain tries to compute. And fails.

Wait—wait, wait, wait.

Darius. My best friend, who's been weird and evasive for weeks. Richard. Alexis's… what *is* he?

Her partner?

Boyfriend?

Husband??

"WHAT. THE. HELL!"

"*You, Creeper!*" Darius yelps before seeing me, practically throwing Richard off him.

Richard, to his credit, remains smooth as ever, adjusting his suit like a man who absolutely did not just get caught in a coat closet scandal.

Meanwhile, Darius is scrambling to fix his hair and tuck in his shirt, like that will somehow erase the fact that I *just saw him making out with our boss's partner.* Darius jerks back like he's been tasered. "Aurora!" he says calmer, but his eyes widen. "Oh my GOD—why—how—WHY?!"

"Why?! I Came In Here To Hang Up A Coat, like a normal person who doesn't destroy lives, You Scandalous Homo Inducer!"

Richard, meanwhile, straightens his suit like he's posing for *GQ*. The man is so composed it's rude. "That's not a real term," he says with a slight smile.

"Don't you dare smile at me," I hissed, pointing a trembling finger. "You're *cheating*. On Alexis, who is hot, powerful, with bone structure like a Greek statue! And *this*—this betrayal during her important gala event—is unforgivable!"

Darius facepalms so hard I hear it. "Okay, can we *not* scream this across the entire venue?! Do you *want* to cause more drama?!"

"Yes!" I hissed. "And I want answers now!"

Richard, absurdly calm, places a hand on my shoulder. "Aurora. Breathe. Alexis and I aren't together."

"Yeah okay, and I'm married to Santa Claus," I snapped.

Darius snorts, Richard smirks, and suddenly, they're *both* laughing, which, to be clear, is *not* the appropriate response to an affair being exposed. And with the potential of all of us losing our jobs and more.

I cross my arms. "I fail to see what's funny about all of this."

He chuckles. I hate that even his laugh is charming. "No. really. We're friends. Old friends. Like you and Darius."

I slowly blink as my brain reboots, my lips part with only air, and my harsh judgment comes out in that exhale.

"Really they are gym buddies and pickleball partners," Darius says.

"But—you—you live together?"

"No. She carpools and we play pickleball every morning," Richard says with an elegant shrug. "This physique doesn't stay ripped without ripping it up on the court. She's my partner."

"Your partner?"

"In pickleball. And crime. And she's more like a sister, besides in what world does a straight man have these abs?"

Darius, with lust still in his eyes, nods.

"But you—" I grasp at straws. "You slapped her butt and topped her!"

"Yeah, well, I also slap Darius's," he says, sending my best friend a wink that earns him an exasperated eye roll.

"Also, he is most definitely the bottom," Darius adds with a chuckle.

I blink. I *blink hard.* I have been *so* dumb.

"But—but—you make her coffee and she has a picture of you in her office."

Richard waves his hand, explaining, "That's from our trip to Mexico when her dad announced she could run the business. Come on, she wears blazers everyday and is obviously not interested in men."

"She gets Darius coffee, too. Do you want to accuse him of an office affair too?"

"She did that already, remember," he says dryly as he finishes dusting off his pants.

"I'm gayer than a drag brunch," Richard ends the discussion and gives a little jazz-hands flourish.

"STOP!" I squeak, smacking my ears. "I can't process this much information while standing in your makeout den!"

Richard grins. Darius smirks. My world tilts.

Oh.

Ohhhhh.

Wait a *minute*. My brain catches up.

My eyes flick between them. Richard. Darius.

So—*Alexis is not dating him*?

She's *single*?

She's...*available*?

Wait... so maybe... maybe there's a chance for... An intense feeling I have been denying races through me. It's not just admiration. It's... something more. Something I can't ignore.

All those weird little lingering glances. All those tiny touches and clues. Alexis rescued me, showed up when I was spiraling, complimented me, and gave me chances. She's in that tux tonight, sparkling in those shoes.

She's not taken.

She's not straight?

She might actually...

I spin on my heel, ignoring the way Darius hisses my name.

"Where are you going?!" he whisper-yells, tripping over a parka.

My heels click against the marble-like war drums.

"To talk to Alexis," I toss back, my insides one part electricity, one part nausea.

"Wait!" he squawks. "At least wait until after the gala, Aurora."

I don't answer.

Because I'm not waiting anymore.

I'm going for it.

For the first time in my romantic disaster of a life, I'm not running. Not playing it safe and small. Not assuming I'm unworthy.

I'm going full heart-first, sparkly-shoe wearing in my very-sexy-business-appropriate Little Black Dress stunning wearing self.

I ignored all the signals.

And suddenly, it's like a dam breaking inside me. Every moment I've brushed off, every stolen glance, every lingering touch—it all crashes over me at once.

Oh, hell.

I *like* Alexis.

I *really* like Alexis.

And for the first time in my romantic disaster of a life, I have the chance to be with someone *suitable* for me. Someone who sees me.

Without another word, I turn on my cute new heels and march out of the coatroom, heels clicking against the marble floors with *purpose.*

Darius calls after me. "Where are you going?!"

I don't stop.

"To find our boss and tell her..." Now that I can say anything—admit my feelings—I'm unsure what to tell her.

My heart swells with an undeniable feeling. And to tell her that I—

This is my chance.

And I'm not wasting it.

I'm not waiting anymore. I'm running *straight toward my feelings* and *to Alexis.*

Chapter 31

So, This Is What L-Word Looks Like

I strut into the hotel ballroom like I haven't been run through an emotional tornado in the coatroom for fifteen minutes. I'm channeling confidence, but my inner monologue is full of panic sirens.

Unfortunately or fortunately, Richard's cologne clings and slowly inhaling it is calming. *Why does that man smell like a designer candle at a seductive ski lodge?*

"Hey, there you are," Lisa giggles as she waves me to an empty seat at her round table. She's fanning himself with the evening's program like she's seconds from catching fire.

"Yep, I'm surviving," I whisper back. "Barely."

"You look like a woman on the brink of kissing someone inappropriate. That LBD is getting you into trouble."

"I'm not ruling it out."

She smirks and mouths, "Trouble looks good on you. I might find some myself tonight."

I press my hands to my cheeks and keep moving.

The ballroom is full of Alaskan glitz, deep green tablecloths, and birch centerpieces wrapped in fairy lights. On stage, a massive screen cycles through old company photos. I spot a blurry, baby-faced Alexis in one—probably still learning to type and break hearts.

And there she is now.

Alexis stands on the raised platform next to her father, spine straight, with a perfectly tailored tux and bright shoes. Like she walked out of a queer businesswomen's dream sequence. Her jawline deserves its own LinkedIn profile.

I stop dead.

Her dad's voice echoes: "And with that, I am officially retiring, leaving the Alaska Temp Agency in the very capable hands of the woman who's not only upheld our family's legacy—but expanded it. My daughter, my pride... Alexis."

I beam with so much pride I might actually float off the ground. Alexis's dad claps her on the back and pulls her into a huge hug, and I just—ugh, I could burst. Everything she's worked for is finally happening. She's not just chasing the dream—she's living it.

Applause explodes around me, warm and thunderous. Alexis stands up there, cool as ever, with that small, composed smile. But I catch it—the flicker in her eyes, the tightness in her jaw. She's not soaking in the spotlight. She's commanding it like she was born to.

And me? I'm over here trying not to sob or faint like some emotional extra in her superhero origin story.

She's not just the woman who gave me a job when I was one bank overdraft from starting an account to sell my foot pics on Only Fans. She's the woman who helped me up after I had a terrible date, got high by accident, and confessed my life story after a gynecologist's visit.

She's seen the messiest parts of me. And still... here she is. Gorgeous. Single. Looking like the lead in my romantic delusion.

I wobble in my heels. I can't confess my true feelings to the CEO of the business I work for. Sit? Flee? Fake a faint and get wheeled out dramatically? The ice sculpture swan is starting to look inviting.

Alexis steps forward and starts speaking into the microphone. "Before we wrap up tonight," she says, calm and clear, "I'd like to announce something new."

Her eyes land on me. And they stay there.

"Alaska Temp Agency is built by people who show up—who try, who grow, who hustle." Her voice drops a degree. Sincere, almost intimate. "People who show us what it means to fight for their future. And we want to fight for them, too."

I blink. Once. Twice. Darius appears, grabs Lisa's arm, and whispers something. Lisa squeals.

"To support that, we're launching a scholarship fund to help young people in our community pursue business, management, and entrepreneurship. And the first recipient has faced challenges most don't see—but she's never stopped showing up."

My heart slams against my ribs.

"Aurora Thompson," Alexis announces, eyes still on me. "Would you please come forward?"

Dead. I'm officially dead. Someone call the EMTs. Tell them to bring a glitter gun to finish me off.

Wait. *What.*

Did she say *my name*?

Lisa screams, not like a polite golf clap squeal. No—she *screams* like someone just told her Channing Tatum's doing a meet-and-greet in the lobby.

I float to the stage, legs jelly, mouth dry, heart loudly thumping. Alexis meets me halfway, and her smile tilts with quiet amusement—like she knows I'm seconds from self-combusting.

I climb the steps on autopilot, my heart doing backflips. The room blurs into sparkles and heat. I reach the podium and take the envelope from Alexis's hand, fingers brushing hers.

Contact.

Electric. Intimate. Yet, completely professional.

She hands me a glass plaque that weighs less than the moment and an envelope. A scholarship. A future. A miracle beyond imagination.

"Congratulations, Aurora." Her voice is quiet now, just for me.

I open my mouth to thank her—say something witty, charming, or literally anything—but my throat closes. The weight I've carried for *months*—rent stress, college bills, grocery math that ends in ramen, and sad bananas—*shatters*.

She did this. She *saw* me. She *chose* me.

"I—uh..." I blink at the microphone. "Is this on? Oh—yep, okay. Cool."

The crowd chuckles gently.

"So. Hi. I wasn't planning to say anything, mostly because I thought the closest I'd get to the stage tonight was spilling a drink on it. But I'm standing here, and my brain said, 'Let's be weird about this.' So. Here we are."

More laughter. I glance at Alexis, who quirks a brow but doesn't interrupt. Her silence is warm. Encouraging.

"This company believed in me when I had no resume, no money, and exactly one pair of office-appropriate pants. I got hired because I was desperate and persistent—and Alexis saw that and didn't run away screaming."

Alexis raises her glass slightly. A small, teasing salute. My chest squeezes.

"So... Thank you. For seeing me. For *believing* in me. And for giving me a chance I didn't think I'd ever get. This scholarship? It's everything. And not because I'm dramatic—which, hi, I am—but because you gave me purpose. Hope. A path forward. Even when I walked in wearing mismatched shoes and without a clue on how to refill paper on a copier."

I inhale slowly. My voice steadies.

"Thank you. Alexis. You believed in me before I believed in myself."

I step back, the applause thunderous. Lisa hoots. Darius throws imaginary roses. Someone yells, "You go, girl!" I blush and pull out my finger guns to show my appreciation.

The crowd claps, and Alexis leans in. "Employees don't usually give speeches," she murmurs, as I follow her, removing myself from the stage and the limelight.

"I'm not a usual employee," I reply, chin high.

She chuckles, soft and low. "Don't I know it."

She hands me the champagne, her fingers brushing mine again. As we step away from the microphone—almost like the universe is in on it—the DJ kicks off some upbeat music. This time, I didn't pull away. I let the warmth settle in.

"You're full of surprises," I whisper.

"So are you," she says, giving me that look again. "Still meeting me after? Ronnie's Sushi?"

She threads her arm through mine and guides me off-stage, through the crowd dancing with their wine and appetizers. I blink fast, trying to stay upright and not do a dramatic swoon. Darius offers a thumbs-up like a proud pageant mom. Lisa mouths "Kiss her!" like a feral cheerleader.

Alexis leads me to the edge of the dance floor, where soft music plays and waiters begin serving tiny cakes I *will* be stealing extras of. She stops under the twinkle lights, right near the faux fireplace and the massive corporate banner that now has Alexis' name on it.

"You didn't have to do that," I murmured. "The scholarship. It's—huge."

She tilts her head, considering me. "You earned it."

"But you didn't have to share your night and make it *about me*."

She nods. "You crushed that speech."

"I blacked out halfway through."

"You said 'duct-taped my life together,' and I thought Darius' sobs might be louder than the mic."

I laugh, leaning on her as the music slows. "Thank you. For everything."

She holds me and looks into my eyes to say, "I didn't do it for thanks." Suddenly, her voice is quieter, less CEO, more... *her*. "You've been all I can think about after that interesting afternoon. I watched you struggle, hustle, and show up, even when no one else would have. You never asked for anything."

"I didn't think I was allowed to," I admit. "You're my boss, and I'm just happy not to get fired."

"You are going to start setting your goals higher." Her lips quirk.

"I know." I swallow hard. "I guess I know a bad ass business woman who might help me with that." I laugh, then add quietly, "... you changed my life."

Her expression softens. Her voice lowers. "You changed mine, too."

We stand there, arms brushing, the silence stretching wide like the stars above the snowy peaks. My brain, usually a swirl of stress—rent, tuition, my mom's voice listing all the things I haven't figured out—goes quiet. And for the first time in months, I don't feel like I'm carrying the world. I feel light. Almost...free.

"Oh, there's karaoke later," Lisa says, dancing into me.

She breaks my trace with her elbow and giggling.

Darius leans in and whispers, "Sorry, besties, but it's time to dance." Then he spins Lisa onto the dance floor with a flair worthy of a rom-com finale and smoothly snatches her moonshine from where she'd tucked it—yep, right out of her cleavage.

The room fills with happy chatter and laughter. Music pulses, the dessert table becomes a crowd magnet, and just like that, everyone's swept up in the chaos. Darius ditches Lisa mid-twirl to strut back to the table and dramatically pull Richard to his feet. They start dancing like they're starring in their own sparkly musical.

I laugh so hard my ribs ache.

And for the first time in what feels like forever, I'm not thinking about next month's rent. Or whether I fit in. Or if I'm too much or not enough. I'm just...here. Happy.

I'm exactly where I want to be. At the edge of a dance floor. Champagne in one hand. My chosen family clinking glasses behind me. Alexis is next to me and keeping me safe like she always does.

"You know," I say casually, "if you wanted to kiss me right now, it'd be, like, thematically appropriate."

Alexis laughs, low and warm. "You're not going to feel taken advantage of by the new CEO."

"Nope. I'm definitely the one taking advantage of you."

She tilts her head. "I knew you'd be trouble, right from the beginning?"

"Always."

She spins me around a potted spruce at the edge of the dance floor, pulling me closer and out of sight. One hand settles on my neck, the other presses firmly against my back. She licks her lips and says, "I've been wanting this since you stole my parking spot and teased me with that kiss last week."

She tugs me behind the ice sculpture display, hiding us from view.

Then she kisses me—soft and certain. Like she's been waiting. Like the universe lined up every star just to make this moment happen.

And maybe it did.

Later that night—after the shock of the scholarship announcement, the champagne-fueled giddiness, and the warm flush still lingering on my cheeks from Alexis's stolen kisses—I slip away from the ballroom on a covert mission to find her alone.

Alexis had been swiftly kidnapped by her father and a swarm of overly enthusiastic businessmen just as karaoke kicked off, right before I could sign up for "Girls Just Wanna Have Fun." I consoled myself with a slice of caramel cheesecake—creamy, rich, and almost distracting enough to forget her smirk.

With my heels in one hand and my tote bag swinging from the other, I seize the moment during Lisa and Darius's chaotic rendition of "Love Shack." The crowd's attention shifts entirely to their impromptu duet, laughter and clapping echoing through the ballroom.

I take my chance.

Dodging waitstaff and slipping past a pair of guests arguing about economic trends, I make my exit through the loading dock, the cool Alaskan night air kissing my bare shoulders like a secret I'm about to tell.

Classy, I know. But desperate girls in borrowed heels don't risk another run-in with any enemies or accidentally make a new one. I was so excited I didn't have a chance to eat. I need sushi. And Alexis. Preferably both, at the same time.

Outside, the summer air hums with that weird Alaskan magic—half-sunlight, half-moon, full chaos.

My phone buzzes, and I glance down, half-expecting Alexis's "*Where are you?*" text.

Instead, I see *Mom.*

Of course.

8:50 p.m.

One new message.

Mom.

Oh no.

My stomach coils. Not the butterflies kind. The oh-god-what-now kind.

I tap it open.

"How could you do this to me? At your work event? You deliberately set me up, ambushed me in front of everyone. After all I've done, this is how you repay me? Don't expect me to be there for you when you inevitably need me again."

My lungs stop cooperating.

Ambushed *her*?

I'm the one who was left with no money and being embarrassed. All while she hissed through her teeth about how *I'm embarrassing* and how I make her *look like a bad mother.*

I reread it once. Then twice. The words stab harder than I expected.

Not because they're new. But because *they're not.* This is predictable behavior from my mother, and she'll never change.

And weirdly, that realization doesn't break me. It frees me.

I stare at the message, blinking back the sting behind my eyes. No more begging for her approval or attention. No more apologizing.

I scroll up to her contact and hover over *Block Caller*.

Then—ping.

One more text. One sentence.

Short. Cruel. Nuclear.

"Seeing as you found your dad, I guess you don't need me anymore anyway."

My thumb freezes.

My breath catches.

I... what?

The world tilts. The gravel lot spins. Or maybe *I* do.

What. Did. She. Say?

My dad?

What dad?

I lock the screen. Then unlock it again. Like, maybe I misread it. Maybe my brain made it up because it's been juggling scholarship stress, hot boss crushes, and secret office drama for three weeks straight.

But it's still there.

That one sentence.

The sentence that detonates everything.

You found your dad.

I don't know who my dad is. She's *never* told me. Ever. Not his name. Not a hint. Not a scrap of truth, even when I begged.

And now, she's texting me in a fit of narcissistic rage to say I *found him?*

My pulse kicks into sprint mode. My hand shakes so hard I almost drop the phone.

I want to scream.

I want to hurl my phone into the nearest pothole and scream until the seagulls file a formal noise complaint. But I don't.

Instead, I walk.

I don't even know where my feet are taking me—just that standing still hurts too much. I drift across the cracked lot, past a drunk guy passionately arguing with a lamppost, and straight toward the glowing red sign of Ronnie's Sushi—the place where Alexis first crashed into my life like a well-dressed hurricane.

I stop outside the door, breathing shallow, heart pounding so loud it drowns out the rest of the city. My mom dropped a bomb tonight, and I don't even know where the shrapnel landed.

"You found your father."

The words won't stop echoing. What does that even mean? Who? When? Was it recent? Was it someone I shook hands with and smiled at like I wasn't completely fatherless my whole life? Was it someone at the gala? Someone who knows and didn't say anything?

My stomach twists with the weight of it.

But still... I don't turn back.

Because behind that door is the one person who makes me feel like the world isn't crumbling beneath my feet. Like I might not fall apart.

She makes me believe I could maybe—possibly—survive this.

I'm about to walk into the arms of someone who makes me question everything I thought I knew about love. And maybe that's terrifying.

But it's also the only thing keeping me from unraveling.

So I square my shoulders, grip the handle, and whisper to no one, "Let's do this."

Because I don't know who to trust.

Because I don't know what's real.

Because I still don't know who the hell my father is.

But I know one thing... I don't want to keep Alexis waiting.

Enjoy Aurora's Bonus epilogue!
Discover the books in the Aurora's Wilderness Love series
at HarmonyNoble.com

Aurora's Wilderness Love: Just a Little Fall Crush
Chapter 1: Unpacking My Mess

Oh my god, I just kissed my therapist.

Donna, my new and first therapist ever, is holding a paper plate, a neat wedge of quiche resting on wax paper. She is dazed and stepping back, like she didn't just give me her bedroom eyes and lean in to ask if I wanted a kiss.

"You—" Donna's words are lost, as I process the situation and realize my mistake.

"Oh my god. I'm mortified and so so *so* sorry," I say, running out of her cozy home office's open door.

Outside, Alaska air slams against my face with an honest clap of cold that I deserve. Sunlight glares judging me.

"Quiche," I mutter to the empty sidewalk, stomping toward my Subaru. "She said quiche, not kiss."

Who kisses their therapist?

I have not gone to therapy before but in movies the sessions usually ended with a big clock buzzing. There was no clock in sight, only knick-knacks, crocheted blankets, and books in a room that looked more like a tv room than a therapy room.

My brain replays the inappropriate moment in horrifying slow motion as I stumble through the sunlight burning my retinas accusatively, unusual for the start of Autumn in Alaska, as if even nature scorns my social misstep.

"Quiche," I mutter, stomping towards my beat-up Subaru. "Who even offers someone quiche at the end of a therapy session?"

"A super-friendly therapist, trying to make a connection and be nice to the mess of a new patient–that's who." I answer myself before I can get mad at Donna, which only makes me more upset at myself.

"Arrrg! Aurora, why do you hate yourself?" I shake my head, look up, and pull my sunglasses out to cover my burning retinas. *Stupid Alaskan weather!*

A passing elderly couple gives me concerned looks as I continue my self-directed tirade, internally. I force a smile and wave, which probably makes me look deranged. Perfect. Add that to today's list of mortifications.

My phone buzzes. *Darius.* Of course, he has a sixth sense for when I've done something monumentally embarrassing.

"So?" he demands without preamble. "Did your therapy fix your life in ninety minutes?"

"I kissed her."

"You... what now?"

"The therapist," I groaned, slumping against my car. "She offered me a kiss–*oh my god*– I mean 'quiche.' I thought she said 'kiss.' And I—ever the compliant-people-pleasing-person—leaned in and gave my therapist a small peck on the lips, Darius."

His laughter erupts so loudly that I have to pull the phone away from my ear. "Oh. My. God. Aurora. You beautiful disaster. This is why we're friends. Only you could turn therapy into a rom-com meet-cute."

"It wasn't a meet-cute! It was a meet-horrifying! And my real meet-cute date is with *Alexis...*" I realize as I say this, that I don't have time to run home and hide in shame under my covers. I'm meeting Alexis for a late lunch and to discuss my schedule. I can't miss it since Alexis graciously gave me the week off to recover.

"And now, I obviously *need therapy* for my therapy. Donna was totally cool, but you can't continue therapy with someone you sexually harassed, right?"

"I have so *many* follow-up questions. Was there any body contact? What did she look like? Did you snap a pic?"

His stream of questions only makes me turn more crimson. I slide into my car, resting my forehead against the steering wheel.

Luckily, he fills in the silence. "Girl, you didn't attack her. You are way too naive to seduce a therapist. I swear every time you are around a powerful woman you melt. You gotta get your libido under control."

"You're right. There was *no* tongue, and I'm sure Donna understood that I had misheard her. It was an honest mistake," I ramble, hoping to believe what I'm saying, because that's the only way I'm going to live down, attacking my super-nice and hot therapist. Darius is right, I'm apparently attracted to hot women who have it together, probably because I'm a hot mess.

He reassures, still chuckling, "O-kayyyy, then. So, besides your failed attempt to seduce your therapist, Donna, did the session help?"

"Actually, yeah. She basically diagnosed my entire personality in fifteen minutes. Apparently, I'm a 'people pleaser' and a 'peacemaker' who will 'do anything to earn the acceptance and love my mother withheld.' She said it all boils down to being raised by a narcissistic single mom."

"Well... she doesn't sound wrong?"

I sigh. "No. And she said I need to stop trying with Mom unless she apologizes, and that I should 'choose me' first."

"Hmm," Darius hums thoughtfully. "Revolutionary concept, and the *same thing* Lisa and I have been telling you. And what about Alexis? Did you tell her about your workplace dumpster fire."

My stomach clenches at the mention of her name. "She said she doesn't give advice, but she had never seen a dating-your-boss situation that didn't go badly. In fact, she thinks I need to look for a new job."

"Now, she's totally wrong there. You *do* need to date Alexis, or this therapist. Whoever is going buy you dinner and pay for your university costs. Besides, you can work summers part-time, since the agency is paying for your business schooling. There's time for Alexis to warm your bed, right?"

"Maybe I should date her before I sleep with her?"

Darius's advice is starting to sound more like the wham-bam queen, Lisa.

Reading my thoughts again, he laments, "I wish Lisa wasn't getting waxed right now. She is going to die when I tell her your new drama."

"Darius, I'll tell her when I get home. Now I have to somehow control myself to meet Alexis."

"To quit? To break up? Or to admit you love her and move into her mansion and be her plaything?

"Not every lesbian owns a U-Haul!" I look in my mirror and wipe my smeared mascara while grabbing my lip gloss. "And yes. And no to the job questions. Just because I got a full-ride scholarship doesn't mean I'm quitting at the temp agency while I take classes. I still need money, and it's a really great job. Why can't I enjoy starting university, keep doing accounting work that'll look good on my resume, *and* having a freaking awesome girlfriend?"

"Aurora—"

"I know, I know," I cut him off. "I'm dreaming and not making a real plan. The therapist basically said the same thing. That it can't be a real relationship if I need emotional support and I'm still figuring out what love is. God, I'm a mess but seriously, Alexis seems like the only unmessy thing in my life."

"You know Alexis will let you take whatever work schedule you want. And the best decision you made was ending feeding your mom's drama. Richard and I totally support whatever you decide. Go talk with Alexis and give me and Lisa the tea tonight. No matter what, you got us all in your corner babe."

Tears prick at my eyes, and I dab them again and sniffle. "Thanks."

Chapter 2: Special SaLmon Kisses

"So thanks again for giving me the week off to process everything," I say as Alexis looks through the Ronnie Sushi weekend specials menu and places her phone on the table.

"Did you use your health benefits to see a professional? Your mom dropping that bombshell about your dad really threw you for a loop." Her brown eyes soften, and I'm starting to think this is a date-date, not a work date.

"I did go to therapy. I still have some self-reflection and work to do. But I'm feeling more... grounded?" I say without conviction.

Alexis doesn't notice and swirls the sake in her tiny ceramic cup. Meanwhile, I'm over here pretending I'm totally fine and wondering if I need to admit to kissing my therapist. Also I'm trying to figure out if this is a date or a work meeting.

She sips and smiles.

I nod and smile, pretending to enjoy sake. Mmm, yes, ancient rice wine, I totally have a refined palate and not the taste buds of someone raised on Costco pizza and Anchorage tap water.

The restaurant mood? Technically romantic. It has low lighting, a lazy jazz playlist, and tiny soy sauce dishes I'm afraid to touch in case I knock one over. But with Alexis' phone on the table and her in a blazer, this has a work lunch vibe.

Alexis checks her phone, so I lift mine as if I'm equally important. What do I get? A highlight reel of how unglamorous my life is:

> Oil change overdue—87 days.
> Doctor's office nagging me.
> Parking ticket waiting to double if not paid asap.
> Trash pickup reminder for tomorrow.
> Low storage. Delete 500 selfies.

My phone doesn't scream successful adult—it heckles me, more my disappointed electronic friend.

"Do you want to discuss your schedule this week? I really need you for our new client since you are our best accounting temp." She shifts to allow the waitress to place edamame in front of us. Her knee brushes mine under the table, casual, confident, electric. I forgot what language is.

My cheeks flush. I think I'd do anything this woman asks. I am a sucker for a powerful woman, especially one wearing a perfectly tailored suit, who is buying me an expensive lunch.

"This edamame is exquisite," Alexis says, lifting a piece to her mouth with chopsticks as precise as a surgeon's scalpel. "Try it."

I reach for mine, but chopsticks are invented by evil spirits to remind me of my fundamental lack of coordination and sophistication. The slippery bean flies off my chopsticks, splatting on the floor. I try to recover my dignity by giggling and sipping my sake, which tastes of warm regret.

Alexis arches an eyebrow. "You don't like Asian cuisine?"

"No, I wasn't really raised eating foods from other cultures, so my chopstick skills are pretty bad," I explain, wondering if I should pick up the bean, but then my cloth napkin would be dirty. I bite my lip and push the offending chopsticks away.

"You're very brave to try. Here," she waves over the waitress and asks for silverware for me. "There. All taken care of now." Her lips twitch in a smirk that borders on affection. "You're lucky you're pretty."

"Thank you," I whisper, and the vibe is bordering on first-date vibes. "Don't forget I also look good in a ball gown, and you said I'm your best accountant."

She grins, and I'm glowing, winning something important—like an Iditarod trophy or her eternal devotion. Either works.

"I like your confidence."

And I was confident with my fork and sass, until... The caviar was served.

I try to lean forward seductively, but my elbow knocks into the little caviar tower. Black pearls rain down onto my dress, my lap, the pristine white napkin I barely used because I didn't want to mess it up.

I freeze. "Oh no. No, no, no... Sorry!"

Alexis blinks, then her grin turns to a laugh. It's that low, warm sound she doesn't give out easily. "You make everything more exciting."

"I am a walking seafood hazard." I try wiping the caviar from my blouse and lap, leaving dark streaks.

"Hold still," she says. Then she shrugs off her actual designer, probably ridiculously expensive, blazer and drapes it over my shoulders.

"Oh my god," I say, clutching it tightly. "I would have spilled something sooner if I knew you'd let me wear your power blazer. Money and boss energy, that's how I smell wearing this blazer," I blurt.

"It's dry-clean only," she deadpans. "Which is code for 'your problem now.' You can wear it at your new assignment."

Then, before I can classify this as a friendly work date, she leans closer, her breath warm against my ear. "Besides, you look good in my clothes."

And now I'm malfunctioning with heat blossoming at my core and making my breath come out in a gasp.

She doesn't move, studying my eyes, then slowly looks down at my stained chest and her blazer on my body.

"Which sashimi do you prefer today, Miss Anders?" The waitress asks while replacing my napkin with a fresh one.

"The sal-mon," she says with authority despite mispronouncing Alaska's biggest export. The waitress says nothing and nods.

"Um. So," I blurt, desperate to change the subject before I melt into a puddle of sexual distress, "did you mean to say 'SaLmon' with the L or—"

"Sal-mon," Alexis replies, crisp and confident.

I squint. "Wait. You really mean Sammon, right?" I am unsure if this is an inside joke because she can't be serious. How does an Alaskan not know how to say salmon?

"It's pronounced the same as it's spelled."

I lean back, eyeing her, and she is totally serious.

The busser stops to clean up the mess around our table—poor guy. I grab him like a lifeline. "Excuse me, how do you pronounce salmon?"

He blinks, his smile tight. "However Miss Anders prefers it."

My eyes dart between Alexis and the poor guy, and something clicks. "Oh my god. Do you own Ronnie's Sushi?"

"Technically, my family owns the building," she says, casual, sipping her sake again. "But yes, the restaurant leases from us."

I throw my hands up. "Alexis, just how rich are you?"

Before she can reply, a crash rings out across the room—a waiter drops a whole tray of drinks and glass scatters everywhere.

I'm up in a heartbeat. "Oh no."

"Aurora—" Alexis starts, but I'm already kneeling, helping to pick up shards, napkins, and glass stems.

The waiter stammers 'thanks' while Alexis stays seated, arms crossed, watching the scene like it's inconvenient rather than a crisis. When I sit back down, brushing off my hands, she hands me her napkin without a word.

"You didn't need to help."

I sip my now lukewarm sake and shrug. "Alexis, tell me, since you are always saving me and have this secret posh life—are you for real? You seem too perfect."

She leans closer again, brushing a loose curl off my cheek, her hand lingering on my blushing face. "I'm real. Would you date the perfect woman?"

"If he were a lesbian with great taste and stilettos? Absolutely."

And then her lips are on mine. Soft, confident, addictive. One of her hands lands gently on my thigh, her blazer still warming my shoulders. I kiss her back—I've been waiting for this exact level of electric, surprising, world-rearranging affection since we met.

I forget about the spilled caviar. I forget whether this is a work date or a real date. I forget how awkward I felt walking into a place where the menu doesn't list prices and where I had one of the worst dates of my life last month. I forget everything except Alexis, her ridiculous smoothness, and her perfectly lipstick-free kisses.

It's unfair how great she looks without needing makeup.

My heart does gymnastics. How is this incredible, controlled powerhouse of a woman attracted to me? Me, with my discount dress and fake confidence.

Before I can spiral too hard into the imposter syndrome abyss, she pulls back slightly, eyes scanning mine. "What's that look for?"

"I'm just surprised and trying not to have a full anxiety attack at this table."

She smiles, and somehow that calms the tornado in my chest.

"I've been thinking," I say, twisting the sake cup between my fingers. Now that I know that Alexis likes me more than as my mentor, I can ask what I was thinking about. "About my mom and the whole family drama situation."

Her expression sharpens, and she lifts a perfectly plucked brow.

"Yeah. She never told me who my dad is, she just ghosted me after saying I knew him. And I know you want me back to work, but all I can think about is finding my dad—finding out where I come from?"

Alexis's hand slides into mine. "Everyone deserves to know their family. I'm sorry you and your mom aren't talking. But I'm sure you can look for your dad and still work."

"I guess," I shrug, realizing that in my week off, I mostly hid in my bed and had my one disastrous counseling appointment. I could have used that time to research who my father was or even hire a private investigator to find him.

Alexis tilts her head. "Why don't we just get your birth certificate?"

I blink. "What?"

"Your birth certificate. It will list your father."

My mouth falls open. "You... you are brilliant."

"You're welcome."

Suddenly, the family stress that's been strangling me all week melts into the soy-scented air. There's a way forward. A clue. A plan. I have a plan.

She squeezes my fingers. "Simple."

I lean in, catch her lips again, quick and sure. My heart pounds, trying to escape my chest, but in a good way this time. The right way.

She leans closer, her woodsy sweet smell invading my body, her fingers warm against my skin. They linger. Not by accident. Not a casual gesture. She's looking at me as if I'm more delicious than her posh sake.

Every nerve in my body flips on. She's found and slammed on my main breaker. The restaurant disappears—waiters, soft music, fish egg trauma—all of it dissolves. The only sound left is the blood roaring behind my ears and maybe the hum of whatever magnetic pull is tugging our mouths together.

Her voice drops low. "Let's call this our official first date."

Already breathless, I whisper, "absolutely."

Her lips catch mine mid-laugh.

There's nothing tentative about it. Alexis kisses to ruin me in the best way possible. Her mouth is soft but focused, warm, and sure. It is as if she mapped out every nerve ending on mine and decided to make each one light up. One of her hands slides behind my neck, fingers threading into my hair, gently tilting my face to deepen the kiss. The other presses firm on my thigh under the table, firmly pinning me here, steadying me, and branding me as hers.

I make a tiny, embarrassing sound. A whimper. A squeak? Definitely not a cool, sophisticated sound.

Her lips curve into a grin against mine. She heard my squeak and it made her smile. Her tongue teases the seam of my lips. I part them without hesitation. And she's kissing me deeper—slower, but with devastating precision. Her mouth tastes faintly of sake and citrus, and she kisses with this blend of heat and control that's wrecking my ability to function. Every pass of her tongue pulls me further under. My whole body leans into hers, chest buzzing, heart tripping over itself drunk on the kiss and Alexis.

I kiss her back like my life is on the line.

This is the only time, the only place, and the only girl who's ever made me think that kissing might actually be the point of being alive.

I lose track of everything except her.

Her scent becomes more defined, a clean and sharp–bergamot, and something so expensive I'll never afford it.

The silk of her blouse against my fingers as I grip her sleeve, desperate for more.

There is a slight hitch in my breath when she bites gently at my bottom lip after the kiss.

That tiny move sets off fireworks inside my ribcage. Her blazer slips off my shoulder as my boss pulls me closer across the table, both half-aware of the sushi casualties being knocked around. Chopsticks clatter. My soy sauce dish tips. Something squishes under my elbow, but I don't care. Nothing matters but her lips on mine.

By the time we come up for air, I'm flushed, dazed, still clutching her sleeve. Alexis's lipstick—usually perfect—is slightly smudged now. There is even color blooming high on her chiseled cheeks, and her eyes are darker, unreadable.

Holy hell.

I did that.

She brushes her thumb over my bottom lip, gentle but possessive, eyes locked on mine. She memorizes the way her kiss breaks me and winks at me.

"You're trouble."

"So are we—"

Alexis's phone buzzes. She hops up–*I guess her legs aren't jelly like mine after our kiss.*

"I have something important," She throws bills down and doesn't even glance up from her phone to say goodbye.

So, are we really officially dating now?

Are we allowed to tell people or is this a sexy secret relationship?

Do you like the way I taste?

These are the questions she ran away from before I could ask.

What call is so important that it ended our first official date?

If you fell for the tension, the longing, and the sparks in Aurora's first sapphic adventure...

her story isn't over yet.

Continue the journey in

Aurora's Wilderness Love: Just a Little Fall Crush

Because some feelings don't fade—they deepen.

Available now.

Chasing that next heart-racing, can't-put-it-down love story?

Find your next escape at HarmonyNoble.com

Join the reader list for exclusive updates, new releases, and special giveaways

COMING NEXT

Aurora's Wilderness Love
Just a Little Fall Crush

In Alaska, the ice is cold, but the workplace tension is scorching.

Aurora's back—and this time, she's juggling college, a corporate job she's barely qualified for, and a secret relationship with her infuriatingly poised boss. (Yes, that boss. The one with cheekbones sharp enough to slice through HR policy.)

After surviving the wilds of Alaskan dating, Aurora thought she knew chaos. But nothing prepared her for office romances, unread syllabi, and learning her absentee father might not be so absent after all. Between quarterly reports and unexpected DNA results, Aurora is forced to confront what it really means to grow up—and who gets to be called family.

With a found-family cast of coworkers, an all-too-supportive best friend, and a boss who kisses like a dream but critiques like a CEO, Aurora's once-simple survival plan turns into a rom-com of epic proportions. Can she keep her job and her heart intact—or will it all crash faster than her GPA?

Tropes you'll love: Secret workplace romance, "we shouldn't be doing this... but we are", found family in unexpected places, college girl chaos meets boss-level confidence, and a big emotional reveal with heartwarming fallout.

In a place where the moose outnumber the men, love was never going to be easy—but Aurora's about to learn that the greatest discoveries happen when you finally stop running and start showing up.

The odds are still good. The feelings? Even messier.

Aurora's Wilderness Love
Christmas Cruise Mistake

Escaping winter in Alaska? Check. Accidentally honeymooning with a stranger? Also check.

When a last-minute tropical Christmas cruise invite saves university student, Aurora, from an awkward post-break-up holiday and the freezing snow of Alaska, she packs her bikinis, her sass, and a plan to have fun and forget her epic break-up.

But a massive booking mix-up later, she's now pretending to be the runaway bride of the woman who left at the altar.

Oops!

Desperate and ready for a second-chance, Aurora's trapped on a couple's cruise filled with love exercises. Aurora's just trying to survive awkward icebreakers, too many trust falls, and the very real sparks flying with her accidental not-wife. *The plan? Fake it 'til they dock.*

A steamy karaoke duet changes everything. Aurora's **heart is reignited** and the cursed cruise might be what her **tender heart needs**.

Tangled in lies, tequila, and tension even a conga line can't break, Aurora's about to learn that running from romance leads her straight into the arms of a woman she never knew she needed.

The odds are still good. The drama? *It's a full-blown shipwreck.*

Snag the latest swoon-worthy read and find upcoming new releases at HarmonyNoble.com

Other Titles by MELODY BEST
& HARMONY NOBLE
For the most up-to-date list visit
www.HarmonyNoble.com

<u>Aurora's Wilderness Love:</u>

Hot Girl Summer Love
Just a Little Fall Crush
Christmas Cruise Mistake

<u>Wilderness Rescue Sapphic Romance Series:</u>

Crashing Into Love
Unthaw My Heart
Winning Love
Stormy Hearts
Scoring Love
Flooded Hearts
Healing Hearts
Tides of Love
Iditarod Love
Frozen Hearts

Coffeehouse Romance Series:

Love, Joy & Lattes (Joy's Story)
Test Driving a Millionaire (Tara's Story)
Shattering Crystal a Bully Romance (Crystal's Story)
Choosing Love, Namaste (Meaghan's Story)
The Wrong Bride for Christmas (Monica's Story)

Coffeehouse Romance Short Stories:

Joy's 4th of July Holidate
Tara's Valentine Holidate
Crystal's Easter Holidate
Meaghan's New Year Holidate
Monica's Halloween Holidate
My Accidental Christmas Fiancé
Joy's Coffeehouse Romance

Snag the latest swoon-worthy reads and stay tuned for upcoming stories at www.HarmonyNoble.com.

About Author –
Harmony Noble & Melody Best

Meet the unstoppable twins from the rugged wilds of Alaska, the writing duo, Harmony & Melody. Fueled by endless lattes, their character-driven stories brim with authenticity, humor, and heart—featuring Alaskan grit, journeys of self-discovery, and swoon-worthy happily-ever-afters.

When they're not crafting adventure romances, these twins can be found hiking trails with breathtaking views, enjoying charming coffee shops, or exploring new worldwide destinations together.

Join the e-newsletter for exclusive content and giveaways at website:

harmonynoble.com

Email: TrueLoveWriters@gmail.com

Instagram/Facebook/TikTok: @truelovewriters

www.ingramcontent.com/pod-product-compliance
Lightning Source LLC
LaVergne TN
LVHW010651110826
845149LV00014B/3034